To
Th

the way for
me at COPA
and all of your
Leadership at
ACEP

Moonstone Hero

MOONSTONE
HERO

A NOVEL BY

David Sklar

ISBN: 978-1-73234843-1 (Paperback)
ISBN: 978-1-73234844-8 (eBook)
ISBN: 978-1-73234845-5 (Audiobook)

Library of Congress Control Number: 2022911887

Any references to historical events, real people, or real places are used ficti-
tiously. All characters, incidents, and dialogue are drawn from the author's
imagination and are not to be construed as real.

Book Design by Stewart A. Williams | www.stewartwilliamsdesign.com

Volcano Cannon Press
355 East Maryland Avenue
Phoenix, Arizona, 85012

This book is dedicated to the doctors, nurses, medical trainees, respiratory therapists, pharmacists, clerks, technicians, janitors, security personnel, and other health workers around the world. In short, everyone who came into contact day after day with COVID-19 infected patients and put their lives at risk, often with inadequate protective equipment. They were the true heroes of the past two years. I was privileged to work with the emergency medicine teams of Valleywise Health Center in Phoenix and University of New Mexico Health Sciences Center in Albuquerque as they cared for COVID-19 patients. This book is particularly dedicated to them. Their courage inspired me to reflect upon heroism, and how it can appear in normal people who confront an abnormal situation and put the welfare of others above their own. Once started, it can spread and grow and create a culture of heroism and a community of heroes. This was the heroism of people who made a difference in spite of their flaws and weaknesses over the past two years—and it's the heroism we will need for the future.

Chapter 1

TANZANIA, AFRICA 1974

H E KNEW THEY were in trouble when Barry started gasping and his lips turned blue. Barry coughed up a wad of clotted blood surrounded by pink foam bubbles, and spit it out onto the snow at Andrew's feet. "Yeah, I feel better now," Barry said.

Andrew closed his eyes for a moment. Partly it was to avoid the swirling snow with bits of volcanic dust blowing into his face, but it was also to avoid looking at Barry's bloody lips and mouth that gurgled as he sucked in air. "Barry, what are you doing?" Andrew asked.

"I can't breathe."

"Would you like some water? Just relax and take normal breaths. Don't suck in air."

"I have to." With each breath, Barry's neck vibrated and honked.

"Just open your mouth and inhale normally, and push out the phlegm when you exhale. Maybe bend forward a little as you walk." Andrew found himself slipping into medical lingo as if he were treating a croup patient on the pediatric ward of the hospital. But Barry was not a child, and he didn't have croup.

They trudged forward together for a few steps, heads bent against the wind like buffalo. Nothing was visible except the dance of snow through stray bursts of sunlight in the gathering darkness ahead of them. Andrew lifted his feet over the scree and snow as his legs shook with each step. It had been three days of uphill climbing, and he was not in shape for such a long hike. His only exercise over the past month had been running between the obstetric wards and the operating room at the Dar es Salaam hospital to help deliver babies, and that was level ground.

This climb up the mountain was supposed to be a vacation from the daily medical drama of life and death decisions that, as a medical student, he had not anticipated would become his responsibility. But when the intern and resident were busy and the faculty supervisor was at home, the nurses came to him with their questions. At first, he had enjoyed the sudden position of authority, the willingness of the nurses to follow his orders without questioning. But later, when the intern and resident returned and scrutinized his decisions, he recognized the gaps in his knowledge and the possible consequences of errors he made. And he realized that the nurses had probably come to him because he was white.

He needed time and distance to reflect on all that had happened since he'd arrived in Africa. Africa's highest mountain would be a test of his dedication and resolve, and it could be his Oracle of Delphi, supplying answers about his future. His quest was supposed to have been a solitary one; he had come alone and did not want to depend on anyone. But somehow he had become attached to a stranger, struggling in the snow, and he felt their fates becoming linked.

Andrew had planned the Kilimanjaro climb with a guidebook and had read about the precautions needed against the cold and the altitude. The guidebook described how groups would assemble spontaneously from all over the world, drawn by the challenge of Africa's highest mountain, and bond during the climb even when they spoke different languages. And that's how it had been at first. There were Germans and Danes, a British guy and his Australian cousin, and two other Americans, with three African guides and porters. Most people came in pairs. He was the only one by himself. Or, at least, he had been alone until Barry became attached to him.

It was a three-day climb to fifteen thousand feet, and a midnight hike up to the summit. And now they were finishing the third day of hiking. He was looking forward to signing the book at the top of the mountain that would document his success at reaching the summit. It had been a long, hard climb, reminiscent of the three days of cross-country races that he had done in high school during the state finals, but the scenery and the companionship with his fellow climbers was a welcome change from the competitiveness of racing. Successfully reaching the summit wouldn't blot out his memories of the past month's medical crises. He knew he wouldn't be able to forget the image of the quivering legs of a breech baby who'd gotten stuck in the birth canal, or the woman who'd gushed buckets of blood after a delivery and almost bled to death. Still, at least his mind would fill temporarily with the grandeur and solitude of the mountain that was his to enjoy.

Unlike at the hospital, where the nurses and residents imbued him with talents and skills that he did not possess, on the mountain no one expected anything special from him. Everyone seemed self-sufficient or counted on their climbing partners in case of an emergency. Andrew didn't mind being responsible for himself. He was twenty-four years old, and used to living and traveling alone. His parents had sent him to outdoor camps as a teenager for two summers, where he had honed his hiking and survival skills.

He actually felt like there was an advantage in not having to look out for a climbing companion who lacked outdoor expedition experience, like the girlfriend he'd broken up with just before the trip to Africa. She'd eaten all of her food rations for a four-day river hike in two days, and then expected Andrew to share his uneaten food with her for the last two. Of course, he did share his food, but with every bite of his cheese and bread that he watched her eat, he felt an ulcer boring into his stomach. If she had slipped on a rock and sprained her ankle, he would have carried her for miles without complaint, but he could not forgive her irresponsibility and lack of discipline in planning her food consumption. What would have happened if he had been equally irresponsible? The hike was a test of compatibility—and when it was over, so was the relationship.

Andrew had been pacing himself as the guidebook recommended, counting his breaths, counting his pulse, counting his steps, marking it all down in his notebook. His physiology teacher in medical school had advised him to look at his fingernails, stop and breathe if they turned blue, stay where he was, and keep breathing until his nails turned pink. The teacher had studied high-altitude illness, and had a theory that the problem was most people did not breathe quickly or deeply enough as the oxygen levels dropped at higher altitudes because their brains did not perceive the low blood oxygen in time. But the fingernail color could be a way to monitor the situation and take corrective action before serious consequences set in.

It was just a theory, but Andrew trusted his professor's intuition. He followed his own pace up the mountain and would abruptly slow down and later start moving forward, following a rhythm that might have suited a drunk trying to navigate a crowded street. Walking with Barry had not been part of his plan. It just happened out of necessity and chance, and now they were yoked together like oxen. The others had disappeared ahead, leaving only footprints in the snow. He couldn't even remember their names—the Germans and Danes, the cousins from England and Australia, the African porters. Except Barry's girlfriend, Eve. He remembered her name, her sculpted face, dark eyes gazing ahead toward the peak, and the upright posture of her body as she walked into the wind, like a statue of a Roman goddess.

But why couldn't he remember the names of the others? He paused for a moment, closed his eyes, and tried to concentrate on the letters of the alphabet. When he reached the letter H, the names Helmut and Helga, two of the German climbers, appeared before him magically. And when he got to R, the third one, Rolph, appeared. Rolph looked like Helmut, except he was a bit taller and a bit more bearded; his hair and beard bobbed and twisted like Tibetan prayer flags in the wind. Helga seemed to be in charge of the two men, because she would shout orders to them in German and they would respond immediately, changing their pace or giving a nod or an obedient glance.

Helga, Rolph, and Helmut. He could remember them now. He could use their help now. They were athletic, muscular, and smelled of sweat. They were the strongest climbers in the group and had planned the expedition to Kilimanjaro to convince investors in a gym they were planning to open that they were serious about fitness. But there was also something self-serving and malignant about them. Andrew would not want to be dangling at the end of a rope that any of them held.

As Andrew and Barry continued up toward the hut, they tested the way forward with their hands and feet. Andrew felt Barry's hand tentatively reaching out, and he paused for a moment to help steady Barry's balance. It was something that had happened with others along the trail, a light touch or something more urgent during a slippery ascent, a bit of subtle intimacy forced upon them by the circumstances. Andrew had walked with everyone in his party at some point in the three days, and they had come to count on each other for a gentle, steadying hand.

Andrew had enjoyed walking with the two Danes. Their names both began with K. The man, Klaus, had long hair to his broad shoulders and over his eyes. Kara, his wife, had hair the color of gold thread that framed her cherubic cheeks. They were like children—naïve, innocent, accepting of whatever obstacles were put in their path—and responded in synchrony as a team. Andrew had never heard them criticize anyone or complain. Andrew felt safe with them, even if they lacked excitement or intrigue. He gravitated toward them during the first two days of the hike as they welcomed him like a cousin or brother, unlike Barry and Eve, who seemed distant and suspicious until this last stretch of the hike, when Barry suddenly became ill.

Barry had been walking with Salaam, one of the African guides, when he began to cough and gasp for air. He had to slow down and was walking too slowly for Salaam to reach the third hut and prepare dinner for all of the climbers. Eve had already disappeared ahead of them, complaining about blisters and a headache. That left Andrew, who was pacing himself based upon the color of his fingernails and was walking at Barry's pace. When Salaam had asked Andrew to walk with Barry for safety's sake, as the temperature was falling and the sun was setting, Andrew agreed without realizing how disabled Barry had become.

"I'm feeling better," said Barry as he tapped Andrew on the shoulder. "I guess I'm out of shape. Four years of beer drinking and partying at Stanford. I thought the two years here in the Peace Corps would wash it all out of my system. But I guess not yet. Thanks for keeping me company." Barry paused and took several breaths and managed a crooked smile on his round face as his lower lip drooped slightly to the left.

Andrew had always been bothered by defects in symmetry, just as he was bothered by defects in discipline and order. He noticed when a page in a book was torn at the edge, or a car was parked outside of the lines in a parking lot. He noticed the signs of a stroke when one hand was weaker than the other or one pupil was dilated. And now he noticed Barry's drooping lip with its blueish tint and the uneven beads of sweat that covered his forehead in spite of the cold. These defects disturbed Andrew's sense of symmetry and pattern and raised his concerns that Barry's body was collapsing.

"It's okay. I think your body is reacting to the altitude. It's not your fault. Anyway, I don't mind walking slow," said Andrew. "I wanted to walk slower once we got up here past the first peak. This is the saddle, a bridge between the two peaks, Mawenzi and Uhuru, where the volcano erupted. I read in the guidebook that it was a spiritual place for the people here, the border between the two gods." The two peaks tilted up into the clouds, the first like a wild younger brother, gray and menacing with jagged edges frosted with snow, while the second, exuding the confidence of the older brother, was smooth with snow coating every piece of stone like white paint. They stood on the bridge between the peaks as the wind attacked in bursts, as if trying to knock them off balance into the vertical drops on either side.

"Yeah. I feel something here. I don't know if it's spiritual," said Barry, "more like terror and awe. It would be nice to be sharing this with Eve. It's what we came for, to be a bit on the edge."

"She passed me. She didn't seem very happy. She was complaining about blisters on her toes and her heavy backpack. She looked kind of miserable with the snow melting on her face," Andrew said. He noticed that Barry did not have his backpack anymore. Salaam was carrying it along with his own backpack, which was something Salaam had told them at the start of the trip was forbidden. "What happened to your backpack?"

"I was dying with that pack on. I couldn't breathe. Salaam suggested it. He was walking with us, pointing out the birds, and then he looked at me, and I guess he noticed how I was breathing and coughing. The next thing I know, he's taking my backpack and putting it on his back. I never asked him. Eve was pissed because she was really tired. I guess she felt like Salaam should have helped her, too. But what am I going to say? I couldn't complain. I needed the help." Barry stretched out his hands as if presenting his arguments to a jury.

Andrew nodded. He had been struggling with his own backpack, which weighed about forty pounds when they started but felt heavier as they reached the higher altitude. Andrew remembered that brief orientation speech from Salaam in the office. Salaam had warned them about not asking for help to carry backpacks, staring at each of them for ten silent seconds through his narrow eyes as if to emphasize his statement. Salaam's high forehead and prominent cheekbones and flared nostrils made his ebony eyes more menacing as they'd peered out from the recesses of his bony skull. He had a British accent and followed a script that seemed to be overly formal for the type of group he was leading. "I am Salaam, your guide for this most wonderful adventure of your life. This will be the climb of Mount Kilimanjaro and the peak is called Uhuru, meaning 'freedom' in Swahili. You are a group from all over the world. Many countries. Germany, Australia, England, Denmark, and the United States of America. We will be speaking to you in English, but if you would like a tour in German, there is one scheduled in one week." Salaam had looked at the Germans and paused until Helga shook her head.

Then Salaam continued, "I will introduce our two porters: Mohammed and Koba. Koba is a trained athlete who can run the entire way up and down this mountain in one day. Mohammed can carry seventy-five kilograms on his back, even though you may see him smoking. They are both accustomed to the high altitude. They speak Swahili, our native language, and will not be able to communicate with you in English. So, I prefer you come to me and do not ask them questions. They are both very strong, but they will only be carrying our food and water and other gear for your accommodations. You must carry your own clothes in your backpack. We are not able to make any exceptions, even for the ladies."

Salaam paused for questions. When there were none, he continued, "So, now you must sign your health forms and the legal release forms that explain the dangers of this tour, which include falls, high-altitude illness, bites from animals, and even death. Remember, this is a natural area. There are wild animals and many dangers. The mountain is very high and not everyone will reach the summit. We are not responsible for that. We are your assistants. But you are the ones who will determine your own fate. Now, please sign the forms, and if you have not completed your payments, please do that now. You may wish to use our toilets here. There are no toilets along the trail. Our truck will depart in a half-hour to take us to the start of the expedition."

The two porters had barely turned to acknowledge their introduction when Salaam identified them, and Andrew had assumed that they were bored and uninterested in Salaam's speech. Later on, after climbing to the second hut, Andrew had come upon Koba doing push-ups and sit-ups on the grass. He was surprised at how thin Koba's arms and legs were for an athlete and how easily they lifted his body into the air. Andrew had tried to start a conversation with Koba by explaining, with a mix of English and Swahili words he'd picked up, that he'd also been a runner in high school and knew about the solitude and peace of long-distance running. Koba stared at him as if he did not understand a word he was saying, and Andrew quickly drifted away.

The hut appeared suddenly out of the dark and fog, and interrupted Andrew's reverie with lights that flickered a hundred yards ahead. They paused for a moment to be sure, and finally Barry said, "I think that's it."

"Yeah," said Andrew. "That's the third hut."

Andrew pushed open the door of the hut and Barry followed. The sudden brightness of the light blinded him. They stood at the open door squinting and trying to get their bearings. Plates were clanging above the din of loud voices. Andrew looked around for someone to take delivery of Barry and lead him to a cot. Barry was tottering and coughing and needed a place to rest, and Andrew felt dizzy and disoriented, too. They stood at the open doorway in the rushes of cold air until Helga came over to them, said something in German, and slammed the door shut. It happened so quickly that Andrew had no time to react.

"What the fuck?" said Barry as the corner of the door struck the side of his ankle. He lost his balance and crumpled to the floor.

Chapter 2

A s BARRY LAY on the narrow wood floor slats encrusted with ice, black mud, and bits of rock, his ankle ached and his toes felt numb. He coughed and felt phlegm filling his throat. Spit dribbled out of his mouth. He tried to cry out, but only a high whistle escaped his lips. He screamed, "Help, help me!" but he only heard an exhaled whisper and felt bits of thick mucus on his tongue. He tried to reach out to one of the people kneeling over him, but his arms barely moved. He felt as if he were a boxer who'd been knocked to the ground and the referee had begun to count. He knew what he needed to do—just get to his feet before the count reached ten—but his feet wouldn't move. As he struggled to understand what had happened, his mind was filled with curiosity and surprise rather than fear. Finally, he willed his foot and his hand to move. Eve held his hand in hers, and he squeezed it with his fingers.

"Squeeze my hand harder," she said.

He tried, but his fingers barely moved.

"Come on Barry, squeeze," she repeated.

He wanted to squeeze, but he liked having Eve hold his hand. He worried that she would loosen her grip if he squeezed harder. She had been angry when she left him behind along the trail, but now that was all forgotten and she was showing that she cared. Barry felt time stretching out as he lay on the floor. It could have been minutes or hours. He had no idea. He lay there against the door, smelling the leather and rubber from the shoes of the three Germans, two Danes, Andrew, and the three Africans who all stared down at him. He tried to move his legs, and they moved back and forth like a scissor kick in swimming. He could feel the soreness in his ankle where the door had struck him. As he stared up at the ceiling, he noticed the odd patterns of swirls, dark circles, and lighter triangles, probably from successive episodes of water damage to the roof over the years.

"Oh my God, what's wrong with him?" whispered Eve. Barry felt her tears drip down onto his hands and shirtsleeves, creating little stains like the water damage on the ceiling. The tears reminded him that people were just bags of water and Eve's tears seemed like a gift to him, almost like she was giving him blood. He noticed how lovely her face was, the tears reflecting the light and revealing the concern she felt for him. The tears meant she cared; maybe she loved him. It also occurred to him that maybe she thought he might die, and the tears were for grief and loss. He shook his head to give a signal to her, even if he could not make a sound.

"I think he just fainted," said Andrew. "The door edge hit him in the leg. Maybe the shock of the pain and dehydration was too much. He's starting to wake up. Look, he's shaking his head."

"Give him air, give him air!" shouted Klaus, waving his hands. His voice was deep and authoritative even if his accent and pronunciation were off, and everyone who had clustered around Barry moved away a few inches. Klaus stretched out his fingers and long arms, like paddles pushing against the crowd.

Barry began to move his head from side to side as his muscles awakened, and then he sat up, which seemed to activate the group. Eve let go of his hand, and Barry felt himself levitating as he was lifted to his feet by several pairs of hands. "Wow, what happened?" he said.

"I think maybe you got dehydrated. Then the door slammed against your foot. It must have scared you, and you fainted. Or maybe it was the pain from the door. How do you feel now?" said Andrew.

"My leg's sore, but it's getting better. It felt like an electric shock all through my body when the door hit me. I'm breathing a little better, but I still feel like I can't get enough air." Barry watched the group's circle begin to break apart as the crisis seemed over. He liked being the center of attention, but he also realized that it was really the mountain that was the center of attention; it was what everyone wanted to discuss, and why they were there. Who would make it to the top, who would give up? He understood that he had been a diversion and now it was time for them to focus on the climb to the top. It was something he'd wanted to do with Eve, the two of them standing together, a picture from the peak that he would send to his family and hers. A signal of triumph together. But as he stood on his cramped legs, each breath an effort, he wasn't sure he would be going anywhere except perhaps to sleep.

Klaus and Rolph, the two strongest men in the group, helped Barry limp to a cot. Barry felt Klaus's hand under his

left armpit, and Rolph had an arm around Barry's chest, allowing Barry to put his right arm on Rolph's shoulder. He could
smell the dampness on their clothes and the sweat on their
arms and hands. When Barry reached the wood slab covered by
his sleeping bag, he sat down and found a comfortable position
leaning against his backpack and the cabin wall.

Salaam came over to check on him. "How are you, Mr. Barry? You should rest now. This may be mountain sickness. Take
tea and rest," said Salaam. "I will get tea for you. I'm sure you
will feel fine soon. This is quite common."

⋇

Andrew was not so sure. There was something about the way
Barry was breathing and the blue tinge of his lips that frightened
him. He had seen this kind of rapid breathing, reminiscent of the
panting of a dog, from patients in the hospital. Severe asthmatics
and pneumonia patients would breathe fast like this until their
muscles tired out and they were placed on oxygen or a ventilator.
But they had no oxygen or ventilators in this mountain hut. They
did not even have electricity or heat. The hut was barely more
than a wooden box with a tin roof, with hard wood ledges for
sleeping bags along the walls and some canvas cots in the middle.

Andrew found an unoccupied wood ledge and rolled out his
sleeping bag. He was not hungry. His head pulsated with pain;
he laid it slowly back on a rumpled shirt and closed his eyes
to rest. A few moments later, Klaus and Kara came over to him
carrying a cup of tea and a bowl of beef soup.

"Would you like dinner?" asked Klaus.

"I'm feeling a little nausea," said Andrew. He tried to smile
at the Danes to show them that he appreciated their effort and

consideration. They were a cute couple, perfect for each other, like matching salt and pepper shakers, and he was grateful for their concern even if he would have preferred to be left alone to rest his eyes. "And I have a headache. I don't think I can eat," Andrew added.

"You should drink tea," said Kara. Her voice carried an edge of maternal authority that surprised him and convinced him to at least try the tea. He took the tea from Kara and sipped it slowly. As he swallowed, the warm liquid seemed to open his throat for more, and he felt a thirst that he had not noticed before. Kara and Klaus looked at each other and smiled as one gulp followed another, as if to say, "I told you so."

"Thanks. I didn't realize that I was so thirsty," Andrew said.

"Yes, it was in our instruction pamphlet to drink tea. We leave for the summit at midnight," said Klaus. "Do you want to walk with us?" Klaus shook his shoulder-length hair as he spoke, and Andrew imagined that Klaus and Kara could have been brother and sister, with their similar hair, fair skin, and ruddy cheeks. Andrew found Kara's sincerity and innocence endearing and unexpectedly attractive as she kept staring at him and smiling. If she had not been married to Klaus, he might have imagined she was flirting and he might have reciprocated.

"I don't know if I'll be able to go any higher," Andrew said.

"But you must reach the summit. We are very close already," Klaus said, "and there is the book at the top for you to write your name. Only those who reach the summit are permitted."

"No. He should rest," said Kara. "And I'm feeling some headache and stomach pains. I think I'm not going to climb to the top. I will stay here with him?" Kara made her statement sound like a question and she stared at Klaus for a moment, waiting for his reaction.

Klaus brought his hands up to his face and held them there, as if he was trying to keep his thoughts from escaping into the atmosphere. "Kara, we have written it all down on our paper. We made a list of everything. We agreed that we will stay together. That was what we decided. I would not want to go to the summit without you," Klaus said.

"I'm feeling cold now," Kara said, and she took off her shoes and guided Klaus to sit next to her on Andrew's sleeping bag. She rubbed Klaus's arm and his shoulder and pulled him close. Klaus turned his head toward her, the surprise on his face replaced by a broad smile as he enveloped her in his long arms. Kara closed her eyes for a few seconds and let her head fall back on Klaus's shoulder. Then she said, "And anyway, I don't think that Barry and Eve will be climbing to the summit either. We will have a nice group here."

Andrew followed Kara's gaze to where Barry sat. Eve was walking back and forth in front of him, chewing on the fingernails of one hand as she twirled her hair with the other.

⊁⊀

Eve could feel each of Barry's breaths shake his body like the rumble of a train. Even the floor was shaking when he coughed, and there was an odor of stale blood with each of his breaths. She looked at the others in the room and wondered what they were thinking. The Danish couple were sitting with Andrew, looking intermittently in her direction. They were probably judging her deficient because she had abandoned Barry on the last part of the hike and gone on ahead without him. They did not know how much pain she was feeling from her backpack and her hiking boots. And now, with Barry worse and the cabin so cold, everyone was suffering and worrying. This problem with Barry was not part of the plan for the climb, and it was disrupting the mood in the cabin.

The truth was, she had no idea what to do. It was not something she wanted to admit, because she was usually the person in a group to provide answers and reassurance. As the oldest child in her family, Eve's brother and sister had always counted on her to deal with bullies at school and negotiate with their parents about punishments. In college, Eve was the dorm advisor and treasurer. But health issues had always been her weakness. She had never been a good nurse to her brother or sister when they were sick. There was something about illness that terrified her, as if a demon took over the body and would not listen to reason. When her mother had her gallbladder removed, Eve would retch when she cleaned her wound dressings.

Perhaps that was why she found herself gravitating to Andrew. He could protect her from the responsibilities that overwhelmed her—that almost infected her with the symptoms of the person she was entrusted to care for. Andrew was in medicine, and she hoped he would be willing to take some responsibility for Barry's health. Andrew was the only person in the group with no connections to anyone else.

In fact, Eve was intrigued with Andrew and curious to know more about him. And he seemed interested in her. Their brief conversations over the past two days, as they occasionally walked together up to the first hut and later to the second, had piqued her interest. He cared about people and so did she. But his type of caring was more personal, more curious about individuals and their physical and mental health. Hers was more general, about how societies and communities can create the best lives possible for their members by working and making decisions together.

If Barry had not been beside her, she would have been able to investigate the origins of Andrew's ideals and share her own with him. And there might have been an opportunity to create the spark of excitement as their ideals converged. But Barry seemed to perceive Andrew as an intrusion, and kept interrupting the conversation with personal questions that cut Andrew out of the discussion. And so, during those brief times with Andrew, she'd limited opportunity to probe beyond the superficialities of his college and medical school life or his preparations for mountain climbing. But now, the calculus had changed, and she needed Andrew's help.

Eve noticed how Andrew had been staring at her when he thought she was not looking, and he was not unattractive. He had an almost angelic face, with curly ringlets of auburn hair and innocent hazel eyes that would dart away and avoid hers anytime their eyes met. He was small, quiet, and thoughtful, and would not be someone that most people would notice. But she liked the intelligence and competence that radiated from him when he spoke, even if he could border on arrogance. She could feel his mind struggling as he looked over at Barry and at her. Was there something he knew that he would not tell her? When his gaze met hers, she could feel his anxiety and vulnerability just before he looked away. She wanted to signal to him, but he turned his head and quickly engaged in a conversation with the two Danes.

Eve twisted her hair into knots, a habit from her childhood that she had long ago broken except in moments of extreme stress. She was watching Barry lean forward with his hands on his knees and look up at the ceiling. It was a posture that seemed unnatural, and Eve worried that Barry was really getting worse, not better, unlike what Salaam had assured her.

Eve rubbed Barry's neck and back to reassure him that she was still there, reflecting on how she had originally hesitated to go on this mountain climb and how she usually trusted her instincts in such matters. She'd never had confidence in her physical prowess, and if she took risks, they were usually of a psychological rather than a physical nature. She felt confident in her ability to judge people, their reliability, and the truth of their commitments and values. She was not afraid of looking inside her own mind through meditation or with a little help from literature, psychology, or the occasional psychedelic stimulant. But her friends and family would never have imagined her climbing any mountain—let alone the highest mountain in Africa.

In fact, she would have preferred a visit to a game park with Barry to see zebras and giraffes and maybe a lion or two from the safety of a Jeep, followed by dinner and comfortable hotel accommodations. She would have been interested in learning about the park's ecology and the politics and economics in the protection of its endangered animals. But Barry had been so enthusiastic about the climb that she eventually warmed to the idea. She even began training with some of the children in the village where she was a volunteer teacher and adviser in the elementary school. The children would run along the dirt paths and up the hills with her, yelling, "Haraka, Haraka!" in Swahili, and she would plod along in her sweats for twenty minutes.

She had read about the various climates on the mountain and the vegetation, birds, and animals they would see. The trail was supposed to be well-worn, with no risk of falling off a cliff. It was just a long uphill walk, and there were huts to rest and sleep in along the way. She imagined heat and a nicely made-up bed in the huts. Even when such dreams had fallen short, she'd remained optimistic that the trip would be an adventure for them both. And though there were warnings in the guidebooks about the altitude causing headaches and pulmonary edema, she assumed those were problems for older people who were in bad physical condition to begin with, not Barry or her or any of the other young people in the group. But something serious was happening in front of her. Barry's illness was becoming a crisis. The adventure was escalating with terrifying speed and becoming dangerously real in ways she never imagined.

She still did not feel that she knew Barry very well, even though they had been in the Peace Corps together in the same region of Tanzania for the past two years. But she thought Barry was interesting and good-looking, and he had graduated from Stanford. He had a sense of humor and made her laugh, and had a twinkle in his eye at times that suggested an openness to adventure. Even though they hadn't yet spent much time together, and had only kissed, she felt that she could trust him, and there was potential for this adventure to lead to more intimacy.

There was something else about Barry that Eve had observed, during a health fair at her village six months ago when they first spent time together. It was a little thing, but it felt like a message. The health fair was organized by a group of volunteer doctors and nurses from Sweden—all blond, sweaty, overweight, and complaining about the heat and the dust. But the Swedish volunteers had a sincere concern about preventing infections in children. They'd come to identify malnourished children and vaccinate them against tetanus, which still afflicted people in the rural area of the country. Eve had been recruited to help with translation, and give explanations to the families about why the doctors and nurses needed to weigh the children and give tetanus shots, and how to use the infant formula and vitamins that the Swedes had brought.

Barry had accompanied the Swedes, picking them up in a Jeep in Dar es Salaam and driving the three hours over dirt roads to reach the village where Eve worked. The first Eve knew about Barry's involvement in the project was when she saw Barry carrying supplies from the Jeep into the converted school building. But there was so much chaos, with children crying and parents asking questions, that Eve had barely been able to do more than wave to Barry as he passed by.

Just after the first children were admitted into the school building for an examination by one of the Swedish pediatricians, an African woman, with a blue-and-black kanga draped over her shoulders, came running to Eve screaming that her boy was missing. The woman was darting about, looking under tables and inside tents and calling out the boy's name. All of the registrations stopped, and villagers along with Eve and the other volunteers began searching for the five-year-old boy named Daudi. "Daudi, Daudi, wapi Daudi?" There were stories of children being stolen, and there was a mistrust of foreigners, so Eve could feel the tension growing as the minutes passed.

Suddenly, Barry appeared, walking toward the school building with a little boy who was crying softly. The boy looked to be about four or five, with thin arms and legs and a protruding belly. He was holding Barry's hand as tears rolled over his ebony cheeks, but he seemed more curious about Barry than frightened. "He's afraid to get his shot," Barry had explained to Eve. "He ran away. I found him crying over by the soccer field when I was unloading the Jeep. At first he was scared of me, but now I've reached the level of a pet dog—a curiosity and a diversion. Soon I'll be his best friend." At that point, the boy's mother rushed over, muttered some curses, and scooped the boy away from Barry with a frightened look on her face. But the boy never stopped staring at Barry as his mother dragged him away.

What Eve remembered was how entranced the boy had been, and Barry's sheepish grin as he stood in the center of all of the chaos. Eve had smiled back at him, grateful for his miraculous appearance with the boy and the excitement he'd contributed to the day. Barry had been so calm and embarrassed at suddenly being thrust into the spotlight as a hero. There was no swagger, no machismo.

Later, as they sipped Cokes together, after the children had all been vaccinated and all the families had left, Barry took her hand in his, traced her palm with his finger, and suggested he could see a line in her hand that was the route for a safari they could take together. She laughed and felt a chill of excitement, imagining being able to let go of the hypervigilance of being a foreign woman alone in Africa, and relaxing enough to do something wild and even a little dangerous knowing that Barry would be there with her. That was when they began to plan to take a vacation together, and when she realized her whole body was feeling alive and tingling as she imagined being with Barry.

When she kissed him, she felt a passion that had been missing from her life during her time in Africa. Later, they became confidants and discussed plans about where they would go when their Peace Corps commitment ended in a few months. Barry encouraged her to move to San Francisco, where he lived, to explore her ideas about community development. She did not immediately reject his suggestion, though it seemed like an unrealistic fantasy.

This adventure of climbing the mountain together was what Barry had divined on her palm. She had been enjoying her solitary life in Africa, but was feeling like it might be the right time to open herself to a new relationship. At the start of the climb, she had been feeling a bit rusty and unsure of herself in the presence of a group of climbers from all over the world, many of whom had known each other for years. Barry was patient with her, but she could sense that he had been anticipating more between them. She was waiting for the right moment that would move them beyond their initial kisses and caresses. But now, all of that was replaced by her responsibility to help Barry, since the Tanzanian guide seemed unprepared or unconcerned about the gravity of the situation. She wanted to help him, but she had no idea what he needed or even what he was thinking.

Barry's mind was a jumble of sensations and fragments of dreams. His chest ached as he tried to breathe and there was so much phlegm that he had to concentrate on clearing his throat and getting enough air. These were not things he usually had to do consciously. He hadn't ever considered his breathing when he slept. Part of him wanted to just go to sleep and see if the natural healing capabilities of his body would activate. Maybe he'd sleep and wake up refreshed, or at least breathing better.

He tried to distract his mind with images of places or people that might help him sleep. He thought about Lake Tahoe and the family vacation there five years ago, when his family stayed at the Stanford summer lodge. The turquoise water surrounded by mile-high mountains shimmered, and seemed to be clear all the way to the bottom. He and his brother had taken two girls who were also there with their families on a hike to a small alpine lake. They had gone skinny-dipping in the freezing cold water and then sat on granite rocks in the sun, warming their bodies.

The image of those girls lying nude next to the pure, clear lake like mountain nymphs usually helped him drift off to sleep, but not on this night. Barry began gasping for air and turned his head to Eve. Her eyes were open wide, intensely staring at him, and he could see his gaping face mirrored in them. For the first time in his life, Barry began to think that he might be about to die, and there was nothing he could do about it...no one to call, no one he could pay to carry him to safety.

Chapter 3

S ALAAM HAD SAID that Barry would feel better with some rest, but he was only getting worse. His eyeballs were floating back in his head as if to escape from the sight of his body. As Eve dribbled water into his mouth, he interrupted the flow of water with disconnected phrases: "Okay, I'll try.... No, I can't breathe.... Yeah, just let me sleep.... No—don't let me fall asleep. I'm too cold."

Helga shuffled over to Eve and said, "He is better? Yah?" Her face showed no emotion as she gazed first at Barry and then at Eve.

"I don't know. I don't think so. I'm not very good with sick people," said Eve. "He seems worse to me."

"Yah, I think he cannot climb to the summit. It's bad luck to come so far and not reach summit. Maybe you come with me? Yah, I valk with you?" Helga said. She pulled the corners of her mouth up into a strained smile that revealed a gap between her two front teeth, and shrugged her large, muscular shoulders.

Helga was a personal trainer in Germany, and the hike up to

the top of the mountain was part of a larger plan to use the climb as marketing for the gym she intended to open with Rolph and Helmut and the rest of her team in Germany. She had donors who would help fund the gym and contribute money to a fund for sick children, and the amount was dependent upon her reaching the summit. The investors had promised to pay for the permits and building rentals that were needed. But it all depended upon her success, and the story that she and her team could tell about how their training had prepared them to meet every challenge—and that the gym would do the same for any German man or woman, regardless of age, who joined her exercise program.

Reaching the summit through the ice, cold, and the altitude was Helga's obsession. It was a necessity. She had been dreaming about the summit. Every day, she would ask Salaam about weather and if there would be clouds that might obscure the view at the top. She would assess the fitness of the other climbers as they progressed up the mountain as competition, because she wanted to be the first. But she also did not want any trouble that might slow her down. It was all part of her plan. Barry was not part of that plan, and now his worsening illness was becoming a distraction, a possible threat to the final ascent and a new topic of conversation that could diminish the importance of reaching the summit.

"I don't think I'll go to the top," said Eve. "I need to stay with Barry. Anyway, I have a headache and upset stomach. Thank you for offering."

⁎⟩Ж⟨⁎

The climb to the top had some theoretical appeal to Eve. It could provide evidence to her family that her years in Africa had

toughened her up, that she really could accomplish a physically demanding task. Her father had tried for years to invite her
on summer backpacking trips, but Eve had chosen music camp
or student government camp. Now she wondered if perhaps she
could have learned some skills from her dad that might have
helped her cope with the current crisis. Her dad always knew
how to bandage a sprain or a cut or a burn. For a moment, she
wondered if perhaps she was overreacting, if perhaps Helga knew
more about the high-altitude sickness than her own meager understanding. If Helga was calm and unconcerned, maybe that
meant something. But Eve had only to look into Barry's bobbing
eyes to shake any doubt from her mind.

"Vell, maybe you change. I can take you. Rolph and Helmut
have extra snowshoes. Now you sleep," said Helga as she walked
away back to her cot.

After Helga left, Salaam returned. "How is Mr. Barry? I think
he is resting now?"

"I don't know; he seems worse to me," Eve said. "His breathing is so rough, and he can't even make sense when he talks.
And look at his eyeballs. They're folded up inside his head. And
when I gave him water, he could barely swallow it."

"No, he is not worse. This is the mountain sickness. Very
common with tourists. Soon he will sleep and be better in the
morning. He just cannot climb to the summit. You can go with
me. And we have our porter, Mohammed. He can be here with
Mr. Barry. No worry."

At that moment, Barry shook his head and spit up the water
he had been drinking onto the floor, spattering Eve and Salaam.
"I'm sorry," Barry said, suddenly awake and alert. Eve tried to
brush the water off of her pants and sweater as she strained
to hear Barry speak. "My stomach has a cramp. I'm sorry. You

don't have to stay here with me. I just need to sleep." And he spit up water mixed with yellow-and-pink phlegm onto the floor.

"Now he be better, get out all the bad water," said Salaam as he turned and walked back to the corner of the hut where his sleeping mat and wool blanket lay piled with those of Koba and Mohammed.

⋆)(⋆

Salaam had seen many tourists with mountain sickness during the two years he had been climbing the mountain as a guide. Some of them would vomit and complain about the cold and the noise in the hut. He found that if he followed a schedule, the tourists would calm down. Once the lights went out, they would become quiet and rest.

Salaam explained the plan to Mohammed and his nephew, Koba, who was on his first trip as a porter, as they unpacked blankets and sleeping mats for a brief nap. None of them would sleep for long because they had to prepare for the final ascent. He reminded them that they would need to do a preliminary scouting walk in an hour. They nodded and said, "Yes, Mzee," as if he was an old man and they were his children. He was not really old, just forty, only ten years more than Mohammed, but it showed respect and gratitude for the job he had given them. God willing, there would be tips and other money to share.

A few minutes later, Salaam shut off the kerosene lantern, plunging the hut into sudden blackness. Sounds of snoring and coughing replaced the shadows and light as sensory anchors. Every movement of a body created noises that were accentuated by the loss of light and visual sensations.

※

Eve was startled at the sudden darkness as she drifted into a purgatory between sleep and hypervigilance. She felt Barry's chest moving, and his forehead was moist with droplets of sweat that had appeared suddenly. She felt her own pulse and noticed that it was skipping beats…or was she imagining it? If something happened to her heart, who would help her? Certainly not Helga, who had only the summit on her mind. Not the cousins, Mickey and John. They were collapsed in exhaustion and would be lucky to get back down the mountain. Andrew would help if she asked him, but he was only a medical student.

She had noticed him staring at her chest on the bus that first day, as if he had never seen a woman's breasts. She did not want to encourage his fantasies by coming to him in the darkness. And she knew where he was—next to the Danes, Kara and Klaus. She wondered if there was something going on between them, some kind of strange threesome that Danish morality encouraged, and she found herself feeling a tinge of jealousy in her forced isolation. She consoled herself that such thoughts were at least a diversion from counting Barry's breaths or her own pulse as she sat leaning against her backpack.

She felt her head resting against something uncomfortable in her backpack—perhaps the sharp edges of her boots or her makeup kit. She knew makeup was a stupid idea for a mountain climb, but she wanted to have the option to look nice for pictures at the summit at dawn. Now that possibility was gone, and her makeup was useless weight. She shifted the objects in her backpack, found a more comfortable position, and gradually drifted off into an uneven sleep.

In the dark, she could be anywhere, even home in her room,

in her bed on the second floor of the house where she grew up. The breaths in the room could be those of her brother or sister when they were little and their parents had gone out for a card game or a concert and left her as the babysitter. They would all fall asleep together in her bed, snuggling, waiting for their parents to return, and she would carry or walk each of them to their beds.

Barry's hand reached out to Eve's face. He found her nose and eyes in the dark and then her mouth and ears. She felt his fingers tracing the outline of her face; at first she was frightened that his fingers were seeking her neck and would strangle her. But they continued over her ears and mouth in an aimless loop. "Yes, yes, I'm here," she reassured him, as she understood now what he wanted, just like she had reassured her brother and sister when they reached for her in the night.

Chapter 4

B ARRY COULD FEEL his muscles straining with each breath as he tried to sleep. He could tell Eve had drifted off, and he did not want to disturb her. He wanted to show Eve that he was not a weakling, even though he was losing control of his body and his mind. He had never been sick like this before, except with the measles as a kid. He remembered how the fever and headache drove him from room to room seeking refuge, and how the rash spread over his arms and legs until he rubbed his back against the cushions of the couch in a vain attempt to ease the itching. His mother would cajole him to eat or drink, watch television, and find some distraction, but nothing she offered helped. He remembered the look on her face, the sadness in her eyes, the pallor of her lips. He came to the realization that his mother could do nothing. He had to endure until the sickness passed, and that was what he was doing now.

He tried to close his eyes and find the refuge of sleep, but his body demanded attention to clear the fluid in his mouth and throat. He coughed and gasped to breathe while trying not to awaken Eve. He tried to bring up the phlegm that was choking him and spit it out onto a tissue without disturbing her. Even tissues were in short supply. Eve had solicited what she could from the others in the group when she realized he needed a supply of them. But their toilet paper was all that they could offer, and no one would part with that easily. Only the Danes had come prepared with packets of tissues, and they would soon be used up. Then he would need to use the shirts and underwear in their backpacks or cough into food basins or onto the floor.

When he spit, he tasted the salty blood and mucous on his tongue as it passed through his mouth, and he smelled the blood on the tissue. It reminded him of the blood he would find in his mouth when he played football in high school and banged heads with kids from East Palo Alto who had something to prove about toughness or race or some other thing that he symbolized for them. He swallowed the blood without complaining in those days, just like his parents swallowed the high taxes they would pay for the garbage collectors and firemen and police because it was the police and firemen and trash collectors who had to clean up the drunks, homeless addicts, and beer cans from the streets every night so that in the morning the streets would sparkle in the sun. Life was not fair.

When he went to Stanford, he decided he was done with football. He volunteered in East Palo Alto at a health clinic for immigrants to help level the playing field for immigrant children, so that they didn't feel the need to bloody the faces of people like him. And they would bring him lettuce from the fields where they worked. He liked the women because they would rub his head and make a big deal about his blond hair. They were tough and worked hard and he respected them even if they had broken the law to get into the US. It was a natural reflex to want to get away from poverty. And he encouraged them to be positive and optimistic about their lives.

There were certain reflexes, like gagging, that no amount of positive thinking could stop. He was comforted to feel Eve's hand on his shoulder, to know that she was there with him, and he was going to turn and thank her but he forgot and drifted off, and then he felt her move and stand up. He wondered where she was going. Perhaps to the bathroom? He watched as she walked across the cabin floor to the door and paused there for a moment, looked over at him, and then she opened the door and walked out.

✴✶✴

On the other side of the hut, Rolph and Helmut were too keyed up to sleep. "Do you want to smoke?" said Helmut.

"Yes," said Rolph. He whispered to Helga the plan to go out of the cabin and smoke a joint, and she nodded. She wanted her team relaxed and focused on their climbing goal. She worried that the problems with the sickness and coughing would be a distraction and a sign of bad luck for the final climb in the night, when one slip could lead to a fall and failure for the team. She worried about Helmut, who was prone to anxiety and superstition. A few moments together sharing marijuana might help.

They walked quietly across the floor, past the snoring and coughing emanating from the various cots. Helga cast a brief look at Barry, sitting up in his cot, coughing and wheezing. But she did not see Eve now. She wondered if perhaps Eve had also left the cabin. The possibility that Eve might be outside excited her.

As she reached the door and opened it, a rush of cold air and snow blew into the cabin before they could get outside and close the door. They walked past the outhouse to a level spot that was shielded from the wind. The snow stopped blowing for a moment, and the moonlight revealed the white cone of mountaintop that loomed directly above them. Helmut pulled out the joint and Rolph lit it before the wind resumed. He inhaled, coughed once, and passed the joint to Helga. She took two puffs before passing the joint to Helmut. "Are you ready?" she said to both of them.

"Yes. I have some headache but I am good," Rolph said. "We are so close now."

Helmut coughed. "I have a headache. I don't feel good. Do you think we have mountain sickness like the American?"

"Everyone has a headache now," said Helga. "You're fine. But that American is ill. He has the severe mountain sickness. It is very bad."

"It's bad luck for him," said Rolph.

"We could carry him down," said Helmut.

"Not now. It's too dark. He can wait until the light. After we reach the summit, there will be light. And maybe he will improve, maybe not," said Helga. "We must reach the top and produce photographs. Sign the book. If we don't reach the top, it could be the end of our gym, and there are the investors who are paying us. Anyway, the guide and the porters are responsible." She reached for the joint and inhaled again.

"Yes, it's bad luck for him," agreed Helmut as he took the joint from Helga. They were looking up toward the mountain and noticed Eve walking back from the outhouse. "And bad luck for her too," he added. Helmut called out to her, "Would you like some smoke?"

Eve came toward them and realized what they were smoking. "Oh, no thanks. My mind is already mixed up enough. I'll just watch you."

Helga came over to Eve and put her arm over her shoulder and rubbed her back and shoulders. "You are very cold," said Helga. "I can feel you shiver. You need some massage." Helga continued to rub Eve's back and she could feel Eve relax and begin to yield to her touch, folding her body toward the manipulations of Helga's hands.

"Yes," said Eve. "It feels good. But I have to go back in. I can't leave him for too long." Eve stiffened her back and moved away from Helga. They stood together, looking up at the snow as the moon poked through the clouds revealing the white cone.

As they were looking up toward the peak, they noticed the three Africans walking down toward them. Helga had not heard them leave the cabin.

"Jambo," said Salaam. Mohammed was smoking a cigarette as he followed behind, and Koba was trailing them.

"Jambo," said Rolph. He shook hands with Salaam and they stood together, silently looking up at the summit. Helga was not sure if smoking marijuana was against the rules for climbers and she hid the joint in her hand, hoping Salaam would not recognize the odor.

"We were scouting the trail," said Salaam. "There is plenty of snow, and we need to select the best route so no one will fall. We are training Koba for his next expedition as a guide." Koba walked over to the three Germans and shook their hands. "He's still young, only a high school boy, but already a strong climber," Salaam continued, as if he needed to justify Koba's presence on the climb. Helga nodded and they waited for Salaam and the porters to continue on into the hut. "We will go back in for some rest. You should come in soon. The hike will start at midnight. It will be very steep and icy. You will need your rest."

"Thank you," said Helga. "We will be going in soon. We will be ready."

The Germans nodded in agreement and watched as the three African guides walked over to the door of the hut, opened it, and disappeared inside.

+>IC+

Andrew was not able to sleep. His mind was cycling with questions about the climb that would begin in a few hours, and he could hear Barry's rapid, noisy breathing. When he saw Eve go outside and leave Barry alone, he wondered what she was doing and why she would abandon Barry in such a moment. Maybe she was going to the bathroom or maybe she was too nervous to sleep. Maybe she needed some reassurance, which he could give her. He had wanted to talk with her about Barry and let her know that he was here to help, but there'd been no time. Then he heard Klaus and Kara rustling about in the cot next to him. He wasn't sure what they were doing, whether trying to find a comfortable position on the hard wooden ledge or making love. But whatever it was, the movements were disturbing his efforts to drift off to sleep. He decided to go outside to find Eve and talk to her. He got up quietly and tiptoed to the door.

When Andrew walked into the freezing, black blindness, his eyes had to adjust for a moment and he stood by the door without moving. He gradually noticed a group of people standing and talking. He could hear the Germans speaking in their language and laughing, and then he recognized Eve returning from the outhouse to join the Germans. The Germans shifted their conversation from German into English when Eve arrived. Helga began rubbing Eve's back and shoulders with alternating swirls of first one hand and then the other. He heard Helga say, "You are cold." And then his vision was obstructed by a swirl of snow. He squinted and finally could distinguish the bodies moving in the shifting darkness. The Germans had coalesced into one group and Eve was moving toward him.

Chapter 5

ve was bundled in her parka, and her body had become an irregular, rounded shadow with her head sticking out like the cone of the peak. Eve curled slightly forward as she walked, her arms folded in front as if she was holding a package.

As she came closer, Andrew called out to her, "Eve, it's me, Andrew."

"Andrew. Oh shit, you scared me. It's so dark. I didn't see you."

"Sorry. I saw you over there, talking with the Germans."

"Yes. They were asking me if I wanted to climb to the summit with them tonight. And they're smoking a joint. Maybe the dope would calm my nerves. I don't know. But as for climbing with them, I can't imagine taking one step further up this mountain. I'm dizzy and all I can think about is getting down now. I'm really worried about Barry."

"Yeah, I don't think they realize how sick Barry is."

"I don't know. They don't seem to be feeling the cold or

the altitude either. There must be something wrong with me. I'm not a wimp, but I feel like I'm eighty years old. Each step is a struggle and my head is pounding with every pulse. I don't know, maybe it's psychological. I watch Barry and some of what he's feeling transfers to me. No one seems to care. Do you care?"

"Of course. I was walking with him. I was worried even before he fell."

"So I'm not crazy?"

"Not at all. You're the only sensible person in the whole group. I wish I could be more helpful. But there's not much we can do. He just needs to hang in there."

"All I can think about is getting Barry down." Eve turned and looked up at the snow-tipped summit, and then back toward the lower peak that the group had passed to reach the third hut. "Except for the snow, I would say we're on the moon. That's what it looks like."

"Yeah," said Andrew, "but the astronauts had better communications than we do."

"Mmm. Not funny. We should have a radio for emergencies. But there's no electricity. Even the outhouse is frozen over, in case you were headed that way. There's nothing alive here except us, and barely us. I'm so cold. I can't think straight. I'm usually the one who pulls everyone together with a plan. But all I can do now is complain and make everyone feel guilty. It's the only way to get their attention. Especially Salaam. He's the one who could turn us all around. But he won't. Am I overreacting?"

"No. You're doing the best you can. Barry's just very sick. I agree. We need to get him down as soon as we can," Andrew said.

"Thank you. I appreciate the validation. I'm not a nurse. I've never been good with sick people or the cold. Or heights. Three strikes for me and I'm out, as my dad would say."

"It's hard to be with sick people, even for me as a medical student. It's hard to watch someone suffer and not be able to do anything. But Barry's strong and he's tough. Now he needs to rest. And so do you. We all need to rest. We're exhausted. But look at all of us out here in the cold. I just saw Salaam and the porters too. Everyone is smoking and talking like it's a party. I guess no one can sleep. We're keyed up. Anxious, worried, excited, guilty. It's the top of the mountain and we're so close, we can feel it like a finish line of a race. No one wants to give up. And we don't want to face what's happening inside the hut with Barry because it's not part of what we signed up for. There's a script, and we don't want to change it."

"It's awkward. Barry and I are really just getting to know each other. We're in the Peace Corps in the same region, and we've been friends but we've only just started dating. This was supposed to be our chance to relax, to get to know each other. I guess we're getting to know each other in ways we never expected. When people are sick they need so much, and I just don't know what to do. I'm sorry. I shouldn't be bothering you with all of this." Eve's voice began to tremble. "But I'm afraid he'll die. And I need your help. I'm really scared."

"Yeah, I'm worried too. I've never seen a case of pulmonary edema before, but I read about it. People can get very sick from it, even die. Even young people like Barry." Andrew watched Eve cover her face and wipe away tears, and he tried to comfort her by coming closer and grasping her shoulders. He pulled her toward him. Eve uncovered her face, and their noses almost touched in the darkness. Her eyes fixed on his, beckoning him closer.

Andrew kissed her softly, their lips barely touching, and then he pressed his lips more firmly against hers. He noticed how cold her lips were and how much warmer the inside of her mouth felt as the heat radiated through. He waited to see if her lips would move away, but they remained pressed against his for several seconds before she finally pulled away. "I'm sorry," he said as he released her shoulders and stepped back. They stood staring at each other in the dark as the wind suddenly gusted against the tin and wood of the hut, bouncing off their ears and blocking any chance for more words to be heard.

"What was that?" Eve finally said.

"I just...sorry," Andrew said.

"No, no, it's...it's fine. We're all somewhat muddled. I need to get back to Barry."

Andrew followed her and opened the door. They shuffled across the floor together toward the cots, with his hand guiding her in the dark. "If Barry gets worse, call me," he whispered. Andrew could hear Barry's gasps and wheezes, and he felt Eve's body tremble before she moved away into the darkness.

Chapter 6

VE HEARD THE snores and muffled voices as she returned to Barry. He was still sitting up, leaning forward with his hands on his knees. "Eve," he whispered to her hoarsely.

"Yes, Barry, I'm here now," she said. "I was outside. Are you feeling any better?"

"No. Where did you go?" he asked.

Eve rubbed her eyes. "Oh, just outside to the bathroom. I had to pee," she said.

"I need you to stay with me. I'm sorry. I'm scared," he said. Barry took five more breaths. "I feel like I could die. And no one cares. "

"You're not going to die. And that's not true. Everyone cares about you. We were talking about you outside. They all want to help carry you. Rolph, Helmut, and Helga. They all want to help, but it's too dark. And Andrew cares about you. He walked with you. He wants to help you, but there's no medicine," she said. "It's just hard because it's night and we're up on the top of this mountain. We have to wait until the light. Now, you just need to rest and when you wake up it'll be morning and we can go down. I promise I won't leave you again." Eve began twirling her hair with her fingers and rubbing her eyes. There was nothing more to say.

Eve heard whispers from the cots behind her and the rustling of sleeping bags along the walls. She tried to find a comfortable position on the cot, bending her neck back to find a soft place on her backpack. High-pitched whistles of wind came through the cracks and holes, like the cries of a pack of coyotes. She sat, listening for the silence that would be her signal to sleep, and she would drift off, and then she would be awakened by Barry's spasmodic coughing. After a particularly serious spasm, Eve asked, "Are you okay?"

Barry took five short breaths and then five more, and he began to sob. "I'm sorry," he said. "I'm just so scared."

Eve held him and felt the tears running down her face as she mopped the tears from Barry's cheeks and eyes. "It's okay," she said. "Now try to rest."

She had never held a crying man in her arms. She felt powerful and monstrous at the same time, as if she were violating one of God's commandments: "Women may not hold men who cry." So she imagined Barry suddenly younger, a five-year-old child who needed to be comforted, just as he had comforted the boy at the health fair who had run away. She rubbed his forehead and felt his breathing calm. He seemed to drift off to sleep. She didn't want to move and break the spell that seemed to have given Barry a few minutes of rest.

When she started the trip with Barry, she had expected him to be a confident Stanford grad who'd come to Africa to lose his innocence and broaden his horizons, even experience the same conditions of the native people to better understand them. He'd been so comfortable and caring when they made their plans for the trip, and she imagined the confidence, fun, and spontaneity he'd exhibited previously would continue. They'd have a good time on the hike up the mountain, maybe have an adventure where they almost got lost or almost got chased by a hyena, and afterward they might celebrate their successful escape by sleeping together. But instead, Eve was massaging Barry's scalp and forehead, worried he might die and praying for each breath to be followed by another. Barry filled every dark space of her imagination, except for a corner where Andrew's kiss lay hidden away for later examination.

⨯

Andrew could hear Eve and Barry talking while others around him were sleeping. He pounded the bottom of his sleeping bag, trying to expand the down so that it would create a cocoon where he could hibernate and reemerge a new and better version of himself. He felt a few down feathers escape through the nylon surface onto his hands. They were soft and fragile, like the snowflakes that had been fluttering in the moonlight.

Andrew had watched people in the hospital intensive care unit struggle to breathe. There would be oxygen, and respiratory therapists and bags with masks and someone in charge. But in this corrugated-metal-and-wood box at the top of the world, no one seemed to be in charge of the impending crisis. Perhaps it was all a bad dream that would dissipate in the night. Perhaps the guides had seen it all before and knew how it ended.

Andrew zipped up his sleeping bag and smelled the nylon and polyester and the down filling as he buried his face deep into the soft, cool fluffiness. There were odors that the bag carried—the smoke of old campfires, the food of late-night snacks, the beer spilled during a night of drinking, and the smell of his body and the bodies of girls who had shared a night with him in the bag. He wondered what had happened to them and if they remembered him and realized that he could not remember most of them either, with the exception of Pam, who had been his first girlfriend.

They met during freshman year, and he remembered how they had started off the night with their clothes on in the sleeping bag at the welcome beach party. They had gotten sand in the bag and into their clothes, and eventually undressed in the sleeping bag. Neither one of them actually slept that first night, and he didn't want to ever clean the bag after that night, until Pam insisted a month later. It wasn't long after he cleaned the bag that they broke up. He had always connected the two events in his mind, and had used that experience as an excuse to delay bathing or showering after sex. This sleeping bag had been with him on overseas adventures in France and Italy and kept him warm in youth hostels that had no heating. It knew him better than anyone, his secret dreams of lovers, adventures, visitations by demons, the terrors of darkness—all images hidden in the recesses of memory that could visit him in the night or perhaps rescue him when his mind was racing and bring him sleep.

The kiss he had given Eve was not anything he had planned. Eve's face had come so close to his that he could smell her sweat and breath on his skin. He felt himself pulled closer by some kind of magnetic force out of his control. Their faces fit perfectly together—their lips and noses and cheeks. When they kissed, it was as if a puzzle was now locked in place, and he could not release her. But it was more than a physical attraction. He also felt that they knew each other. He wanted to protect her and he wanted to follow her. His eyes had been open, and he'd studied her. He noticed that her cheeks had small, tan freckles that he hadn't noticed before. Her nose had a slight bump along the bridge, and her nostrils flared as she breathed in through them. Her eyes were closed as she kissed him and her lips fluttered slightly, at first unsure of their commitment to the kiss. He'd felt her lips pushing back against his almost like the undulations of a wave, first the top lip and then the bottom one.

Even if the kiss had not been planned, it wasn't as if she had resisted it. Perhaps she even anticipated it. His mind turned over the kiss like a surgical specimen with clues about the prognosis of a disease. Was it a test? Like tasting a new food and then deciding if you would taste it again? Or some random event, like a seed that falls from a tree and could land on grass or on a table? A random event that would determine their future. Would the seed germinate and grow? How was he to know? The question lingered in his mind until he felt the sleeping bag carry him away past the old campfires and the summer songs and begin to warm his shivering arms and legs.

Salaam was resting as he prepared for the ascent to the summit. He tried to remember the names and faces of the tourists, but to him they all looked the same, so how was he to attach a different name to so many duplicate faces? He was supposed to remember each one and their home countries and even something about the country, like the biggest city, a few words in the language, or the kind of food they liked—pizza, hamburgers, beef stew. That was what the other guides suggested would yield big tips, and everyone needed tips because otherwise the salary was too low. Salaam had his wife and three little children to feed, and their small piece of land was not enough. He had taken on the guide job even though it meant leaving his wife and children for one week every month and having to take care of the foreigners.

He noticed how the foreigners would become easily lost on a trail and veer off in the wrong direction, even though there were footprints and signs that provided obvious direction, even for a child. That was what they emphasized in the training: The Mzungu is like a child. Even worse than a child. You cannot assume that they can do anything correctly, and just like a child, they will complain about being tired and thirsty and hungry and want someone to carry their backpack and eventually carry them up to the top of the mountain. This was why they required a guide.

The guide had to remember that the foreigners were also like a herd of cattle. They were his valuable property and would feed him and his family, but at times he would need to force them to walk when they wanted to rest, and drink water when they wanted to sleep. And he could not let any of them become lost or injured. The greatest danger was during the climb to the summit, when the tourists might stumble or collapse from exhaustion.

Salaam was worried about the climb to the summit. But he was also worried about the sick tourist, Mr. Barry. Salaam had seen other tourists with mountain sickness improve with a few hours of sleep. He hoped that would be the case for Mr. Barry. But there was something different that worried him. Something in the blueness of Mr. Barry's lips, and the sound of his breaths, that Salaam had not experienced before. And because of that, he could not sleep.

Chapter 7

NDREW TRIED TO sleep by melding the noises of snoring and coughing into images of water rushing over gray rocks in a stream sparkling in the sun. He drifted away into sleep, then woke up and had drifted off again when he was awakened by a flashlight shining into his face.

"Andrew, Andrew, wake up," Eve said.

"What? Who...Eve? What's wrong?"

"It's Barry. He's coughing up blood. He can't breathe," she said. "Could you come over and look at him?"

"Okay...Okay. I'll be right there," Andrew said. He pulled himself out of his sleeping bag quietly, pulled on his pants, and noticed that only two hours had passed since he lay down to sleep. There were still three hours to go before they would get up and begin the final ascent through the snow to the top to see the sunrise and gaze a hundred miles in every direction. His head ached, but it was less of a throbbing. Now it was more of a dull pain in the back of his neck and behind his eyes. All around him, the hut was dark and cold and there were various sounds of snoring, mumbling, bodies moving, coughing, and whistling wind. In the dark, Andrew could not remember where Barry and Eve had been sleeping or the medical questions he should be asking. Eve grabbed his shoulder and directed him with her flashlight along the wood plank floor, past one bed and then another.

Andrew could hear the gurgles of air and water passing through Barry's clogged throat as he got closer to where Barry crouched on a cot, rocking forward and backward, holding his knees with his hands. The shaky light from Eve's flashlight revealed clusters of translucent bubbles of pink froth that had dripped from Barry's mouth onto his sleeping bag. Barry's forehead was drenched in sweat, and his eyes alternated between a prayerful upward gaze at the ceiling and an anxious scanning of the room. Andrew felt Barry's pulse; it was irregular and too fast to count. His shallow, rapid breaths were barely moving any air through his congested lungs.

Andrew knew that Barry was worse, even if he did not know why or what to do about it. The only solution seemed to be to get Barry down the mountain to a hospital immediately, where he could receive oxygen and perhaps drain off the excess fluid flooding his lungs. But it was the middle of the night and they were at the top of the highest mountain in Africa, with no way to get down except to walk.

"Barry? Barry, can you hear me?" Andrew whispered to see whether Barry could talk.

Barry nodded.

"I think we need to go down. I think you have mountain sickness—pulmonary edema. It's very serious. It's getting worse. That blood that you're coughing up is from your lungs. You could die if we don't go back down now."

Barry nodded. He was too breathless to speak. The hut was dark except for the flashlight in Eve's hands that provided glimpses of the others in the hut, sleeping or turning over on their cots. Andrew wanted to wake everyone up and explain the situation, but he hesitated. He was not really a doctor, and he might be wrong about his diagnosis. "It's dark now...probably darker than before...the middle of the night. We probably need to wait 'till there's light. Then I'll help carry you down. Is that okay? Can you make it till morning?"

Barry nodded again.

Andrew realized that Barry was too out of breath to talk or think clearly. He looked over at Eve. "What do you think? What should we do?"

"I...I don't know. I'm sorry. I don't feel well...at all myself." Then she vomited on the floor near Andrew's feet. "Oh, excuse me," she said. "That was...disgusting." Andrew bent down to help clean up the vomit with a paper towel from his pocket. "Okay, I feel a little better," she said. "What was it that you were asking me?"

"About taking Barry down now. His lungs are filled with fluid and blood. He has pulmonary edema and we need to get him down, but maybe we should wait. I don't know. I don't know if he can make it 'till morning." Andrew was beginning to feel the same type of anxiety that he had felt in the African obstetrics ward where he was in over his head, but here there was no one else to help him.

"If he really needs to go now, then we should find Salaam and tell him," Eve said. "Maybe he has some oxygen or maybe he can call someone. Maybe he has a radio that he's hidden away. Or maybe they carry little cans of oxygen for an emergency? Let's go talk to Salaam," Eve said, and she began rubbing her forehead and her eyes.

"Why don't you stay here with Barry. I'll find Salaam and come right back," Andrew said. He walked through the hut, pointing the flashlight at the cots, the walls, and the floor, looking for Salaam and the African porters. The narrow flashlight beam cast shadows that made everything on the floor look like boxes and piles of clothes.

Salaam, Koba, and Mohammed lay huddled in the corner of the hut near the door. They were sleeping on the floor on mats and blankets. Parts of three dark bodies poked out from olive green wool blankets, first an arm on one side, a leg on another, another arm.

"Salaam, Salaam," Andrew said, "we need some help." When no one stood up, Andrew began shaking the bodies. One of the figures began to move under the blankets, and then Salaam was standing in front of him. "Salaam, we have a big problem with one of the people in our group," said Andrew. "It's Barry. He can't breathe. I think we need to take him down now. We need your help."

⇥✹⇤

Salaam yawned and shook his head. This was not what he had been planning, but it was what he had feared. To put the fear out of his mind, he'd been imagining the hike up the last part of the mountain in the cold wind and the final burst up to the top with the hugs and celebrations, the signing of the book, photographs, the descent back to the hut, and a breakfast before they would continue down to the second hut. This problem was not part of the plan.

The tourists wanted to reach the summit. They had all paid

for the complete trip. He knew of tourists who got sick on these climbs. Some would have headaches; others would be too tired. That was to be expected. There would always be a few who would wait in the hut while the others continued the climb through the snow to the summit. But Salaam had never heard of taking a foreigner back down the mountain in the night. That would be dangerous, and what would he do about the others who wanted to complete the hike?

Salaam moved to Mr. Barry and looked at the man's face in the orange glow of the flashlight. He could see the sweat covering the man's pale forehead and the blue color of the man's lips. Salaam had seen a similar look on the face of his uncle just before he died from malaria, and he had seen it in the face of a man killed on a bicycle by a bus. An animal in the jaws of a lion had such a look before it died.

"Mr. Barry," Salaam said, "you are not well. Your friend has informed me that you wish to go back. But as you can see, it is night, and it is not possible to go back in the night. There are no lights and it will be very cold. There is ice on the trail. You must rest here until the morning. By that time, the others who wish to climb to the top of the mountain will return, and they can help you walk or carry you if you cannot walk."

Salaam felt satisfied that he had found an acceptable solution. He was preparing to turn and go back for some more rest to prepare for the hike to the top. But the American woman, Miss Eve, began to argue. Salaam had enjoyed watching how she walked, with a strong, upright posture like an African woman carrying a jug of water on her head. Most white women walked hunched over and would never have been able to balance anything on their heads. But Miss Eve had an African posture, and she spoke out even though there was a man who had already spoken for Mr. Barry. Her speech was like a strong pepper spice that burned his mouth and made him sweat.

"I don't think Barry will be able to last until the morning. If we wait here, it will be too late. He could die," said Eve. "And it will be your fault. You're the guide."

"Ah, but Miss Eve, there are others who have come so far for this climb of Kibo to reach Uhuru Peak. They come to cure a sick parent or to fulfill a pledge to God or a pledge to a charity or to see the future. We do not know who will reach the top or who will fulfill a pledge. We do not ask them. That is their destiny. They will write their names in the book and their words to the gods. I cannot deny them their destiny," Salaam said, using the words that guides memorize in their training.

"I think we should talk to the others in the group. Maybe they would be willing to change plans. Maybe if we all went back now together, we could use the lights that you would have used to hike to the summit. I think that if you explain to the group how serious the problem is, they would all agree."

"Yes, Miss Eve, you seem very worried," said Salaam, "but I can assure you that Mr. Barry will be safer if we wait until the sun will rise. But if you wish, we can discuss this with the others."

Salaam had never heard of a group meeting in the middle of the night. It would disturb the sleep of all of the climbers who were preparing for their final ascent, and then if they failed to reach the summit, they would blame him for the interruption of their sleep and the disruption of their concentration. Guides were in charge, but they also had to be responsive to the clients. Salaam thought it would be unfair to the foreigners who had paid a high price to reach the summit to return now. Besides, all of the foreigners had signed an agreement at the beginning that the hiking company was not responsible for illnesses or injuries. And yet, he was also thinking of the look on Mr. Barry's face, and the strong voice of Miss Eve and her excellent posture, so he agreed to convene the group.

※

Eve and Andrew walked through the hut, shaking sleeping bags until a head poked out, shining a flashlight into their faces and explaining that there was an emergency. There was a rustling of sleeping bags and a mix of German, English, and Danish filled the room as the group assembled in a circle of cots in groups of twos and threes. Barry was in the center, sitting up and gasping for air. Salaam began the meeting. "I am very sorry to awaken all of you in the middle of the night before the final climb. But we have an emergency that we must discuss. As you can see, Mr. Barry is very sick. He needs to go to the hospital. Mr. Andrew is a medical student and he can explain this problem to you."

Andrew looked at the group. He had walked with each of them on the three days they'd climbed from the jungle, up through the trees and grasslands, to the barren volcanic top. He knew that, for each of them, the summit had a special meaning and that he was going to ask them to abandon that goal. But he was going to offer them something more important—the chance to be a hero and save a life. He needed to be clear and confident in his advisement, even though he had no experience with high-altitude illness.

He cleared his throat so that his voice would come out with a strong, resonant tone. "I'm not a doctor. I'm a second-year medical student. But I think one of our group has become critically ill with pulmonary edema. He has fluid in his lungs. He's spitting up blood. He may die if we don't take him down to the bottom. At first, I thought that maybe we could wait until the morning. But when I looked at him a few minutes ago, I realized we need to take him immediately. I don't think he can wait. That's why I woke you all up—so we could decide if you're willing to carry him back down now instead of going up to the summit." As if on cue, Barry produced bubbly pink froth that he coughed into a napkin for everyone to see.

Several conversations began in different languages at different parts of the circle. Helga got to her feet. Her voice was loud and high-pitched. "How are you certain of the man's condition? You are not a doctor."

"No, I'm a medical student."

"Have you ever treated anyone with this condition before?"

"No."

"And yet you are certain that he must be taken down tonight? If he can rest tonight, we can take him in the morning. If we carry him in the night, we can fall and then we can all be injured. I think we should wait until the morning. That is safer."

Salaam got up and nodded. "Yes, it is much safer in the morning. In the night is very difficult."

John, one of the British cousins who had been sitting silently, got up, and Andrew was surprised to hear him speak. He had a round face with curly brown hair and a small, pointed nose. He was from Newcastle, England, and worked in a tavern. Andrew knew that he and his cousin Mickey, from Australia, had saved for this expedition for the past three years. John's voice cracked as he began to speak and he apologized, "Sorry, sorry. I'm not much for giving speeches. Mickey and me, we're probably the two least fit blokes among you and we're not even capable of any further climbing up to the top. We can see our mate,

Barry, here breathing hard and we want to help. But we are too exhausted ourselves to be of any use tonight. We're sorry, but it will be up to those who are most fit. So, they should decide. We'll come along with whatever the group decides." Mickey stood up next to his cousin and nodded in agreement.

Eve stood up. "Look, someone needs to make a decision. We can't be debating about this all night. We're all feeling a bit ill, but not like Barry. I agree with John. It's really up to those of you who are in shape and could carry him to decide. I'm not strong enough. So, who is willing to carry him down now?"

Rolph got up from his chair, rubbed his face a few times, and then said, "This is a big problem. We would like to help. But we have come so far, all the way from Germany. We have been training for one year at the gym, and in the field with running and climbing. We are part of a team, and people in Germany have contributed money for the children with cancer in Berlin. But only if we reach the top. I hope you will understand. I think Barry will be okay here. I think so. And then in the morning we will carry him down to hospital. I can promise that."

Helga stood up when Rolph finished. "Rolph is right. Even though I want to help Eve, and I would go now with her and Barry tonight, it is better if we wait until the morning. Yes. I think that is the best for all of us."

Mickey went over to look at Barry. Then he said, "We're spent. That's the truth. John has the runs. He didn't want to complain. He's been shitting his brains out. And my head's about to explode. We'd like to help. But we're not in any condition. Maybe in the morning we'll be feeling more up to it. I think we should try and rest now, even though John said we are willing to go down now if the group decides to do that."

Andrew looked over to Klaus and Kara. Kara was waving her

hands and raising her voice at Klaus. Andrew could not understand the Danish, but he could see the emotion on both of their faces. Klaus listened and shook his head as Kara began to pound her hands. Finally, Klaus bent down and whispered to Andrew, "Kara is feeling sick. She wants me to go down now with you and she can come with the others later, but I cannot go without her."

Kara was almost crying. "I'm sorry. Klaus and I promised we would stay together. We promised our parents before our trip. We are both feeling sick. I want Klaus to go with you now. He is very stubborn. He will not leave me here, and I am too sick to go with you now. You would have to carry me also. I'm so sorry."

Andrew did not know what to do. He had imagined that, after Eve spoke, the group would come together to build a stretcher for Barry that they would all carry. He expected at least Rolph and Helmut and Klaus would volunteer, and perhaps one of the Africans. But now he felt trapped and would have to sit with Eve, watching Barry gasp for air as they waited for the group to leave for the summit and then return to carry him down. Then Andrew noticed that Eve was putting on her down jacket. "What are you doing?" he asked her.

"I'll take him myself if I have to. Damn it. Even if no one else will go. I can help carry him," she said.

"No, no," said Andrew. "I just saw you vomit. You're too sick. I don't think that would be a good idea."

"Why? Because I'm a woman?"

"No, it's not that. It's just not safe. You've heard them. Barry's better off here, where we can watch him, keep him warm, and prepare some equipment for the morning," said Andrew, trying to convince himself as he convinced Eve.

"Just look at him," said Eve. "He's getting worse by the

minute. He's shaking. His fingers are cold and purple. His lips are blue. He's coughing up blood." Eve rubbed her eyes and her forehead, then she vomited again. "Oh shit," she said. "I'm sorry."

Andrew knew Eve was right about Barry. He would probably not survive the night. But the walk back in the dark could be as dangerous as waiting. Maybe even worse. If it was just the two of them, they could die on the trail of the cold, or from falling over a cliff, and that assumed that Barry would even be able to walk. Was he willing to risk his life for Barry? He hardly knew Barry. He didn't even like Barry. From what he could tell, Barry was a spoiled rich kid, a Stanford frat boy who had never faced real adversity. Why would he risk his life for someone he hardly knew and didn't like, someone who was with the girl he had just kissed? But if he was going to be a doctor, this would be what he would have to do. Even for people who were unpleasant or stupid. If it was the right thing to do, that was all that mattered.

Andrew decided to talk with Salaam. He walked past the cots to the corner of the room where Salaam was rearranging his sleeping bag and mat on the floor. "Salaam," said Andrew, "I think we need to take Barry down now. I'll walk with him. But I need you to help me. If you don't help me, Eve will try to come along. And she's sick."

Salaam nodded and scratched his ear. He looked down at the sleeping forms of the two porters. "I cannot leave the others," Salaam said, "but maybe Koba, my nephew, can help you if you are determined to go now. Are you?"

Andrew nodded.

Salaam shook Koba until he poked his head out from his blanket. Their conversation was brief, with one- or two-word responses from Koba, who was shaking his head to clear his mind and twisting his body as he went from sitting to standing. Andrew could smell the smoke from the cooking fire and the rice and meat on his clothes.

⇥✠⇤

Salaam had known Koba since he was a small boy, his sister's youngest son now grown up. Koba had always been the baby, protected by his parents and excuses made for his failures in school. It was not a lack of intelligence but a willful disregard for the rules and completion of assignments. Koba preferred to spend his time drawing pictures or running on the track at school when he should have been studying. Salaam had heard the stories about how Koba would lose things—his jacket, his wallet, even the family cow. What if Koba lost the two Americans? Then it would be up to him, Salaam, to take responsibility and maybe lose his job. But he had also heard how Koba was winning races. He was the fastest boy in his school and he ran up and down the mountain like an antelope.

Salaam's sister had begged him to take Koba along on this climb because Koba needed the money for his athletic training and for the travel to races. She assured Salaam that Koba could be trusted and that he was no longer the irresponsible child that Salaam remembered. But from what he had seen, Koba was only interested in doing the minimum to complete his tasks. He disappeared when he should have been cleaning plates or packing food, leaving the work to Mohammed, who was always going behind the hut to smoke or rest.

Salaam watched Koba move through the hut, picking up clothes and food and stuffing them into Barry's backpack. His movements were sudden and jerky. His hair was disheveled from sleep and his eyes were red from rubbing. Salaam was worried about whether this boy, who had not always been reliable as a child, could guide the two men down to the second hut in the dark. But Koba also knew the trail and the mountain and he had more endurance than any of them. He would have to do. He watched Koba silently move near Andrew and Barry, slip his arms into his jacket, and wait for further instructions.

Salaam shook his head to register his displeasure at the situation to Andrew. He did not like breaking the group up. But he had no choice. "This is a very dangerous plan to walk in the night. It is better to wait until the morning. But if you are certain that you must go now, Koba will lead you. Koba is a strong boy. He knows this mountain well from his training. He can guide the two of you on the trail to the second hut. You can rest there and we will catch up to you. Maybe the lower altitude will be helpful. Maybe not." Salaam turned to his nephew and said, "Koba, can you introduce yourself to Mr. Andrew and Mr. Barry, please?"

Koba came forward and stood next to Salaam. He tried to force a smile and raised his hand. "Habari. Mimi ni Koba," he announced his name simply in Swahili. After a silence of five seconds, he looked down at the floor and then hoisted Barry's backpack onto his shoulders. A few seconds later, he walked toward the door and stood there waiting.

→❏←

With the addition of Koba, the trip down the mountain in the middle of the night was no longer theoretical. Andrew had a porter and a patient to evacuate for emergency care and permission to proceed. But at that moment, Andrew began to have doubts. He was exhausted and cold, feeling the pulsations of a headache and neck pain like everyone else. He asked himself why this problem was his to solve. Why not Salaam or perhaps the entire group? They should abort the summit climb and come with him. But there was no purpose in such argument.

Koba was waiting expectantly. Barry gazed up at Andrew, fighting for each breath as Eve helped him pull on his parka and hat. Somehow, the plan that Andrew and Eve had forced upon Salaam had been put into motion, with little thought about details. Now on the threshold of leaving, Andrew began to consider the risks and the alternatives. But it was too late to stop. It was like diving. Once you climbed the steps and walked out onto the diving board, you could look down for only so long. At some point you had to jump or crawl back down, and no one wanted to do that even if their legs were shaking, particularly in front of a crowd who would remember the moment.

Andrew stooped down to face Barry. "Are you ready to go?" he asked.

"I feel a little better already," Barry said as he coughed up a glob of bloody phlegm.

Eve shook her head. "You'll never make it, just the three of you. I want to come with you."

"No," said Andrew, "you're sick. Koba is strong. He's an athlete. I'm a cross-country runner. We'll be okay."

"It's so cold out there," she said.

"We'll be fine," Andrew said. He was surprised at how easily Eve could be convinced. He wondered if she might kiss him again for good luck, perhaps kiss all of them and hug them, but he dismissed the thought as he watched Eve put Barry's hiking boots on his feet and tie the laces for him. Then she pulled his heavy wool cap down over his ears. Finally, she looked at Andrew. "Where's your wool cap?"

"I have a hood on my parka," he said.

"That's not enough. Here, take mine." Eve started to hand him her blue-and-pink stocking cap and then decided to pull the cap down over Andrew's head herself. Andrew felt her hands trace the contour of his scalp and move down his neck until the cap was covering his ears. He rotated his neck, moving his head in her hands to make sure the cap was secure. "Perfect fit," Eve added. Andrew nodded as Barry got unsteadily to his feet.

The other foreigners, who had listened to the argument for stopping the climb and had rejected it, were now gathered around the three men who were about to venture out into the dark. Rolph began clapping as if he were at a sporting event. First a solitary beat of one pair of hands, the clapping spread like a contagion. Now that it was clear who was going out into the cold and who would remain in the cabin, it was easy to cheer the team on. Barry managed a brief smile as he acknowledged the clapping and took a tentative step. Even Andrew felt a burst of optimism. Only Koba ignored the clapping, slowly stepping forward with Barry's pack on his shoulders containing water, clothes, and food. He pushed open the door, lowered his head, and stumbled forward into the cold night, like a pack animal whose only goal was its own survival.

Chapter 8

WHEN KOBA WAS a child, his mother gave him brown and white beads to wear around his neck to protect him from the spirits that wandered in the dark. His older sister and brother would scare him at night with stories of lions and hyenas, and he would hold on to his beads. Now he had grown five inches in the last year and was taller than his brother and sister. He was a man, no longer a boy. Girls looked at him when he walked by them at school, calling out his name and smiling. But even though he was now taller than his brother and even his father, he still felt for his beads when he stepped out into the night.

He remembered a story his mother told him about a wandering white woman who tried to scoop African children up into her arms when the wind was whistling at night. The white woman would carry the children to a cave, cover them with dirt and water, and take away any memories they had of their families. Koba and his brother and sister would shiver in fright, listening to their mother tell the story as they lay on a mat on the floor of their kitchen.

"You will forget me," their mother said, and they had cried, "No, no, Mama."

"But you will," said their mother. Then she continued the story. "The next day, the children who had been covered with dirt and water woke up from sleep and roots sprouted from their legs, digging into the earth, and leaves grew from their ears."

"We will run away," Koba had told his mother.

"Ah, but the white woman would feed you sweets if you stay with her. If the children did not run away on that first day, they would be become ferns and bamboo, stuck to the ground where the white men and women drove in cars and trucks." Then his mother gave him and his brother and sister beads to wear around their neck to help them remember where their family lived, so that they could run back if ever they were taken by the white woman or the other spirits that wander in the dark. Koba thought about this story when he saw white men and women visiting his school to recruit students for scholarships, and even though he no longer believed the story, it made him hesitant about being too close to whites. Now, as he began his walk on the path to the second hut, he felt his skin shivering with cold and fear to be alone in the night with these two white men.

But Koba also felt some sadness as he watched how the white men walked, with their heads bent down, searching the ground for the place to put their feet. Without him, they would become lost and die. He had heard their conversations as he rested in the hut, and he understood what they said, how they tried to decide whether to go down in the night. He had waited to see what they would decide. He agreed with the plan to go down even though it meant he would be sent out into the night with them, because he could feel the sickness growing in the hut, becoming too big to be contained inside. He would have to lead it outside.

Koba had heard of spirits and animals that hunted in the dark—leopards and hyenas and the spirts of the dead. If some spirit reached out in the dark and pulled him away, these two white men who walked with him would not be able to help. They would watch him struggle and perhaps take a photograph of him as the whites had a habit of doing during their safaris, but they would not help. If the sick American died on the trail at night, Salaam had instructed him to return with the other one to the third hut and leave the dead body on the trail. They would collect it later.

Koba had seen how weak the whites were. He had run races against white boys from the international school in Dar es Salaam, and he had seen how easily they would tire and give up. He could always run past them at the end of the race. He expected that these whites with him now would give up, and he would have to turn around and bring them back up the hill to the hut. Or maybe they would become terrified in the dark and die like cattle surrounded by lions, paralyzed by fear and unable to move in any direction. He would try to help them if he could, but the paralysis of fear was not easily broken.

Koba shone his flashlight on the ground. The light created a weak glow that barely illuminated the trail with its black lava rock sprinkled with snow. Koba's feet slipped on ice as he followed the trail downhill. He moved the flashlight in front and behind and waited, pretending he did not understand the English words when the whites said "wait" or "slow down" or "please." He pretended not to understand, even though he had top scores in his

English studies in school, because he did not want to speak with the whites. He had heard that they could hypnotize Africans with their words. In school, the teachers said that whites captured Africans and made them slaves by speaking words and even singing songs in English. The whites had chained the Africans they caught like animals and whipped them.

Koba just kept walking a few steps and then waiting...walking and waiting...flashing the ground behind and in front with his light...walking and waiting. One of the whites reached out his trembling hand like a ghost and grasped Koba's shoulder and neck, and Koba shook free so that the hand fell away. The fingers of the hand had felt like claws scratching him, about to grab hold of him just like a night spirit might.

As he continued ahead with his flashlight, he wondered why the hand had clutched at his neck. Even as he feared the poisonous touch of a white, he also wondered what they wanted. They walked like holy men on a pilgrimage blindly following his light as if he were an apostle, and Koba was confused enough to wonder if they might actually be men of God. Intermittent gusts of wind were coming from different directions, pushing him from side to side. Koba had noticed how the wind at the top of the mountain would often move in circles at night, returning night walkers back to where they had come from.

⚜

The wind was twisting all of them as they tried to follow the flashlight's glow. Barry slid off the trail onto the scree and ice near the edge. He did not know how far he would be able to walk. His feet felt numb and heavy, and he was not sure where he was putting them. The first few steps were downhill, and he let gravity carry him. Each breath took all of his strength, and he felt that his chest was about to collapse inward from the pressure. He tried to follow the light that the young African porter carried, but the porter was moving the light from side to side too quickly, like a fluttering moth.

Barry would have yelled at the young man, but he had no breath left to speak even a word. He tried to steady himself by reaching out for the young man's back or shoulder, but even that small effort was too exhausting to sustain and the man brushed his hand away.

In the past, so many of Barry's problems could be solved with a clever quip or a fistful of money. But now he could not speak at all and had no money to give away. He could feel his legs moving at odd angles, as if he were skiing, not walking.

→)|(←

Andrew felt Barry's arm clawing at him and slowed his pace to allow Barry to lean on him. Andrew's eyes were still attempting to adjust to the darkness and the blowing snow, and his mind was back in the hut. Andrew could not see the path forward, though he could feel it under his feet. Barry was initially ahead of him, then slowed and fell back behind him, wheezing and coughing. Andrew might have turned back, but Koba was urging them forward with a small flashlight, intermittently illuminating the gravel, black rock, and snow on the path ahead. Barry was taking steps on his own with just an occasional hand on Andrew's shoulder to steady himself, and Andrew did not want to disturb what seemed to be a successful walking pattern.

Andrew walked down the hill trying to find the right pace that Barry could tolerate and still keep up with Koba's moving flashlight. The first ten minutes had been all downhill into the bottom of the saddle before they began to climb again. The third hut had disappeared into the darkness and blowing snow, and Andrew began to feel increasingly optimistic as they progressed along the trail. Maybe Barry would be able to manage as they dropped to a lower altitude and walked down to the next hut. They would stop every few minutes to give Barry a rest and a chance to take more breaths and cough out phlegm.

"How are you doing?" Andrew asked during one of those stops.

"Okay," said Barry, "but my feet are so cold. I can barely feel them. I'm so exhausted."

"Just try to keep going. The more progress we make downhill, the better you'll feel," said Andrew. He decided not to remind Barry that soon the trail would turn uphill as they ascended the saddle on the way to Mawenzi, the lower peak, where the oxygen content would get lower and gravity would pull them back.

⊁⊀

Koba watched for a signal for when to pause, and he shut off the flashlight to save the battery when they rested. It was like the pacing that runners did during a long-distance race. Koba knew that the purpose was to set a good pace that could be sustained and would allow them to reach the second hut without wearing out the sick American man, who walked like a pregnant cow about to give birth.

Koba would pause and listen to the conversations of the two whites. He heard them complain about their feet and the cold. He wanted to tell them to curl their toes and then stretch them out. But that would break his silence, and they would ask him more questions until they hypnotized him with their words. As he waited and listened, he noticed the swirling of snow reflected in the flashlight's glow. It reminded him of flies and mosquitoes around a night campfire in the bush. The snow on the ground was illuminated in the moonlight that occasionally penetrated through the clouds, creating unexpected moments of visibility. In the brief glow of moonlight, he could see both of their faces with mouths gaping open and slits of eyeball visible between their eyelids, tracking him like starving baby birds followed their mother. And he made sure not to allow them to come too close.

>I<

Andrew noticed that Barry was slowing his pace, his head bent and his arm trembling. Barry teetered and veered off the trail for a moment as the clouds covered the moon. Only the sounds of Barry's breathing indicated where he was walking. Andrew felt Barry's hand on his shoulder, probing and seeking reassurance.

"Yeah, yeah. I've got you. It's okay. Keep going," Andrew said.

Gradually the downward slope leveled and the trail began going uphill. This was the part of the hike where they needed to go up past the lower peak that reached seventeen thousand feet. It was a slow, gradual climb, but Koba still paused. "You wish to continue?" he asked.

Andrew was surprised at the words, pronounced so distinctly with a British accent in excellent English. At first he wondered where they had come from, perhaps God? They were the first words in English he had heard from Koba.

"You can speak English?" he asked.

"A little," said Koba, his secret revealed.

There was a silence as Andrew considered the implications of the question. He did not know how to answer, since it was really Barry whose life hung in the balance. Finally, Koba repeated, "You wish to continue, sir? It will be uphill."

Andrew waited for Barry to answer. There was no point in continuing if Barry wished to turn around. Then Barry's answer came in almost a whisper. "Yes."

As Koba began the climb up the steep part of the trail, the flashlight caught parts of the lower peak. Andrew and Barry followed in halting progression, as if held together by an elastic band. Spikes of rock jutted out at odd angles from the trail, poking them in the head and shoulder. The wind pushed them back down the trail while Koba accelerated up the saddle toward the peak, intermittently pausing as the group coalesced again and proceeded up the trail.

Andrew could feel the difference in his own breathing as they trudged uphill. Barry was stopping more frequently, and Andrew stopped with him. First it was after thirty steps, then twenty-five, then twenty. Then ten steps and finally Barry stopped completely.

"I can't go anymore," said Barry. "I need to rest."

"Okay. Rest and we'll get going when you're ready," Andrew said. Barry moved five steps and then stopped again.

"Just leave me here. I can't feel my hands or my feet. I want to sleep. I'm so cold," Barry said.

"No, we can't do that," said Andrew. "We can't stop. I won't leave you. It's just a little farther up the saddle and then we'll be over the top and it'll be all downhill after that."

"Just leave me. Why do you care? You don't even know me."

"We have plenty of time," said Andrew, and then added,

"you're right. I don't really know you. Tell me about yourself."

"Are you fucking kidding?" Barry paused to catch his breath. "We're dying out here. What's the difference? You don't want to know about me. You hate me now, because I'm slowing you down. And because I made you go with me." Barry paused again and took five breaths and then coughed. "No one cares about us. The ones in the hut...they all want to climb to the top. So do you. Why don't you turn around, and you can still make it? And take this freak with the flashlight too. All he does is make me dizzy."

"I'm not going to leave you," said Andrew. "So why don't you tell me something. Where are you from?"

"Oh fuck. What does it matter? I'm from the moon. I'm from Hades. That's what this looks like. We're all going to die here," said Barry.

"No, we're not."

"Okay, I'm from San Francisco...I joined Peace Corps because...because...I didn't know what to do after college.... I guess because...I thought I'd go to Italy...or Spain...but I ended up in fucking Africa...Tanzania.... And that's where...I'll die... THE END."

"What about Eve?" Andrew said.

"Yeah...I noticed...you looking at her...everyone does...even women."

"Really?"

"Yeah, haven't you noticed...that German dyke?"

"You mean Helga?"

"Yeah. Goddamn it." Barry said and he paused and took four quick breaths, opening his mouth into the wind. "I can't breathe...I can't fucking breathe.... And I can't keep up with that guy with the light. He's going to leave us here."

"Calm down. He's just trying to help you. He's waiting. All right? Now take some steps and you'll feel better," said Andrew.

Barry took ten steps and stopped again, gasping. "You're trying to kill me. Both of you. Is that why you're here? Do you think I'll pay you some reward?"

"No. We're just trying to help you."

"You want to show Eve that you're better than me. You're going to push me off the mountain," Barry said.

Andrew wondered if he was hearing the words of a paranoid, crazy man who was not getting enough oxygen to his brain. He should ignore them, but the words stung. Even if they came from a disturbed mind, they still hurt. The truth was that he didn't want to be there with Barry at all. But once the plan had gained momentum, it had carried him along like a landslide, and he could not control it or stop it. Now, as they stood together, teetering, Andrew did wonder if he could continue. The memory of the breech baby that he could not pull free haunted him. If he could not do that, perhaps he did not have the stamina to continue with Barry. Perhaps he did not have the stamina for medical school or to be a doctor. Better to find that out now, before he caused any more damage than he had already.

They stood there for a few minutes as Barry tried to catch his breath. Then Koba came back and went over to Andrew. He pointed to Andrew's backpack and asked him to take it off. Then Koba positioned Barry behind Andrew. He looped Barry's arms over Andrew's head and around his neck in a sort of swimmer's rescue embrace and pushed Barry forward. "You walk and he hold your neck," said Koba.

Andrew took a few steps forward and could feel Barry's weight on his neck and shoulders as he dragged Barry's body forward, Barry taking tiny steps behind him. Koba carried both backpacks looped over his shoulders as they continued up the hill for twenty more steps.

"Whew. That's better," said Barry. "I'm sorry for being a jerk. You're dragging me over this fucking mountain and I'm shitting on you. And that African kid too. I'm an asshole."

"You're just sick. People say things when they're sick... things they don't mean," said Andrew, and he wondered what Barry did believe. Did Barry know that Eve had kissed him outside the hut? Did she tell him? It didn't matter now. Barry had his hands around Andrew's neck.

Andrew looked out at the peak ahead of them, and he imagined death up there on the peak. He wondered how it would be to freeze beneath the lower peak with its slabs of stone slicing into the air. His heart would begin to slow, his body would eventually stop shivering, and he would enter some realm between sleep and death and float suspended for hours before the end would come. What would his last thoughts be? Would there be a sense of peace and acceptance? Would he see faces like in a dream? His parents; brother; sister; former girlfriends; favorite professors; favorite places; foods? Maybe it would be odor that his frontal lobe would notice just before shutting down. Or perhaps profanity might be flashing in neon. That was what happened to stroke victims who lost the ability to speak, except for some profane words buried deep in the subconscious mind. His last thoughts might be, "Shit, fuck, damn."

But he was not ready to die. He had not decided what type of doctor he would be or even if he had the ability to respond in a crisis. He had no idea, and he had to find out before he died. Otherwise his death would just be one more failure, the ultimate failure. He had not even ever fallen in love. He'd only had sex a few dozen times. How could he die without finding his soulmate and the mother of his children? How could he die with nothing meaningful to put on his grave? Just "Medical Student." That was better than nothing, but would not be enough. He needed more time to write a better epithet. If he believed in God, he might be able to convince himself that the voice of God was in the wind, urging him on. He was trying. Really trying with every bit of strength he had. He was trying to do what the African boy had suggested. But the truth was that each step only meant that Barry was still holding onto him, leaning on him, suffocating him.

Andrew could hear each of Barry's breaths and feel the drool down his neck. He had never felt a man so close to him before. It was an odd intimacy to have another body so vulnerable and so spent against his own back and shoulders, as if they were locked in love or deadly combat. Barry's body was heavy and throwing off Andrew's steps. Each move forward reminded Andrew of rescuing a drowning swimmer. He had learned how to perform the swimmer's rescue maneuver in summer camp when he was twelve years old. They told you that when people were drowning, they would do anything to get a breath, even if they drowned the person trying to save them. The first rule in rescuing someone in the water was to keep yourself safe and control the other person. You should never let them squeeze your neck. But Andrew was violating that rule. They moved twenty steps more and rested. How much more could he endure before he would collapse, carrying Barry down on top of him?

>✠<

Koba continued up the hill with two backpacks hanging from his shoulders, stopping intermittently to light the way with the flashlight. He watched the two whites with a mix of curiosity and surprise. He had not expected them to continue so long. Their end seemed inevitable. But now he wanted to see what they were capable of doing before they collapsed. They had to fall, then he would check to see if they were breathing, and after that he would run back to the hut and inform Salaam and Mohammed. But the two whites continued forward.

Koba could not understand what force was holding them up. They were not like the white boys who gave up in races before the finish line. He could see it in those boys' faces before their legs slowed, because they had already decided that the pain was too much. But the faces of these two white men showed no acceptance of defeat. Perhaps there were ghosts walking about, carrying them for some unknown purpose that only ghosts could understand. And if that were the case, he would walk with the ghosts, respect them, and see what they wanted from him.

⇥✳⇤

Andrew had not really considered Koba before they left the hut. Koba had been invisible, like the ropes and ground cloths of the tents where he stayed, and Andrew could barely describe his face or height. He did not even know how much English Koba could speak. Now he realized how foolish he had been to undertake this rescue mission without talking to Koba and learning more about him. Andrew realized that all their lives were connected, and he needed to know more about Koba now. They were three in the equation. If they were to reach the second hut successfully, Koba would probably be the reason. He was stronger than either of them, and he was familiar with the mountain and the places where they could find shelter.

When they rested to catch their breath, Andrew turned and, for the first time, looked carefully at Koba, whose face glowed in the dim light. He noticed Koba's high forehead, narrow eyes. There was an intensity in the way his eyes and forehead fused together. The lower part of Koba's face was smooth, shiny ebony covering high cheekbones, with narrow, thin nostrils above the first wisps of a mustache, and a narrow bowstring of lips over perfectly-aligned ivory teeth. When he smiled, his mouth and eyes sparkled as one. His broad, powerful shoulders and short torso sitting on long, thin legs carried the two backpacks with little evidence of strain.

As he looked at Koba, Andrew wondered why he had not noticed how handsome he was. The fact was, he had not noticed him at all. He knew nothing of what was inside Koba—his heart and his will to overcome the cold and the fatigue. He sensed that there was something powerful, though, hidden beneath the layers of protective surface, something that Koba had not shared during the climb. And just as important as his heart was Koba's mind. Did Koba understand how sick Barry was, that he might die? Andrew wanted to know what Koba was thinking. He tried a few words of Swahili.

"Jambo, Koba, mgonjwa sana," Andrew said, trying to explain that Barry was very sick. Koba nodded. "Yes, I know he is sick. You can speak me in English."

"Good," said Andrew, "because I only know a little Swahili. I learned it in the hospital in Dar es Salaam. Thank you for coming with us. We could not find our way without you. I'm sorry we never talked before we left. Everything happened so fast, and now it's so dark, I can't see the path. How much farther up the hill do we go before we can start to go downhill? I think that will help."

"Not so far," said Koba. "But he is big man. Big body. Too big to carry. If he was cattle we would hit him with a stick and make him move his legs. Maybe that is the only way."

"No, we can't do that," said Andrew. "He's not being stubborn or lazy. It's just his lungs that are too full of water. I think I can keep carrying him."

Koba nodded and they continued another twenty steps. Now Andrew needed the rest almost as much as Barry. Andrew was gasping and could feel his heart pounding. The path had not seemed so rough when they walked it the day before in the light, but now, in the night, there were rocks and ice that made him slide and almost tumble over with Barry's extra weight.

Barry stumbled, lost his footing, and fell on top of Andrew, pushing them both to the ground and almost over the edge of the trail. They lay on the ground, chests heaving and wheezing. Andrew felt the pressure of Barry's weight constricting his chest as he tried to breathe deeply. Barry did not move as they lay on the ground, with Andrew twisting and trying to roll out from under him. Andrew wondered if Barry's immobility meant that he had slipped into a coma.

"Let me sleep," Barry finally whispered into Andrew's ear. "Just for a minute. I feel warm here. Then I will go again. I promise." So, they lay there together, with Barry seeking Andrew's warmth with his hands. "Just one more minute. I'm so tired," Barry said.

"Come on, Barry, we have to go. Just another twenty steps. Get up, you're crushing me," said Andrew as he moved under Barry's weight and felt Barry's resistance holding him down.

"Fuck you, asshole," Barry said as Andrew rolled away, freeing himself from Barry's arms and then yanking at Barry's neck and shoulders to pull him up. "Asshole," Barry muttered as he grasped at Andrew's legs, almost tackling him. Andrew kicked at Barry's hands and arms that were entangling his own feet.

"Now you are kicking him like he was cattle. It's what I told you," said Koba.

"I didn't mean to do that. But he was holding my legs," said Andrew as he pulled Barry up. Barry's arms encircled Andrew's neck again and they walked on another twenty steps and then another, with Andrew dragging Barry behind him. "Come on, Barry. Just take some fucking steps. Don't make me drag you over this damn mountain. Just take steps. Even baby steps. Just don't make me drag you." Andrew felt tears coming out of his eyes as the anger and fear and exhaustion coursed through his body. He could feel himself giving up, just as he had with that baby. He was a failure and he would always be a failure when it most counted. Barry's arms around his neck were strangling him, and he was about to lose consciousness.

"I hate you," said Barry as they began to walk.

Now, Andrew noticed the jagged peak ahead of them in more detail. There were small pockets in the rock that looked like the sockets of two eyes, rectangular and triangular, glowing in the moonlight. Below an outcrop of smooth, black rock could be a long, broad nose, and farther down were two horizontal ridges that could be the lips and the chin. It was the type of cubist face Picasso might have painted.

Andrew imagined the face watching them with curiosity and sadness and he realized that the face was now in front of him. It was Koba's face staring into his eyes. Andrew teetered, almost falling backward as Barry pulled on his neck with all of his weight, and then Koba reached out his hand, helping Andrew regain his balance and bend forward.

"My hand, my arm," said Koba. "Just hold them like a rope."

Chapter 9

K OBA'S PALM WAS thick with calluses and his forearm bulged with muscles. Andrew imagined it was a hand familiar with tools: machetes to cut away bush; shovels to dig irrigation ditches; hammers to pound nails into wood planks; spears to kill animals. Andrew could sense it was a hand that would not let go of anything it grasped.

Andrew felt Koba's strength as their hands connected, like an electrical jolt running through his body. What he felt from Koba was more than the muscles of his hand. There was commitment, power, and solidarity. Koba's hand was an assertion of brotherhood in struggle that would not be broken. Andrew was not sure why Koba offered himself in this way to someone he did not know. Perhaps it was the gravity of the situation or perhaps it was just what Maasai did, because Andrew knew that the Maasai had to depend on each other to survive. Heroism was not a choice; it was built into their genes and their blood. Andrew squeezed back with his own hand to create the bond that Koba was offering.

As Barry and Andrew slid over the snow and dirt moving up the trail, Barry said, "She wanted to come with us. She's a little crazy, temperamental, and unpredictable. It's what I love about her. You know, I've never had sex with her. I sure wish I had before I died."

"We're not going to die. We just need to keep going," Andrew responded, ignoring Barry's provocative comments.

"But if we died, if I die, I wouldn't mind it so much if I'd had sex with her," said Barry.

"Then maybe that thought will keep you going. Something to live for," said Andrew.

"You're thinking of sex with her, too."

"Barry, your mind is messed up from lack of oxygen. I never thought of having sex with her."

"You're lying. I can tell because your breathing just changed. I can feel it with my hands. You stopped breathing for a few seconds."

"When we make it off the mountain, you can tell her how embarrassed you feel about discussing this with me, but now we just need to keep going. If my breathing changed, it's because I'm fucking exhausted pulling you up this hill. I can't catch my breath."

"It's true. I can't think straight. I'm all fucked up. But I can tell that you're thinking about her, too. Actually, I don't mind. When I think of her I feel better. Maybe it's the same for you, so you'll be able to pull me."

"Fine, then go ahead. Think about her. If that helps you walk better. She's worth it."

"You see. You do want her."

"Just walk."

"I can't walk straight. I can't feel my hands or my feet. I'm not even sure if they are my feet. Tell me the truth—are we going to die?"

"Just keep moving your feet. We just have to go a little further up the hill. Hold on to my neck. Koba's helping to pull me now."

"Am I dying?"

"No. We're all going to be okay. Look at Koba. He's pulling all of us like a train engine pulls all the cars up the mountain. Your feet are wheels. Keep moving them."

"Am I dying? Goddamn it. Tell me."

"I don't know."

"Why is that man kicking me? He was in front of us and now he's behind me, kicking me."

"It's Koba. He's not kicking you. He's trying to push you now from behind and then he'll pull you forward like he does with his cattle. Like a cow that won't walk through a gate."

"A cow?"

"Or any animal...a sheep...a donkey. He's trying to herd you over the mountain."

They made slow progress up the hill, closer to the peak and past small caves and pockmarks in the rock face. As they got closer to the top, the wind became ferocious and Barry dangled like a kite attached to Andrew's neck. They might have fallen back, but Andrew was anchored to Koba's arms that now pulled with greater strength to counter the wind. Andrew shook his head to loosen Barry's grasp on his neck and provide a bit of a passage for the air to enter his throat. He made guttural animal sounds, *"Chaaa, gaaa, chaaa."*

Koba went behind them again, and now he grabbed Barry's feet in his hands and lifted as Andrew pulled. They grunted and coughed and Andrew could see what looked like the top of the ridge through the moonlight and dust. He stumbled and heaved himself over the ridge and fell face forward onto the snow and dirt and lay panting as he felt the others pile on top of him. There was the warmth of their three bodies stacked like poker chips. Andrew lost track of the time as he continued to pant. It could have been fifteen minutes or it could have been an hour. He could hear them coughing and breathing above him, and their bodies moved and burrowed into each other. The breathing and the movements of the bodies made him feel like they were becoming one mind, one body, and as if Koba and Barry's thoughts merged with his.

They lay there frozen against the volcanic ash at the precipice, their feet pointed back to the third hut. Their heads pointed down toward the second hut, and more oxygen and more heat, if only they could move toward it. They lay still, just breathing and feeling each other's bodies, their blood circulating between them, and waited. Light from the sunrise illuminated the rocks and the peak and began to warm their skin. It was the moment when the others must have reached the upper peak's summit, seen the glorious view, and written their names in the book and taken their pictures to prove their accomplishment to the rest of the world. It was when Andrew pushed Barry and Koba off his back and they all shuffled to their feet. They could see one hundred miles in every direction from Mawenzi Peak, and they could see the sunlight reflecting off the snow on Kibo.

Chapter 10

OR A FEW seconds, Barry, Andrew, and Koba stood motionless, taking in the expanse below and looming above the third hut where they had been. The snow covering the pink-gray volcanic rock ahead of them merged into light green clusters of bushes. Morning sunlight poked through the clouds, creating intermittent sparkles on the snow and distant trees. In the far distance, brown plains traversed by green strips of river valleys extended all the way out to the horizon.

"Damn," said Barry, scanning the panorama around them. "Where are we? Is this heaven or the top of the fucking world?" When he turned back toward the saddle between the two peaks, a gust of wind forced him to grab for Andrew's arm to keep from falling.

"I've got you," said Andrew. "We're on the second peak."

"Did we die and go to heaven?" asked Barry.

"You're alive. We're all alive. You did it. It's all downhill now," said Andrew.

Another blast of cold wind pushed Barry off balance again. It was only Koba's quick reflexes this time and the strength of his arms that kept Barry on his feet, as he teetered on the edge of the path and a thirty-foot drop-off into a gulley. "Who are you?" Barry asked as he gazed at the fingers holding his jacket, appearing confused.

"I keep your *uhai*, your life, in my hands," said Koba, showing the whiteness of his palms against the blackness of his face. Barry closed his eyes, bent his knees, and lowered himself to the ground.

Andrew and Koba pulled Barry back up to his feet. Andrew had imagined that once they reached the top of the rise that marked the lower peak, they would be able to coast down to the lower hut, powered by gravitational forces, as if there were a slide that would deliver them all the way down to the hut. He imagined Barry gaining strength and becoming more alert with each step as oxygen flooded into his thirsty lungs, replacing the fluid that he was coughing up, and then the oxygen would be delivered to his brain. They would arrive at the hut, walk in together like champions basking in the glory of their triumph. But Barry's body seemed to have reached its limit.

Andrew and Koba stood on either side of Barry, trying to guide him and hold on to his shoulders as he walked slowly downhill. Barry placed one foot and then the other on the trail. As he gained momentum, he came loose from Andrew's grip and then his foot slipped on wet rocks. He tumbled down a small incline, bounced off a large boulder, and lay there motionless on a ledge, blood trickling from his nose.

Koba turned to Andrew. "Maybe dead now?"

"No!" Andrew screamed, and he felt tears running down his face as his whole body shook. They had come so far. How could it end here like this? The journey had seemed hopeless in the darkness, until they had all stood up at dawn with the horizon stretching out ahead of them. For that brief moment, everything seemed possible. Now Andrew could not see Barry's chest moving at all. Andrew's legs had no strength left to climb down to check on Barry. In the hospital, this would be the moment when the resuscitation team would begin to compress the chest and the electrical defibrillator would be wheeled over to shock the heart into beating. Or perhaps a gray-haired senior physician would walk by and decide that any further actions would be futile, and he would look at his watch and determine the time of death. Andrew stood motionless for a few seconds, when suddenly he thought he saw Barry's hand flicker and move and heard him moan.

Andrew steadied his legs then sat down on the ground and slid over the dirt and snow down to where Barry lay. He grabbed Barry's jacket and tugged at it. "Barry, are you okay? Can you hear me? Get up, Barry. Damn it." But Barry rolled away from him and swatted at his face. "Come on. Just grab my hands. We'll walk up to the path. Then we'll roll down the hill like two logs tied together. Come on." He pulled Barry slowly to his feet. There was bloody drool on Barry's beard and lips and a gash on his forehead.

Barry swatted at Andrew's face with his bloody hands. Andrew wanted to wipe the blood away but he was afraid that with even slight pressure on his face, Barry would tip over and fall into the gulley ten feet below. So instead he grabbed Barry's arms as if they were dancing. "Yeah, that's it," he said as they stepped sideways and forward together back up to the path. Andrew noticed that Koba was watching them intently.

"Koba, he's still alive. Help me pull him up."

Koba knelt on the ground, reached his hands down, grabbed under Barry's arm and yanked him up to the path.

"Great," Andrew said as he scurried up to Koba. "We're going to walk down the path a little further together and then start rolling down the mountain. Do you want to roll with us, all three together?" he asked Koba.

"No, I walk. I run. I catch you if you fall. I do not crawl on the ground like a snake or insect."

After stumbling forward another fifty yards, Andrew found a patch of grass on the gray volcanic scree that was soft enough to lay down with Barry in his arms, and they stretched out. Barry's face was a disgusting mass of blood and drool, and the smell made Andrew vomit in uncontrollable spasms. He wanted to release Barry and regain his composure. But before he could do so, they began to roll. At first, they just moved a few feet before being stopped by a boulder. There were sharp spikes of rock, and the snow covered the ground unevenly. Andrew shivered from the cold and wanted to lay where they had come to rest, to stop the bruises and scrapes of his back and chest. But then he heard Barry's gasping, and knew he had to keep them moving. They rolled a few more feet, picking up speed, bounced, and stopped again.

Barry vomited on the snow. "No more. Let me die here. No more," he said. His body had twisted and now his head lay down below his feet as if he were diving down the mountain. Barry pounded at Andrew's face and chest with his hands. "Let go of me," he said.

Andrew stood up and tried to pull Barry up with him, but Barry rolled into a ball and tumbled several more feet down the hill into a hole. Andrew stumbled after him and checked to make sure that Barry was still breathing. He grasped Barry's collar and waist and pulled him out of the hole, resting him on his back at the start of another steep slope. Barry was now covered with dirt, rocks, vomit, and bloody drool. "I'm sorry," Andrew said, apologizing as much to Koba for Barry's frightful condition as to Barry.

He lay next to Barry again, pushed with his legs and hips to orient their bodies toward a promising slope, and they started to roll again. This time they gained so much speed that Andrew became frightened and tried to slow their progress with his hands and feet. Their bodies bounced into the air and flew ten feet before sliding to a stop on a pile of ice and rocks. Koba hurried after them, traversing switchbacks, and bent down to check on them. Andrew felt Koba's cold fingers on his forehead and neck, and when he turned his head, he noticed Koba's eyeballs darting wildly. Andrew stuck his hands inside his shirt and could feel blood seeping from the scrapes and cuts on his chest. He showed his bloody hand to Koba.

"You are bleeding," said Koba.

"Yes," said Andrew. "I guess so." He licked his fingers to get the blood off. "I don't think I can roll like this anymore. It's too dangerous."

"Ouch, ow, ow," Barry moaned as he turned and grabbed his head with his hands. "What did you do to me?"

"We hit some rocks. We need to walk now. Can you walk?" said Andrew.

"I'm all broken. My bones are broken in pieces. I can't feel my feet. I can't walk."

"Then you'll just have to keep rolling down the hill. I'll push you."

"Take your hands off of me. Where's Eve?"

"She's up on the mountain. She'll be coming down soon."

"Who are you?"

"I'm Andrew. We're trying to get down the mountain. Do you remember?"

"Who's he?" asked Barry as he pointed to Koba.

"That's Koba...our guide."

"Are we lost? Oh God, we're lost. Help, help." Barry got up, stumbled, and lurched at Koba, catching Koba's neck in a desperate grasp.

Koba let Barry hang from his neck for a moment, considering what to do. As Barry slid further down toward the ground, Koba twisted his body, dropped the backpacks on the trail, reached down with his left arm, and hoisted Barry up onto his shoulders and back like a sack of corn, supporting Barry's legs with his arms.

"Salaam will collect backpacks. We can walk without water and food," Koba said as he stepped forward, bouncing Barry's body against his shoulders. Andrew noticed the veins on Koba's neck and forehead, swollen with the strain of carrying Barry in his arms. Andrew estimated that Barry weighed at least 160 pounds. Koba was probably no more than 135 or 140. It was hard to imagine how he could carry the weight, but Koba continued down the trail without looking back, his eyes glaring, steadfast and determined. As Andrew watched Koba carrying Barry, he looked at the backpacks left on the trail, and he thought about their stupidity in not abandoning the backpacks sooner to conserve their strength for carrying Barry.

"Are you sure?" Andrew said.

Koba nodded. "Sure."

With Koba carrying Barry down the trail, they made better progress. The sun was warming the air, and with the completion of each switchback, Andrew could feel the air become thicker and more nourishing. The scrub bushes and trees that appeared along the trail gave off a pungent odor that reminded Andrew of the balm that he would use in the gym for treating sore muscles. And like the balm, the bushes offered a hope of relief from the exhaustion that Andrew felt with each step. With the appearance of trees came more evidence that they were descending to a lower altitude—the sound of birds and insects and the disappearance of the snow.

Barry should have been feeling better as they zigzagged down the mountain trail, but his breathing had become noisy again, as if the phlegm was getting stuck in his throat as he hung over Koba's shoulder. Andrew looked for some message in Koba's face, some explanation of his strength, his determination, or a recognition of the impossibility and an admission of defeat. He looked more closely at Koba's face for a sign, and noticed only the fire in his eyes and the whiteness of his teeth when he grimaced with each step. But he could find no explanation of how or why Koba continued the hopeless task. The transformation of Koba from distant, unmotivated, unwilling to speak or touch them to a lifesaving superhero was breathtaking. And Andrew could not understand it.

While Andrew watched Koba negotiating the hairpin turns on the switchback down the mountain train, he noticed that Barry had begun to choke and gasp and his face had turned blue. "Koba," said Andrew, "Barry's not breathing well. I think you need to put him down."

Koba nodded, and grunted as he lowered Barry down into low scrub bushes and acrid gray dirt. Barry coughed and vomited up pink-and-yellow phlegm onto the dirt as he lay suspended from the olive bushes. Andrew bent down to look at what had come out. There were streaks of red-and-brown blood and air bubbles. As Andrew was wiping away the vomit from Barry's face, Barry vomited again, this time onto Andrew's arms and face.

"Damn it. Goddamn it," Andrew said as he wiped the vomit off his mouth and nose with his shirt and the leaves of a bush, then felt his own stomach burp and heave. "Koba, I think we need to find some water. We should wash the vomit from Barry's throat so he doesn't choke on it. I need to get it off of me too. It's making me sick. Do you have any water?"

"Sorry. I left in the backpack. I was too much in a hurry," Koba explained. He paused and looked around. "Maybe there is some water down there," said Koba, pointing to a cluster of bushes and trees near a gray rock cliff about two hundred yards ahead.

"Are you sure? I don't remember any water on the way up."

"Yes, it's water we can use to clean the face. Not water to drink. It smells bad." Without waiting for Andrew's agreement, Koba bent down and lifted Barry, then carried him over some rocks onto a partially-obscured trail leading to the water. Along the path was evidence that other hikers had found this place: toilet paper and the smell of human waste; a glove that had fallen from someone's pocket; a plastic bag with a chocolate bar. Andrew scooped up the chocolate bar, still with its wrapping intact. Andrew was suddenly overtaken by a hunger for sugar, and he unwrapped the chocolate bar. He was about to put it into his mouth when he stopped. If Koba was going to carry Barry, he needed the energy from the sugar.

"Koba, here, take this," he said, offering the chocolate. Koba took it and broke it in half, took his piece, and handed the other half back to Andrew. Then he broke off a small corner of the bar and put it into Barry's mouth. Koba continued to feed the chocolate to Barry until it was gone.

The water hole was dusty and had a faint smell of sulfur. The water came out from between two rocks and there were green fringes of small plants growing along the edges. Two birds flew up from the bushes as they arrived, and there were also the tracks of a small animal in the mud. Koba lowered Barry down and watched as Barry lay there, partially folded like a sclerotic lawn chair, flapping his hands across his neck and face. Barry's breathing whistled and echoed as it passed through his mouth.

Andrew scooped up some water from the spring and washed the residue of vomit off his face, hands, and shirt. The water felt warm, and Andrew noticed steam drifting out from behind one of the rocks. Andrew dribbled some of the water onto Barry's face and beard. The vomit was drying and Andrew washed and rubbed Barry's mouth and nose with his hands until the vomit dissolved as Barry lapped at the water with his tongue. Koba had said the water was not safe to drink, but Andrew wanted to wash the vomit off Barry's mouth and lips and figured that any water Barry might swallow would be of little consequence.

Andrew removed his jacket and shirt, then wet the corner of his shirt and used it as a washcloth. There was melted chocolate on Barry's lips, along with the vomit, and Andrew washed them both away. He opened Barry's mouth and washed it with his wet shirt as Barry sucked at the wet cloth. Barry coughed and vomited more pink froth mixed with chocolate. Andrew wet his shirt again and repeated the cleaning. The sulfur, steam, and the green plants felt like some strange combination of toxins and herbs that Andrew hoped would kill any germs that Barry might swallow.

Koba stripped off his shirt and dripped water over his head and neck and across his chest, causing the muscles of his chest

and neck to glow in the sunlight. There was an expression of relief on Koba's face as the water dripped over him, as if the water was soothing or rejuvenating him.

"Koba," Andrew said, "how are you feeling? Maybe I can try
to help carry him."

"I feel better now. This is medicine water," Koba said.

"Can you drink it?" Andrew asked, hoping that he had mis-
understood what Koba had told him about the water.

Koba raised his eyebrows. "This is not water for drinking. It
is *dawa*. It is Maasai medicine for a shaman, strong medicine,
not for whites."

"What kind of medicine?" asked Andrew.

"It is for poison, and sickness."

"I put some in Barry's mouth."

"Maybe help him. Maybe make more sick. Not for whites."

"Have you been here before?"

"Mohammed is my brother. He is my uncle but I call him
my brother. He took me here for my malaria one time. I went
all the way in the pool until the heat cured my fever. But now
the tourists make this place dirty. This water makes my arm
strong again so I can carry him now. Mohammed and Salaam
may be coming soon. Meet us in the next hut."

"Koba, what you're doing. It's amazing. You're saving him.
It's more than I could do as a doctor. I'm sorry I can't help you
more. I never realized how strong you were," Andrew said.

Koba nodded, rubbed his face and his arms for a moment
and said, "We cannot be weak here. Not like whites. Not like
tourists. Or we would be dead. No one will carry us if we fall
down. We are all strong here. Now we go meet Salaam."

"Yes, of course. I guess they've already been to the summit.
I wonder if any of them made it to the top. Have you been there

to the top of the mountain?"

"Only Salaam can go there with the whites. I go one time with my father."

"You can run all the way to the top?"

"Maybe yes. Not yet try. Usually just to the second hut. I go there and then turn around and run back same day.

"Wow, all in one day?"

Koba smiled briefly, and Andrew realized that it was the first time he had seen Koba smile. It was an innocent display of youthful pride, quickly hidden. Koba looked back at the trail they had traversed and said, "In America you learn how to spell words and how to add and subtract big numbers. You smart in America. You learn about the dates when important people are born and when they die, when they come to America, just white people. In my school the teachers hit you if you are late, and they hit you if you do not know the right date of famous white people. Our books go missing; teachers disappear; electricity goes off; the food is not enough. So we are not able to learn like in America. Or be smart like Americans. But in Africa we learn how to be strong." Koba bent down and hoisted Barry back up into his arms and began walking back to the trail.

Chapter 11

HEY REACHED THE second hut in the late afternoon. Andrew had imagined a crowd waiting for them with food and water and many arms lifting Barry onto a bed. But the hut was empty, cold, lifeless. No one was there. Just empty cots and the lingering odors of previous meals, old socks, and underwear.

Koba laid Barry down on an olive canvas cot, and Andrew noticed that Koba was drenched in sweat and teetering, about to pass out. Koba had been struggling in the minutes before they arrived at the hut, grimacing, grunting, stumbling, almost dropping Barry. Somehow, he had been able to hold on. But now it was obvious that Koba was near collapse, sweat dripping from his face and a wild, disoriented look in his eyes. Koba's eyes rolled back in his head just before he dropped onto another cot, eyes closed, legs twitching, taking deep breaths.

"Koba, are you okay?" Andrew asked. He waited for an answer and when there was none, he repeated, "Are you okay?"

"Okay. Okay," Koba answered weakly and waved wildly into

the air then tried to get up. Andrew held Koba down so that he would not get up. He felt Koba's matted hair with his hands, and held his head as if it were a glass globe, fragile and breakable, dangling loosely from his neck. Andrew could feel the pulsations of the arteries of Koba's forehead and the softness of his eyes fluttering beneath the lids. Andrew left his hands on Koba's eyelids for a moment, lightly massaging them and the forehead, down his cheeks to his lips, but Koba brushed Andrew's hands away, opened his eyes, and stared at Andrew's face as if surprised or embarrassed.

"Okay, okay," he repeated, waving away Andrew's hands.

Andrew sighed, released Koba's head gently onto the cot, and moved over to check on Barry, whose face and neck were gray and mottled. Barry's eyes bobbed aimlessly in circles, unable to focus. Andrew had no idea what to do. He had no medicine or water for Barry. The hut had been all he could think about as they stumbled down the trail. It was the finish line where the race was supposed to end. But now Andrew realized the finish line was all a mirage; the race would continue, and there was nothing more to do but wait. He slid onto the rough canvas of the adjacent cot, rolled his body into a ball, and closed his eyes.

Andrew was awakened by footsteps and voices at the doorway. Hands helped him sit up while other hands dripped water into his mouth, and he barely had time to identify who the hands belonged to—the rough, callused fingers of Helga or the soft, fleshy hands of Kara. He kept his eyes closed as he sipped the water to prolong the sense of relief and to appreciate the gentle massage of his neck. But he could hear the voices with increasingly frantic questions. Eve was there and Kara and Klaus.

Salaam squatted down next to where he lay. "Mr. Andrew, this was a very difficult journey for you, was it?" Salaam squeezed Andrew's hands and Andrew squeezed back. "Very good. Yes, you are fine. Just tired, is it?"

Andrew nodded and said, "I'm okay. I'm okay." He sat up and then stood tentatively, testing his legs to see if they would hold him, and felt hands on his shoulders and hands that stabilized him as if he were a plaster statue being placed on an uneven pedestal. He stood in front of them for a moment as they waited to see if he would fall over. Andrew felt dizzy and closed his eyes to see if his brain would reset in a more stable state. He was surprised that he could take small steps. His muscles had recovered enough to support his weight without buckling. As he walked around the hut, the hands that had been on his body gradually disappeared, and the attention of the group shifted to Barry and Koba.

Eve called out Barry's name, but Barry's only responses were gurgles and moans. "Oh my God," Eve said. "What's wrong with him?" And then after a pause she added, "He's dying. Can't you all see? We have to carry him down to the hospital. Now."

Helga nodded. "Yes, we must all carry him down to the hospital. Is truth." Helga organized Helmut, Rolph, and Klaus to find rope and tree branches to convert a cot to a stretcher to carry Barry down the mountain. Helga assigned everyone a task. She asked Mickey and John to use the rope to tie the branches to the cot so that they could all carry the cot down the trail. John nodded, pulled Mickey up from a cot, and they got to work.

Salaam and Mohammed spoke to Koba in Swahili and brought a cup of water for him to drink. Koba stood up shakily, his hands pressed over his eyeballs as he sipped water. He turned his head a few times and shook his arms. Salaam hugged Koba and rubbed Koba's arms and shoulders with his hands as if to be sure that nothing was broken. Once he assured himself that Koba was fine, Salaam returned to Andrew. "So sorry," he said. "It was a very hard trip, was it?"

"Yes," said Andrew. "It was hard, but Koba saved us. He carried Barry by himself for the last part."

"Yes. He is a very strong boy, a good boy," said Salaam as he rubbed his hand over Koba's head. "He is my nephew. He is a champion runner," he added as if that explained everything. "Now we will make a stretcher to carry Mr. Barry. You can walk down to the next hut, now?" he asked Andrew.

At first Andrew thought that the question was some kind of joke. How could anyone ask him to get up and hike now? But as Salaam continued to wait and stare at him, Andrew realized that the question was part of an actual plan. Kara came over to him and asked, "Can you walk now with me to the first hut? Helga and Salaam think it would be best if we went ahead and got help. The others will stay with Barry and carry him right after us. We will go to the first hut and arrange for a Jeep to meet them when they get to the hut."

"I'm so tired. But yes, I can try," Andrew said. "What about Koba? Can he come with us? He probably would know the way."

"No, we will need him to help carry Mr. Barry," said Salaam. "Anyway, the trail is well marked. You cannot get lost. You can take a flashlight."

"It's good," Kara said. "I will help you walk. Just walking. No one to carry."

Eve came over to Andrew, her lips trembling, tears running down her face. "Are you okay? What happened to Barry? He has blood all over his face."

"I'm okay, just exhausted. We had to carry him. Koba and me. He fell down. But I think he just has a few scrapes."

"We found the backpacks. We thought all of you fell over the cliff. We looked down expecting to see your bodies."

"No. We had to leave the backpacks. They were too heavy. We should have left them sooner, but we were stupid. We had to carry Barry. He couldn't walk. First, I dragged him over the lower peak, and then Koba picked him up and carried him. That was where we left the backpacks on the trail. Really, Koba carried Barry most of the way down."

"This is terrible. I'm sorry. He's so sick. He can't even talk. I think he's in a coma. I can't believe there aren't any medical kits. How can you have a famous mountain like Kilimanjaro with tourists climbing every day and not have medical supplies?!" She glared at Salaam as if he had caused the crisis, or was responsible for Barry's plight. Salaam shook his head, turned, and walked outside, calling out directives to Mohammed.

"I don't know," Andrew said. "It's Africa. Yeah, I wish there was a first aid kit or some oxygen. But there isn't any."

"I'm sorry to be yelling. It's not your fault. I'm just so upset," said Eve, then she put her hands over her face and sobbed. "We should have all gone down with you." The eyeliner she had applied when she got up that morning was now smudged over her cheeks and nose. Kara put her arms around Eve's neck and cleaned Eve's face with a tissue, and they held each other. Andrew walked over to them, and they opened their embrace to include him in their little circle. He could feel their faces wet against his, their legs swaying.

Kara said to Eve, "Salaam said that Andrew and I will go now to get help. You will stay with Barry and Klaus. Helga and

Salaam will organize everyone to carry him as soon as they finish to make a stretcher." Eve nodded her agreement with the
plan. "Come with me," said Kara as she tugged Andrew toward
the door.

Before he left the hut, Andrew pulled a clean shirt from
his newly-arrived backpack. The shirt he had been wearing still
smelled of vomit and the sweat of all of their bodies. Then Salaam made him drink a cup of water and instructed Kara and
Andrew to send for a Jeep as soon as they arrived at the first
hut. The Jeep would have to come up from the base of the trail
and meet the group carrying Barry, then drive Barry to the missionary hospital at the base of the mountain. Salaam walked
back and forth among the group, rubbing Koba's neck, saying
some kind of prayer when he was in front of Barry, and giving
instructions about the construction of the stretcher.

Andrew gulped down the cup of water and was about to lift
his backpack onto his shoulders, but Kara grasped his hand and
pushed it away from the pack. "No, they will carry it," she said
and gestured outside.

"But my passport," he said weakly.

"We must go now. Before the dark. No need for a passport."
Kara pushed open the door, revealing Klaus and Rolph working on converting a cot into a stretcher. Helga was pulling at
the canvas and the poles to make sure they were tight. Mickey
and John were passing food and water to the group. Andrew accepted a stale biscuit, almost choking as he swallowed the hard
chunks.

As Andrew started off walking down toward the trail, the air
was cooler than what he remembered from his arrival, and the
sun had almost set. He paused and looked over at Helga and the
group working on the stretcher. "Did you make it?" he asked.

"Did you see one hundred miles? Did you see Kenya?"

Helga came over to him and patted him on the back several times. "I wrote your name in the book on the top of mountain. Not my name," she said. "Just your name in the book."

Andrew smiled at the idea of his name in the logbook as having reached the summit, even though it was not true. "Really? You wrote my name in the book?"

"Is truth," Helga said. "Only your name."

The sun had set and the trail was already fading into the darkness. "Do you have a flashlight?" Andrew asked Kara as they began walking.

Kara pulled a small light from her pocket. "Do you want more water?" she said as she pulled out her canteen from her backpack and took a sip.

"Okay." He gulped down the water and let some drip onto his chin and neck and down his shirt. He felt a strange intimacy sharing the water from her canteen.

They passed from the grasslands with long, open vistas into the canopy of dense trees and vines and mud. In the deepening darkness, the vines felt ominous as they appeared without warning, tripping him. The muscles of Andrew's legs were sore and cramping as he tried to slow his downward slide through the mud. Kara reached out to steady him, and he noticed how strong her grasp was and how tightly she held him. He sensed something more than her strength in the grasp of her hand, as if she were also sending him the message that she cared about him. He used his hands to grab branches and the base of bushes and trees and felt the sting of thorns that he had not seen. There were tiny drops of blood on his fingers that tasted salty when he licked them. Kara handed him a yellow-and-green bandanna that had been in her pocket to dry his fingers.

"Thorns, on the bushes," he said, and she nodded. "So, did you reach the top of the mountain?" he asked.

"The top? Oh no. I stayed in the hut. Anyway, Klaus went up almost to the top. Just only thirty meters more. But he stopped. I don't know why. He wouldn't tell me. Only Helga and Salaam reached the top. Even Helmut and Rolph stopped before the top."

"Yes, Helga told me she made it. What about Eve? Did she try?"

"Oh no, she stayed with me. She worried about you and Barry all the time. She was not happy. She was crying. She had headache. She thought you both can be dead. She told me that she was very scared of hyena and snakes when she walked in the jungle. And I told her the same for me and lions even more, and we both laughed."

In the dark, the trail had holes and roots that appeared suddenly and there were sounds of movement in the bushes. Andrew had the sense that animals were just away from the trail, lurking and waiting. He had heard that a hyena could bite off an arm in a few seconds. There were poisonous snakes that could be dangling like a vine from a tree. A bite could be fatal. Or poisonous insects, scorpions, centipedes, bees, and ants. But he could not examine every bush or tree. They needed to keep moving and get help so that a car could be waiting for Barry to transport him to the hospital.

Hours later, when it was very dark, Andrew saw lights flickering through the trees. He thought they might be people with flashlights on the trail looking for them, but the lights did not move and got bigger and outlined the hut, where voices and music replaced the slosh of mud and the swish of the leaves and branches against their bodies. Kara's profile became visible, her golden threads of hair reflecting the light.

At first, their arrival at the hut did not provoke any reaction. No one knew who they were. They might have been any late arrival wandering up to the cabin from the base camp at the beginning of their adventure. But then Kara began to call out that there was an emergency, that they needed help. The other climbers and guides in the hut gathered around to hear her story. As Kara explained about Barry, people began moving in different directions, activated by the emergency and possible death, some rushing down the hill to get a car while others hurried up the trail to meet the stretcher and help carry it.

Andrew followed Kara into the hut. They drank hot tea with milk and lay on cots next to each other, legs extended stiffly and arms by their sides, as if they had been placed in coffins and their life's journey was finally complete.

Chapter 12

NDREW AND KARA woke up as the group carrying Barry arrived at the first hut. Koba, Klaus, Rolph, Helga, and Mohammed carried Barry to the Jeep that had arrived while Andrew and Kara slept. Andrew was rubbing his eyes and trying to find his way through the crowd surrounding Barry, when Eve suddenly appeared in front of him. He had not seen her with the others.

"Can you come to the hospital with me? You're the best person to explain to the doctors at the hospital what happened to Barry," she said.

"The hospital? Now?" Andrew's mind felt jumbled from the recent nap and it took him a few seconds to orient himself. "Yeah, the hospital, okay, sure, I'll go."

He looked for Kara to tell her what he was doing, as if they were still on a mission together, but Eve took his hand and pulled him through the crowd to the Jeep before he could find Kara to say anything. Andrew twisted his body into the back of the Jeep next to where Barry lay, and Eve sat up front with the African driver, who started the engine immediately and began racing down the trail, bouncing over the roots and potholes. Andrew wanted to ask Eve what they would do when they found the hospital, but it was too noisy to say much in the Jeep as tree branches brushed by the windows with high-pitched squeals. There was not much that he could do for Barry in the dark except listen to the sounds of his breaths and make sure the breaths didn't stop.

As Andrew's mind drifted away from the sound of Barry's breathing, he thought of all the people who had helped get Barry to the hospital. The people who had carried Barry in the makeshift stretcher in the dark must have struggled to navigate the narrow path, and they had been climbing since midnight. It was a group effort now, even if it had not felt that way at the start. They all contributed what they could, even if they had been selfish about their goal to reach the top. Now he would be the interpreter for the doctors at the hospital and explain how Barry had developed pulmonary edema. There was no reason for him to be angry now that they were in the Jeep. Maybe it was just his fatigue. But he was angry and he did blame them, all of them, for forcing him and Barry to almost die.

The Jeep reached the paved road and passed a sign indicating the missionary hospital. Andrew looked back at Barry and could see that he was still struggling for air, but at least he was breathing. "He's doing better!" Andrew yelled to Eve through the engine noise.

Eve reached back and touched Andrew's shoulder to let him know she had heard his voice, even if she could not make out his words. Her face had hardened into a dark mask without any sign of emotion. Andrew could sense the tension that she was feeling. He imagined she was rehearsing the story she would tell at the hospital and how she would cope with her own anxieties and he wanted to reassure her that he would help. But the tenuous touch on his shoulder provided little opportunity for reassurance. He tried to grasp her hand with his, but her hand was gone before he could reach it.

When the Jeep arrived at the hospital, an elderly white nurse in a gray-and-white uniform greeted them at the entrance. Andrew jumped out of the Jeep and pointed at Barry in the stretcher. "We were climbing and he got high-altitude pulmonary edema. We carried him, down from sixteen thousand feet. He's an American Peace Corps, twenty-four years old without any other medical problems," he explained, hoping that the use of medical terminology would expedite the triage process.

The nurse noticed the blood on Barry's face and kept asking if Barry had fallen, and Andrew had to explain that Barry's cuts and scrapes were from rolling down the hill. They were not the cause of his sickness. The real problem was his lungs, which were full of fluid. The nurse finally called two African orderlies to carry Barry into the casualty room and told Andrew and Eve to go to the waiting room and sign the information forms. A half hour later, they were still filling out forms when a British doctor with a ruddy face, thin black mustache, and receding gray hair came out to the waiting room, waving a chest X-ray.

"Hello. I'm Dr. Burns," he announced. "You are with this American Peace Corps?"

"Yes," said Eve, "I'm his...wife, Eve Vigil."

"Very well, Mrs. Vigil. As you can see from this X-ray, your husband has pulmonary edema. We see this quite commonly from European travelers who climb too quickly without adequate acclimatization. By the time they arrive here, it's often too late." The doctor pointed out the abnormal pattern of excessive fluid in the lungs. "Fortunately, you were able to get him down the mountain in time. That was what saved his life. Our altitude here at the hospital is about seven hundred meters. He should recover fully in the next few days with oxygen and diuretics. But we will need to keep him here for at least five days, because the strain on his heart and lungs has been substantial. We've had a few coronary events during recovery. But he is young. The oxygen we have given him has had a remarkable effect already."

"Can we see him?" said Eve.

"We don't allow visitors in the casualty area, but since you're family, we can make an exception for a few minutes. We will be bringing him to a hospital room soon and you'll be able to visit him there during normal visiting hours tomorrow."

"Thank you," said Eve.

The doctor led them past the door and the yellow-and-black checked curtain that separated the emergency care area from the waiting room. Barry lay propped up on a hospital gurney, with an oxygen mask on his face. His eyes were closed. Eve reached over and grabbed his hand, and Barry opened his eyes.

"Where am I?" he said.

"The hospital," said Eve. "By the way, I told them we were married. Otherwise, they wouldn't let us in to see you."

"Cool, do I get a kiss?"

"You must be feeling better, dear," said Eve as she laughed and gave him a peck on the cheek.

"If I'm your husband, it seems like I would get a more serious kiss," he said.

"Don't push it," said Eve.

"Okay, so where am I?"

Eve looked at Andrew and waved her hand at him, directing

him to answer. "Hi, Barry," Andrew said. "This is one of the best hospitals in Tanzania. We're at the bottom of the mountain...we got you down to the hospital. It's run by European missionaries. I read all about it when I was trying to decide where to do my obstetrics and gynecology rotation in Africa."

"That's fine. They can even baptize me as long as they keep this oxygen going. I never appreciated oxygen. I just took it for granted."

"You're going to be fine. We talked to the doctor. You just need to be here for a few days until the fluid goes out of your lungs," Andrew said.

Barry smiled weakly. "Thank you. You saved my life. Both of you. And that African guy. What's his name?"

"Koba," Andrew said.

"Did he carry me? Or was I dreaming?"

"Yes. He did. It was amazing. A miracle. I don't know how he did it."

"I wasn't sure. I remembered you dragging me. And I remember being upside down and falling in a hole. Everything was so mixed up. I've never been so sick."

"You never gave up," said Andrew. "You're pretty tough."

Barry closed his eyes. "I don't remember that. I wanted to give up. I was so cold. I just wanted to sleep. That African guy carried me on his back, like I was a sack of dirty laundry. I couldn't breathe. Do you have any idea what that feels like?"

Eve came over to Barry and gently rubbed his hair and his forehead. "It must have been terrible. You can rest now. Just breathe the oxygen. We'll take care of everything else. Who do you want us to call?"

"I don't know. I guess just call Peace Corps. I don't want to freak out my parents."

"All right," said Eve. "Just try to rest."

"Okay, I will. I wish I'd had this oxygen up on the mountain. Shit, I'm sorry I ruined everyone's trip," said Barry. Then, looking at Andrew, he added, "You never made it to the top. That's a bummer. Hey, you don't have to stay here with me if you want to try to climb it again."

"No way. I'm done with climbing," said Andrew. "Actually, I'm supposed to be leaving tomorrow for Malindi. I have bus tickets. It's on the Kenyan coast, a little beach town. I got a package deal tour. Kilimanjaro and then Malindi Beach. Sounded good at the time. Exercise and adventure followed by relaxation. But now I'm so tired, I don't know if I can go. I just want to sleep. I definitely would not want to climb that mountain again. Once was enough. Helga said she wrote my name in the book they have on the summit, so I'm covered. I'll be able to tell my children the story someday, if I ever have any. Maybe they'll see my name in the book. Anyway, I think I should stick around here and make sure you're okay."

"I'll be fine," said Barry. "You deserve some R&R. You both do." Some of the oxygen escaped the mask as he talked, creating a smoky cloud of humidified air. He paused as Eve wiped the sweat from his forehead, then turned and looked at Andrew. "Why don't you take Eve with you? She knows Swahili, and you shouldn't go to Kenya by yourself, particularly that bus station in Nairobi. By the time you get back, I'll be more presentable. I don't want to seem like an invalid."

Andrew suspected that Barry had made the suggestion in jest, but as he watched Eve and Barry looking at each other, he realized Barry was serious, and was curious about how Eve would react. When Eve hesitated to respond, Barry took a deep breath from the oxygen mask and seemed to drift off in some kind of dream for a few seconds.

"No," said Eve. "I just want to rest. I'm not ready for any more trips, even to one of the most beautiful beaches in the world. I've heard of Malindi. Andrew, you should definitely go," said Eve, and she stared into his eyes as if they were alone in the room. "But I want to stay around here with Barry and make sure everything is okay. And what would the missionaries think if I went off with Andrew?" she laughed awkwardly.

As they were talking, Kara's face poked through the curtain. She and Klaus had just arrived in a van with the others from the group. She waited quietly for a moment as if to make sure that she was in the right place. Her face was flushed and sweaty. "Klaus, Klaus," she called back through the curtain. "I've found them all here. Barry is alive." A few seconds later, Klaus walked through the curtain and stood with Kara for a moment before coming over to Barry to watch him breathe through the oxygen mask.

"Wonderful," said Klaus. "They told us that you had died. Kara asked the nurse in the front and she must not have understood our English."

"No, I'm feeling good now. It's amazing what a little oxygen can do for you. And a lower altitude," said Barry. "But they want to keep me here for five days so that my lungs will get better."

Salaam and Helga walked in and waved. Salaam bowed his head as if he were offering a prayer of gratitude. "Mr. Barry, I am so happy to see you. Your journey was very difficult. We were all praying for you. The whole group is in the waiting room, but they would not allow so many people to come into your room," said Salaam.

"I would like to see Koba and thank him. He carried me on his shoulders," said Barry.

"Oh, I am very sorry, Mr. Barry. Koba met some other guides in the first hut after we arrived. They asked if he would accompany them back up the mountain, and he went with them," said Salaam.

"Really?" said Barry. "Back up the mountain? Wasn't he tired? I don't remember much but I remember him. He carried me. Upside down."

"Yes, he is a very strong runner. He goes up and down the mountain all the time," said Salaam. "Miss Helga and her friends have agreed to sponsor him for his track team. It is a very good chance for Koba."

"Great idea," said Barry. "Maybe we all could help him. Why not? As long as I don't have to run," and his mouth opened into a big grin.

"Your lips are pink now," said Kara. "That's a much better color." Andrew, Klaus, and Eve all bent down to look at Barry's lips and then his tongue and throat.

"Hey, this is weird," said Barry. "I feel like you're all going to kiss me or smother me. While I wouldn't mind a little closeness of the female persuasion, I've already had too much close contact from Andrew and all those guys carrying me in the stretcher. I don't need any more."

A tall nurse, wearing a curved white hat like a crown on her blond hair, rushed into the room as they were all bending over Barry. "This is not allowed. This is a sterile area. You may not touch our patients here. You must all go to the waiting room immediately. We cannot have visitors here. Even the wife. You can infect the other patients. Thank you," said the nurse, and she began herding the group out of the room.

"Oh well," said Kara, "we will come back to tomorrow. Will he be in a hospital room?"

"You can consult the patient information office," said the nurse. "And the visiting hours."

"Maybe you should go to Malindi," Eve said to Andrew as they walked out past the curtains. "We can take care of Barry, if they will allow us to do that. They won't even let me stay, and I'm supposed to be his wife. Now that Klaus and Kara and the others are here, I'll have lots of company." Eve smiled at Kara. "I guess there are some advantages to being married."

Andrew felt a wave of fatigue and yawned. "I don't know. I'm exhausted. I need to sleep. I can't imagine how Koba could have gone back up the mountain. Anyway, I don't want to leave until I know that Barry is going to be fine."

"But you should go. I can take care of Barry and there are the doctors and nurses. After all that you have done, you deserve to lie on the beach," said Eve. "Barry wants you to go."

As Andrew listened to Eve, persisting in her encouragement for him to go to Malindi, he began to wonder if she was the one who wanted to go to the beach. Perhaps, unconsciously, she also wanted to be with him. But maybe she needed to know that he felt the same way about her before she could consider going with him.

"I don't really want to go by myself. I'd rather stay here with all of you," said Andrew. "We're a team."

Kara came over to Andrew and stood close to him. "You should go. Klaus and I will be here until you come back. Our plane is not for a week. We would like to do this. Maybe Eve can go with you?" said Kara with a subtle wink.

Eve seemed surprised at Kara's suggestion. "Oh no. I couldn't relax knowing that Barry was here in the hospital. Even tempting me with Malindi Beach won't change my mind."

Andrew could feel Eve searching his face for some kind of

signal even as she declined Kara's offer. He felt like she was asking him if he really wanted her companionship. If he was regretting that kiss at the top of the mountain. Or, perhaps, if he was not regretting it at all. If he would think that she was being irresponsible to even consider leaving Barry with Klaus and Kara. Andrew returned her stare by opening his eyes wide to the possibility, nodding his head, moving his lips slightly to indicate that yes, he truly wanted her to come with him, even as he remained silent. She seemed to understand and smiled.

"It would be different," she said. "I have a bathing suit in my pack. But I don't know. This sounds crazy."

Andrew had not imagined that Eve would seriously consider going off with him to a beach. They hardly knew each other, and he didn't think Eve would want to be with him alone. But there had been that kiss, and in the Jeep she had touched his shoulder. He was not sure what tectonic force was shaking them and pushing them together with tremors barely perceptible at first but increasing in intensity, and now the possibility had opened up like a giant unexpected crack in the earth. Kara had noticed. Even Barry seemed to have become aware of it and seemed to have given his tacit blessing.

"That would be great," said Andrew. "We'd be back in a few days. It's just a bus ride to Nairobi and over to Mombasa and then up the coast an hour or two. But only if Kara and Klaus are able to stay here with Barry."

"We are like family now," said Kara. "We are brothers and sisters. And Helga and Rolph and Helmut are here, and I'm sure Salaam can help if we need anything. Please go to Malindi. Do this for us and let us help you. Andrew has done so much that we failed to do. Andrew should not go alone."

Andrew looked at Eve to see if she would back out and tell

him she was just joking, just like her claim to be married to Barry. "Will you do it?" Andrew asked her.

"Yes, why not, if Klaus and Kara can stay with Barry. I'll go. I've never been very comfortable in hospitals. And you deserve this."

"Okay, then. I'll get your bus tickets now," said Andrew. "For the morning bus?"

"I'll be ready," she said. "I'll bring along a little surprise."

"Really," he said. "What kind of surprise?"

"If I told you, it wouldn't be a surprise," she said and smiled with her eyes opened wide, shook her dark hair, and gave a secretive grin that Andrew had never seen from her before.

Chapter 13

THE BUS RIDE to Malindi was longer than Andrew imagined. His knees banged against the seat in front of him, and burlap bags with vegetables and dried fish prevented him from angling his legs toward the aisle. Mosquitoes buzzed in Andrew's ears when he tried to rest his eyes and drift off to sleep.

Eve was next to him, wearing safari clothes with hat netting to cover her ears. She rested her head against the window of the bus and her legs pushed against his knees. With her head against the window and eyes closed, he could study her face as he might study a painting in a museum. First, he focused on her mouth, the bows on both sides that met in the middle with a small V. The bowstring that met the lower lip, and then the lower lip, round and full. He noticed a tiny scar at the corner of her mouth. Perhaps it had been from a fall when she was a child, or a rock thrown by another child. No one would notice it without having the time he had to look closely, but now he thought about how rather than ruining the perfection of her mouth, it gave it character, a certain toughness.

When Eve changed position, her back practically pushed Andrew off the seat into the aisle and he had to stop his voyeurism. At other times, Eve would turn and rest her head against his shoulder for a few minutes. When she did, he tried to move his arm slightly to create space in the mesh of his shoulder muscles—the teres minor, supraspinatus, infraspinatus, subscapularis, all muscles of the rotator cuff whose names he had memorized for his anatomy test. But after a few minutes, Eve would move her head away and change her position again.

Andrew wanted to ask Eve what had prompted her to get on the bus with him. Was it the lure of Malindi Beach and the opportunity to escape the memories of Barry's illness? Or were there some feelings for him, some attraction, either physical or mental, perhaps enhanced by his new status as a "hero" that had convinced her? Did she actually calculate his positives— the income he would earn as a physician, his intelligence, his overall attractiveness, which he would estimate at better than average, and then subtract his negatives—his short stature, his inability to grow a decent beard, the crookedness of his teeth, and his eyes that barely passed the vision test for his driver's license? Perhaps she suspected deficiencies in his social class, or an ancestry of poor, uneducated immigrants, which they had never discussed, but sometimes bubbled up in his skin color or language usage. Maybe Eve did not go by such an analytic, quantitative inventory and went by gut feeling or other sensory stimulation—his voice, the odor of his body, the feel of his skin, the taste of his kiss. He could ask her, but such questions might raise to the conscious level the subtle, unconscious feelings that probably had encouraged her to come with him on the trip to Malindi. And once conscious, she might dismiss them.

Andrew felt some guilt to be taking advantage of Barry's convalescence. He and Barry had been about as physically close as two men could be, almost dying together. Barry had trusted Andrew with his life. And it was likely that the trust had extended to encouraging Eve to go with him to Malindi. Andrew did not want to betray that trust with his romantic musings that could grow into actions he would regret. But what if Eve did feel an attraction to him? She wasn't, after all, married to Barry as they had suggested to the hospital to get past the security. In fact, Eve had said they were friends just beginning to date, and Barry had admitted they'd never slept together. Eve had been eager to take this trip to Malindi Beach with him. So what was the problem?

And Eve's feelings and desires were only one side of the equation. What were his feelings? He had invited Eve on a whim, but was he prepared to reciprocate attractions that he imagined Eve might be feeling? He had kissed her outside of the third hut when both of them were frightened and feeling isolated and ill from the effects of mountain sickness. Was the kiss more than a spontaneous physical moment? Or was it something deeper, the first tentative expression of feelings that had been building over the three days they had observed each other from a distance and then thrown together in a crisis?

Andrew also wondered about the surprise that Eve had promised. He wanted to ask her, but with the noise of the bus engine and the bumps in the road, he would have to scream for Eve to hear him. What if it was all a joke or something silly, like a piece of African chocolate? Or maybe she would forget about the surprise altogether. But the way she had been smiling when she said it suggested something dangerous or conspiratorial, and against the rules. Andrew had generally been a rule follower all of his life. He turned in assignments on time, washed his hands before eating, did not speed or go through yellow lights. But there were also times when he said, "What the fuck," ran naked through the streets, or rode on an elephant's back, and this surprise felt like one of those times.

Andrew shifted his thoughts to his family at home. They would be surprised at his adventure on Kilimanjaro. His dad would take credit for encouraging Andrew to run cross country and maintain a high level of fitness that probably saved him on the mountain. And his dad would probably be right. Left to his own devices, Andrew might have chosen the high school chess club rather than cross country. His mother would worry that after surviving one near-death experience, he'd be encouraged to pursue other dangerous activities, like parachuting from an airplane or deep sea diving, and get injured in the process. She needn't worry. He had no interest in challenging death. He'd already seen how unfair that battle could be.

Neither of his parents had been to Africa, and their imaginations of Africa were fueled by movies and television that showed starving babies, lions killing zebras, or the leeches that Humphrey Bogart had to pull from his body in the movie *African Queen*. His dad had only traveled out of the US during World War II as part of the invasion of France. What his father remembered was the hand-to-hand combat with German soldiers and the burns he suffered when there was a gas explosion. Andrew had seen the scars on his dad's chest and back, though his dad did not talk much about them. His mother worried about all the tropical diseases, like malaria or elephantiasis, that could kill or disfigure him. They had looked at pictures together in his medical books of men with legs the size of tree trunks, and his mother had frowned and closed the book.

He loved his parents, but they were from another generation that did not understand how much the world was changing and that there were cures or vaccines for most diseases, like tuberculosis and polio, that used to kill. His dad's major concern about Andrew practicing medicine in the US was the way hospitals and doctors were driving the country and patients to bankruptcy. His dad had worked on the staff of one of the US Senate committees in charge of Medicare. His dad had likened Medicare to an open checkbook for doctors and hospitals. With people living longer, there was no end to the operations and treatments that doctors and hospitals could devise to keep old people alive and keep the checks rolling in.

When Andrew had gotten into medical school, his dad joked that it was probably some hospital lobbyist's final attempt to bribe him to shut up by admitting his son into the belly of the beast. But his parents were proud of him, and actually a bit surprised that he was willing to go to Africa for his obstetrics clerkship rather than selecting a more comfortable clerkship in an American hospital. And they were probably right that Andrew would not have ventured out to Africa on his own. But there had been a presentation at medical school from one of the obstetrics faculty, who showed pictures of Tanzania and offered a scholarship for a student who would go to the hospital in Dar es Salaam as part of an exchange program that was starting. Andrew had been the only student who applied. It was that simple.

As the bus accelerated into a long, straight stretch of road, Andrew would fall asleep for a few minutes then would be jerked awake as the bus braked for a slow truck or animal, throwing him and Eve against the seat in front of them. As they bumped along the road, Andrew practiced what he would say when they arrived in Malindi. He would tell Eve how glad he was that she had come along, and discuss all the activities they could do that he had read in the guidebook: snorkeling in Malindi Marine National Park; walks along the beach; shopping in the market. Then he would assure her that he would give her personal space after all she'd suffered on Kilimanjaro, and they'd get separate rooms, hopefully next to each other at a hotel near the beach. That would avoid any awkwardness or assumptions that either of them might have, and would leave the door open to other options later.

"This is sure different from climbing a mountain," Andrew observed after the bus unexpectedly pulled over to the side of the road and idled for several minutes. The others in the bus seemed unconcerned about the reason for the delay or its possible duration, but Andrew and Eve fidgeted and counted the minutes, worried about a mechanical breakdown that would delay them. Now that it was quiet enough for a conversation, they could not figure out what to say. Finally, to open the conversation, Andrew asked Eve how she compared the bus trip to hiking up the mountain.

"On the mountain I got blisters on my toes, and on the bus, I'm getting them on my knees and my head," she said. "Your shoulder's not very soft."

"I'm sorry," he said. "It's difficult to find a stable position. I've been trying to rearrange the muscles of my rotator cuff to create a cushion, but they're not anatomically created for that purpose. I feel like every muscle in my body has been stretched and pounded. I'm not sure what size person these buses were built for, but you and I are not the ones. But the Africans don't seem to be bothered by the bumps or the stops. You'd think we'd be happy to have all of the bouncing around stop for a few minutes, but I'm even more anxious than when we were moving," he said. "I'm worried the bus is broken and we'll be out on the road walking."

"This is Africa. The surprises are part of the experience," said Eve and she smiled. Then she continued, "I have no idea what a rotator cuff is or if it's part of your shirt or what. But now that we're not moving, we have another problem. We're an easy target for the mosquitoes. They're biting right through my jeans. And these are new jeans. Who ever heard of mosquitoes that could do that? They'll probably give us malaria as a bonus. We didn't have mosquitoes up on that mountain. In the village where I worked, we had netting and mosquito repellent, and they weren't this bad."

"What were you doing in the village?" Andrew asked.

"I worked at a school, kids of all ages. I was teaching English and African history. Fortunately, I could read ahead of the kids in the African history book, because I knew nothing about the history of Julius Nyerere and how the revolution occurred. That would have been nice to include in my Peace Corps training."

"What did you think about the Peace Corps? It's the US government and I always worry that the government might be trying to mix propaganda with the aid work. And from what I know of Nyerere, he's a bit of a socialist and not very interested in capitalism. So being an American Peace Corps could be tricky."

"Oh, in the rural areas no one cares about the politics. They're happy to have American money and food. Sometimes there have been some Cuban volunteers and they can be a bit nasty, but the truth is that over here we're all just trying to survive. I would even help the Cuban doctors who came to the village by translating Swahili into Spanish. My Spanish is not great, but it was better than nothing. Now that I'm just about finished, it's strange to be thinking about returning to the US, where we all hate the Cubans and are suspicious of Tanzania. 'Course, who would have thought that Nixon would go to China two years ago and suddenly we're friends with the Chinese... or at least not enemies anymore? That's what makes politics so fascinating. Well, I'm going on and on and you probably want to rest. I was hoping to catch up on some sleep too, but you're the one who must be exhausted. You had to carry Barry all night," Eve said.

"Fortunately, I had Koba. We could never have survived without him," said Andrew. "You'd never know he was that strong by looking at him. He's just a kid. I wish I could have thanked him, but he headed back up the mountain right away. Fortunately, he's used to climbing up and down the mountain."

"I never really noticed him until he was just about out the door with you," said Eve. "Just that he was the youngest one and quiet. The only one who talked was Salaam. Up there in that cabin, I wasn't thinking clearly. Maybe it was the lack of oxygen. Besides, when you're in pain and feeling sick, you don't notice much else. I'm ashamed of what we did, practically pushing the three of you out of the hut to walk down the mountain in the dark. I guess we all felt sick and even though I wanted to help, I was actually relieved not to have to go." Eve swiped at a mosquito on her thigh and showed the dead bug to Andrew. "Got it," she added triumphantly.

"Good job," he said. He paused and looked around the bus and then swatted at a mosquito. "Damn. Missed. Where was I? Oh yeah, I remember. You were talking about how you were sick. I remember you were vomiting when we left. I don't think any of us realized how sick Barry was or how we all had mountain sickness, even the Germans, who were probably in the best shape. And Helga was the only one to make it to the top."

"I feel stupid. I was sort of delirious. I really wanted to help and go with you."

"There was no way you would have made it. You were too sick, but even so I knew you wanted to go."

"Well, I don't give up easily. That's something about me. I'm not willing to accept bad news. But that night, I just felt so sick I couldn't think straight. Maybe that's what happened to everybody: Group mentality. Group helplessness. Group suffering. Vulnerability. Only Klaus and the Germans even tried to reach the summit. When you left with Barry, it was sort of a relief. We didn't have to hear him wheezing and coughing. We didn't have to think about Barry. You solved our problem. That's the sad truth. We could rest, recuperate, take care of ourselves. I guess we were hoping that once you got lower down the mountain, Barry would be better. When I saw him lying half dead in the second hut, I felt sick. We all did. We realized what we had done to you and to him. We abandoned you. I'm so sorry. I know I can be selfish, a bit of a prima donna sometimes. But I think we all just convinced ourselves that everything would be okay. I'm really not a bad person."

"I know that. None of us knew how bad he would get. I've only read about high-altitude pulmonary edema in books. I was really scared he was going to die when we were trying to go up the saddle to the lower peak. I thought we all would die. It was so cold and dark. But I wasn't really scared. That probably sounds strange. It was so beautiful up there. If I were religious, I would say that I felt like God was up there with us. Or maybe it was ghosts or mountain spirits, or probably just the wind. But I did feel like something was out there. Some presence, some power. Anyway, I was okay with whatever happened to me."

"Mmm," she said. "I didn't realize you were religious."

"I'm not. In fact, I'm sort of surprised at what I'm saying. I don't really believe in God or that we are really here for some religious purpose. But I think we are part of something bigger and we've been given this gift of life and the ability to think and feel to do something more than eat, fuck, and fight."

Eve smiled and shook her head. "Don't leave out shopping. That's the way I distract my mind when I'm bored or anxious. I make lists of what I'll buy."

Andrew laughed. "That's not something guys would ever distract themselves with. We think about sports or sex."

"Yes, the most important priorities in life," said Eve. "Well, we're really in the middle of the jungle here. I sure hope we haven't run out of gas. The vines from the trees are already trying to climb into the windows." Eve reached her arm out of the window and pulled in a vine with large, flat leaves. "See."

"Yeah. Make sure you didn't grab some spiders with the vine. You never know. There's so much randomness that knocks us off the path we think we're on. Even something as simple as pulling the bus over to the side of the road. Who knows what that might do? What if someone got off the bus to go to the bathroom and got lost or hurt or left behind?"

Andrew paused. "Each day follows the one before, just like when you're driving in traffic, like this bus. You don't realize that one day there will be an accident, and someone in another car who you have never met will also be in the accident. That other person will become the most important person in your life, and both of your lives will become connected and change, maybe forever. You might die or lose a leg or go into a coma and the other person might be who decides what will happen to you. We figure life will continue on the way it has always gone, and that gives us some sense of confidence and peace of mind, but the truth is that it won't. There's eventually going to be an accident. The effects of that accident can change our lives for good or bad. They will happen. We just don't know when."

Eve took a deep breath then pulled the leaves off of the vine she had been holding and gave them to Andrew. "So are you saying these leaves are an accident? After all, I just killed them. I've changed their life. Or I'm an accident? Or this trip is an accident? Maybe it's fate or just God's will. And it might change your life and mine forever. Don't I have any say in all that?" Eve said. "Maybe I have a plan in mind but just haven't told you yet." She was joking, but it took Andrew a few moments to realize that she wasn't being serious when she began to smile and laugh. Eve moved closer to Andrew and touched his arm, and Andrew's arm jumped reflexively.

"Sorry," Andrew said. "I thought your hand was a mosquito. Anyway, sometimes both people can affect what happens. Up on that mountain, I had a glimpse of my own accident and Barry was the other car. Our lives were suddenly linked and maybe our deaths. Barry was the most important person in my life at that moment. I hardly knew him before, but that night I knew his heartbeat, his lungs, his body, even his mind, and I'm sure he knew mine. And Koba's too. We were three bodies joined together. Before that, Koba had been an African porter whose purpose had been to carry our food. But then suddenly our lives depended upon him and trusting him. It was just chance that we were together, like the two cars on the highway. And we were so vulnerable. I should have been afraid, but I wasn't."

The bus began to move again, and the reason for the delay became clear as a new passenger moved down the aisle, a woman in a brightly-colored tube of cloth, with red and black stripes

down the sides and a yellow circle in the center. She had ringlets of hair extending out in all directions and a wooden stick
in her hand, and Andrew could smell breast milk as she passed
him. Then he noticed the baby on her breast under her robe.
Andrew stared at the woman and she met his eyes with a smile,
as if they knew each other. As she continued to stare, he almost
felt that she was putting him under a spell. She hesitated for a
moment, gazed over at Eve, and continued down the aisle.

Andrew wanted to ask Eve if she had the same feeling that
he did about the strangeness of the woman with the baby. How
had the bus known to stop and pick up this African woman on
this road in the middle of the jungle? Had someone arranged
for the pickup or was it an accident? Andrew turned toward Eve,
but her eyes were already closed and her head was against the
window. He turned to see if perhaps there was someone waiting
for the woman in the rear of the bus, a husband or brother. But
she was alone, sitting on a burlap sack filled with grain. She
smiled at him again when their eyes met, and he noticed a gold
tooth in the front of her mouth.

They passed trees and animals who appeared suddenly in
the lights of the bus like fragmentary dreams then disappeared.
Eve's knee banged against Andrew's thigh, and her hand touched
his elbow. Andrew realized that all of the sudden touches were
probably from the movements of the bus, the bumps in the
road, and the sudden stops. But who could know for sure? The
question was a good distraction from the uncomfortable jerking
of his head and neck. Andrew closed his eyes and let his mind
wander.

Andrew found himself drifting back to the mountain—the
physical sensations of cold and exhaustion, and the touching
of bodies on the mountain and now on the bus. He had always

resisted close physical touch, feeling it an intrusion against his personal boundaries, but in the last few days he had lowered his guard and allowed Barry and Koba and Kara and now Eve to be touching him, leaning against him. He struggled against the sense of suffocation versus the liberation of a nakedness and connectedness when he allowed his walls to fall. He listened to Eve's breathing and felt the rise and fall of her chest, and the movements of her hands and her head that all seemed involuntary but also demonstrated that she was allowing herself to be vulnerable, and felt safe to lean against him. As he let his thoughts move between sleep and consciousness, Andrew also continued to reflect on the woman with the wild hair holding the baby, who had gotten on the bus so mysteriously and seemed to know him, seemed to know some secret between him and Eve that had not yet been shared with him.

They both were jolted from their half-sleep when they came to the Kenyan border, where they had to show their passports and get them stamped. Everyone got off the bus and stood around waiting for the border guards to call for them. Eve became impatient and walked over to the small shack where the two border guards were playing cards. Andrew could see how the guards studied her as she came up to them, how they noticed every movement of her body and her face. She was both their entertainment and a challenge to their authority.

Andrew watched with trepidation as the two wiry men in fading blue uniforms considered their next move. One of them reached out his hand and said something to Eve. She put her passport into the man's hand, and he began turning the pages, examining each one and asking questions as if he might find some fraudulent entry. Then the other guard took the passport and examined it. He grinned at Eve and said something. Eve answered with Swahili words that Andrew could not understand, then the guard pulled an immigration stamp from his pocket and pressed it onto Eve's passport with a loud thump and returned it to her. He waved the rest of the bus passengers forward and began stamping passports one after another. Andrew got himself into line and by the time they had gotten to him, the guards were bored and barely examined the page that they stamped. When Andrew returned to the bus and sat down next to Eve, he asked her why she had gone up to the guards and what they had said to her.

"He asked me if I was traveling alone. He said that it was not safe for a woman to travel to Nairobi alone."

"So, what did you say to him?"

"I told him that I was traveling with my husband, that you were my husband."

"Ha ha, your second husband in two days. What did he say to that?"

"He took my passport and began to study all my stamps. There are a lot of places: France; England; Italy; Guatemala. I've traveled a lot during vacations. The border guard looked at all the places on my passport and then asked why I wanted to go to Nairobi and if I was CIA."

"They think every American is CIA. I used to get asked that question at the hospital in Dar. So, what did you say?"

"I just said that if we were CIA we would not tell him. I also told him the CIA had a height requirement, and we were not tall enough."

"Seriously? Is that true? Am I too short for the CIA?" asked Andrew. He had never wanted to be in the CIA, but now that he might be excluded due to his height, he began to feel the echoes of being disqualified from the high school basketball team, football team, even the baseball team. It was only track and cross country for him. He had also read that he was too short to be a pilot, and that most US presidents were over six feet tall. It was an embarrassment that he'd hoped to avoid discussing with Eve.

"No," she said. "I made that up. I'm sure you'd make a fine spy. I just had to come up with a reason that the guard would believe."

"And he did? He thought we were too short to be CIA?"

"Who knows? It's not important. Anyway, I told him that you might be short in height but were very large in another area. That was when he laughed and began taking all the passports and stamping them. He just wanted some entertainment, a laugh to break up the boredom. No harm in that," she said. "Anyway, it will give you something to live up to." Andrew blushed and covered his eyes with his hand.

The bus soon began moving again into Kenya, stopping at a gas station with bathrooms and a café for everyone to get a quick meal while it refueled. Some people came back to the bus carrying food, sandwiches, and Cokes, but most just used the bathroom. Andrew stood by the men's room and watched for the woman from the bus with the baby, drawn by some unexplained curiosity. She went into the women's bathroom and when she came back out, she peered deep into his eyes with some unexpressed question or secret. He thought at first she was about to ask for food or money, but no words followed. They stood for a moment, waiting, looking at each other as if there would suddenly be an explanation for this odd sense of recognition, or some exchange of information or wisdom before they climbed back onto the bus without speaking.

They continued on to the bus station in Nairobi, where

beggars gathered around the arriving buses. As each passenger descended from the bus, random hands and fingers pulled at the passengers' luggage, and shadowy faces asked for money and shouted directions to hotels and connecting buses. Andrew and Eve tried to find their connection to Malindi as a large, muscular, bearded man in a torn gray t-shirt and red cap tried to pull one of Andrew's bags away from him.

"No, no," said Andrew. "Leave them alone."

"Come. I help you. Carry bag."

"No. No," said Andrew, shaking his head. They struggled over the bag and Andrew could feel it loosening from his grasp. In the dark, he could not see how many other men were there, watching and waiting to join the attack like wolves. Then the lady with the wild hair and the baby came over and began to shout at the bearded man and wave her arms at him. She struck him with a wooden stick on his head and neck. Andrew pulled his bags free and rushed away to find Eve. He turned and looked back for a moment and saw the woman still beating the man with one hand and holding her baby with the other. He remembered the fearsome look on her face as she pummeled the man, just before she was swallowed up by the crowd.

Eve was waiting by a bus with a sign for Malindi. She had the tickets in her hand and showed them to the driver as Andrew gave him their bags to store in the luggage compartment. This bus was more luxurious than the one they had taken from Tanzania, with cushioned seats that could be tilted to allow for stretching out hips and knees and leaning back. The people on the bus were a mix of Europeans and Africans. Even the African riders wore western clothes and carried radios. The aisles were free of baskets or bags. Gradually, Andrew began to relax as the danger and confusion of the bus station receded. He laid his head back on the soft, cushioned seat and his face was hidden from the outside by the tinted windows of the bus. Eve asked him what had happened, and he mentioned the scuffle with beggars, the thieves waiting to ambush him in the dark. "The woman from our bus, the one who got on when our bus pulled over, hit the man over the head with a stick."

"The woman with the baby?" asked Eve.

"Yes. She held the baby in one arm and hit the man with a stick with her other arm."

"Seriously? Was anyone with her? Did anyone help her?"

"I don't know. I didn't see anyone. It was dark. I felt bad. But I didn't know what else to do. There were so many of them around me. It was crazy."

"I should have stayed with you. I didn't realize. That was crazy, what she did," Eve said.

She stretched out her legs. Finally, in the darkness and the comfort of a cushioned seat, she felt the exhaustion of the bus ride washing over her.

She looked at Andrew in the seat next to her, and he seemed small and vulnerable. She wanted to touch him, partly to surprise him and partly to show him that she was thinking of him in a sexual way and that her joke about his height at the border was not a commentary about his attractiveness. Usually she was attracted to bigger men, but Andrew had a curious charm. She had joked about his size to the border guide, but now she wondered about how body type, and the details of hands, face, and eyes all fit into attraction.

She had noticed Andrew's hands—the fine curve of his fingers and even the delicacy and tapering of his fingertips that suggested sensitivity. Her hands were broader and her fingertips blunter, like the head of a hammer. She noticed that his chin created a solid foundation for lips that opened slightly as she touched him. His eyes were closed and his lids fluttered occasionally, as if perhaps he was dreaming. She liked his eyes, their eagerness and curiosity. His light-brown curls hung down in spirals and ringlets that framed his face with a soft gentleness. He smelled of sweat, and he had the beginnings of brown stubble on his chin.

He was not exactly handsome, but he was cute, which meant that he still had some of the naiveté, softness, and inexperience of an adolescent. He did not wear his sexuality as armor to protect himself from any innuendo of softness. In fact, his sexuality was just like his heroism—hidden and mysterious. She had chosen to come with him on this trip because he was different and safe and respectful of her individuality, and because she found the differences he expressed to be intriguing and attractive. She was also not ready to take on the role of Barry's caretaker at the hospital. She needed to get away and Barry would be there waiting when she returned, and they could sort things out. This trip with Andrew was spontaneous and a diversion from her life as a Peace Corps teacher, and she wanted to make the most of it. She let her hand slide down his belly and fall softly on his thigh as if by accident as she shifted in her seat, and could feel him stiffen beneath her hand.

→)K←

The bus was soon on a smooth highway and Andrew closed his eyes and was drifting off to sleep when he felt Eve's hand brush across his stomach and his leg and land on his lap. He opened his mouth and exhaled softly. He did not want to move lest he dislodge her hand, and so he lay still as his mind raced, waiting to see what might follow. But nothing did. He noticed her shoulders and chest expanding as she began to breathe faster. Through his half-closed eyes, he noticed that her eyes were open wide and her pupils were dilated black, leaving only a small rim of brown iris. And the skin of her neck and cheeks had begun to blush strawberry red.

The bus stopped at a station where they could eat some eggs and use the bathroom. Andrew got off first and Eve reached for his hand as she jumped off the bus step to the sidewalk. Andrew laughed as Eve stumbled slightly, and helped her regain her balance. "I guess my leg fell asleep," she said, smiling back at him.

The restaurant was noisy and humid, suffused with the moisture from the ocean. Andrew could feel his lungs filling with the rich, dense air. He felt himself regaining his equilibrium and his mind had stopped racing. He was curious about how to interpret Eve's hand and her obvious excitement. Was it innocent and inadvertent, or intentional? A test, perhaps?

Andrew felt a burst of energy as he regained his seat on the bus, perhaps from the early morning light and the breeze off of the ocean, or perhaps the hints of possibility to come. As the bus moved back onto the road, he could see the ocean shimmering blue and green in the light. He pointed out the water to Eve, and she smiled, the first time he had seen her whole face relax into a broad grin.

"Oh my God, I've never seen the ocean like this. It's such a deep blue-green and turquoise," she said, and he felt her squeeze his arm. After a moment of indecision, he decided to reach his arm over her shoulder and pull her toward him, and she came without any resistance. He might have kissed her then, but he was afraid to ruin the gradual, growing excitement.

Instead, they lay back on their seats in a half embrace for ten or fifteen minutes until his arm became sore, and he had to remove it.

⇥✦⇤

The bus pulled into Malindi as they were both drifting in and out of sleep. As the bus stopped, Andrew noticed the old hotels and restaurants near the bus station, with pink paint peeling off the walls. Foreigners in shorts and straw hats walked along the street, carrying bottles of Coke, as others sat at wooden tables on the sidewalk sipping beer and eating sandwiches. Andrew and Eve picked up their backpacks and walked toward the beach. After a few blocks, they found the Rafiki Hotel, with a vacancy sign in the window. The owner was a middle-aged East Indian man wearing a yellow-and-black dashiki, drinking a Coke and reading a newspaper.

"Hello, my friends. I'm Mr. Patel. Welcome to the Rafiki Hotel. Rafiki means 'friend' in Swahili. We are the friendliest hotel in all of Malindi. This is my promise to you. You are Americans? Yes?"

Andrew and Eve nodded. "How did you know?" said Andrew.

"Ah, that is my business, to know my clients. But the hint was the Levi jeans that the lady is wearing. Those are the real Levi's. Not an imitation. May I offer you a room?" said Mr. Patel. "I have one with a queen for you. That is the only one I have, but I think you will find it quite to your liking. It has a private bathroom. Only fifty dollars American. And it comes with a free breakfast and we will also drive you to the Malindi Marine National Park, which is our underwater park."

Andrew looked at Eve and she nodded. He thought for a

second about how he had intended to suggest separate rooms to protect the friendship he had with Barry, to honor their trust and all that had happened on the mountain. "Yes," said Andrew. "That will be fine."

Chapter 14

FTER THEY CHECKED in, they went into the room and Andrew laid his pack at the foot of the bed. Eve turned on the fan and closed the curtains. She was tempted to take off her clothes and lay naked in front of him, but she felt sweaty and dirty from the long bus ride. They were exhausted and discussed taking a short nap, but Eve decided to shower first. When she came out of the bathroom, she said, "Let's see the beach. We can sleep later. It's too beautiful to sleep now."

She went back into the bathroom to put on her bathing suit and Andrew pulled on nylon shorts. He took off his shoes and found sandals for his feet. His head and eyes were sore, but he wanted to see the beach so he took a Tylenol from his backpack and drank half a glass of water from a plastic bottle on the bureau. Eve emerged from the bathroom in a blue-and-yellow bikini, and Andrew tried not to stare at her, until she asked him to put sunscreen on her back and shoulders. He rubbed the white cream as she directed, far down her back, almost to where the bikini bottom began.

"Do you want me to put some on you?"

"What? Put what on?"

"Do you want some sunscreen? You should. We're on the equator. You'll need to take off your t-shirt."

"Oh yeah, sure. Good idea. Thanks, yeah, it would be ironic to get a sunburn after almost freezing to death a few days ago," he said.

"Yes, well, we've gone from Africa's highest mountain to sea level," she said. "I'm trying to look out for you."

"Thanks," he said. "I'm not used to that."

Andrew closed his eyes as he felt Eve's hands rubbing the lotion in. At first he felt anxious as he tried to relax and allow Eve to touch his body. Her strong fingers found the spaces between his muscles, kneading them and pressing on the sore spots. He tried to ignore the pain and lay still, hoping not to discourage her massage, but she noticed his pulling away.

"Sorry, too much?"

"Yeah, I guess there are some sore spots from all the lifting and carrying I did. But it feels good. Really. Just a little softer." He did not want to explain that he was always sensitive to any deep touch. He did not know why.

"Okay," she said. "I want you to enjoy," and she rubbed his skin gently all over. He could have drifted off to those delicious sensations, but Eve soon finished putting on the sunscreen and began to walk to the door, forcing Andrew to jump off the bed and follow her. "All right, let's go," she said.

They walked past two young African boys kicking a ball in the street. They found the sidewalk with grass on both sides, and a rusted green sign and small cement monument describing this spot to be the exact location of a visit from the Portuguese explorer Vasco de Gama in 1498. Just past the sign was a long stretch of white sand beach with a few umbrellas in the distance. The blue-green water lapped the sand gently.

Andrew took off his sandals when he reached the sand and his feet sank into the warm powder up to his ankles. He curled his toes into the sand, feeling the soft warmth rush between them. Eve ran ahead into the water and stood looking out into the distance. After a moment, Andrew pulled his feet out of the deep sand and followed her. They stood together, looking east toward India as the gentle waves brushed against their ankles and calves. There were rocks mixed with the sand in the water and bleached white pieces of coral at the waterline.

Eve turned and grinned at Andrew in an odd, intimate way. "What?" he said as she continued to stare at him and grin.

"Andrew, I have a surprise. I brought something for you."

"Really? What kind of surprise?"

"I brought some acid for us. Do you want to take some with me?"

"You mean LSD? I've never had it," he admitted.

"Really? A virgin?"

"I guess."

"I'll go slow," she said, and he could feel himself blushing. "It's windowpane. It's the best. We can take half and see how we feel."

"Now? We're going to take it now?" He looked at his watch. It was 10:00 a.m.

He had heard stories about bad experiences with LSD. There was a lecture in medical school during orientation about people hallucinating and jumping out of windows or getting lost or staring at the sun and going blind. Some people never recovered from a bad trip. His idea for the trip to Malindi was to lie on the beach and snorkel in the coral with the tropical fish. He wanted to see a place he had never seen and might never see again. Eve had been an unexpected addition to the trip, and his imagination had already created romantic possibilities. He thought she had given hints of similar romantic feelings, though he hesitated to assume that there was a hidden meaning from a squeeze of the hands or some innocent touching on the bus. But he had not imagined she would suggest LSD.

He worried about what it might do to him or both of them. Andrew also worried about betraying the trust that Barry had bestowed upon him by encouraging Eve to accompany him on the trip to Malindi. Barry would never have encouraged Eve if he imagined that they would take drugs together and share a bed. Andrew wasn't sure if the drug would be like alcohol and remove the inhibitions that were preventing him from doing something he might regret later. Or if the drug would make him see things that he did not want to see about himself or Eve, some dark or evil hallucinations that would not stop.

In college, he had been tempted to try LSD, but most of his friends smoked marijuana or drank beer and he had already gotten into enough trouble without LSD, almost losing his admission to medical school over a drunken party at his apartment where the police had been called. He'd had to go into alcohol and drug counseling to get charges dropped, and his dad had to call the dean of students, who made him spend two weekends watching films and listening to lectures. What he remembered from those sessions was that he had to avoid temptation and "say no" before he started, because he had a genetic vulnerability to the abuse of alcohol. That was a secret his father had shared with him. But now he was being asked to say yes.

⟶✠⟵

"Yes," said Eve. "This is a good time to take it. We'll be coming down just in time to have dinner and go to sleep."

Eve had brought along the LSD to help both of them discard the memories of what had happened on the mountain and plunge into an adventure on the beach with a clean slate. She'd found that LSD could shorten the process of stripping away the protective layers that prevented people from truly seeing and understanding each other. You could not lie or hide your fears and secrets on acid. Everything you were afraid to see about yourself was spread out in front of you in the ocean waves or the clouds that played out as your own private, recurring movie. You could not move on until you accepted it and shared it. And Eve wanted to know what Andrew was really like, inside and out. She would be his guide and protector as he had been for her on the mountain, but he would have to trust her.

"How long does it last?"

"About twelve hours, but the first hour or two are the most intense."

"Will we be able to swim and snorkel? I wouldn't do either if I was drunk."

"It's not the same at all. We'll be able to do whatever you want in the afternoon, just not for the next few hours. Open your mouth now, and I'll put half of the windowpane on your tongue." Eve pulled out a piece of foil and unwrapped it and pulled the thin clear square out and split it in half. "Okay, stick out your tongue."

"Are you sure about this?" he said.

"Yes, trust me," she said.

※

Andrew opened his mouth slowly, in stages, first the separation of his lips, then the gradual depression of his jaw, and finally the exposure of his teeth and tongue to the air.

"Good, now stick out your tongue," Eve said.

Andrew stuck out his tongue, closed his eyes, and Eve put half of the windowpane carefully on the middle of his tongue then pushed his jaw up to close his mouth. Then she put the other half on her own tongue and let it dissolve.

"Now what do we do?" Andrew asked.

"Oh, we can just walk along the beach and watch the waves and the sand for a while. I think you'll notice something unusual about the waves soon. We'll see what we feel like doing after that." For Eve, the LSD was a way to cut through all of the rules and red tape of life, to open her mind to the possibility that a wave could become a mermaid, and a human face could become a dog's face. Her friends had been surprised that she had taken LSD, because in most parts of her life she was well-organized and attentive to the rules and expectations of others. But there was something about an occasional foray into the world of LSD that felt liberating.

She'd first tried it with two friends from high school just before graduation. They took LSD and then walked along a river. For the first time in her life, she felt free of the constraints of her parents, and her mind leapt into realms of fantasy and imagination. Her friends had become fellow travelers in space, and they had forged a bond that was deeper than anything she'd felt before. She still called them, and when they talked their conversations had a special basis in their shared LSD experience.

Ever since, she'd found LSD to be a good way to reshuffle

the deck of cards that she had been dealt and to imagine a new hand with new cards. She hoped now that the world would become filled with love that was overflowing into the street for them to share. And for a time, her perceptions would sharpen and she could recognize the possibility of love between people that was usually hidden from view. She was curious about what mysteries would be revealed about Andrew; what were his secrets and fears? The hallucinations might provide answers, and in any case, there would be the opportunity to experience the beach and the coral with altered consciousness together with Andrew.

⊹❈⊹

Andrew did not feel anything for a few minutes. He thought perhaps he was immune to the effects of the drug or that Eve was playing a joke on him. He was holding Eve's hand as they walked on the beach when he noticed something odd: there were faces in the waves, faces that appeared and disappeared, old men with beards like presidents or kings of a hundred years before, and these faces were moving and turning into animals—lions, giraffes, and elephants all tumbling round and round in the water. He pointed them out to Eve and she smiled and her face became an animal's face, just like the animals in the water—the face of a monkey and then the face of a deer and then the face of a zebra. It frightened him. Why was he seeing these animals when he looked at Eve? What did that mean? Were these hidden attributes of Eve that were now becoming visible?

He decided to look away and stared at the sand and mud to make the faces go away, but that did not stop the faces from appearing in front of him, and the more he tried to stop them, the more they multiplied. He saw the Queen of England, the King of Hearts, and Alice in Wonderland, and Snow White, and Sylvia Weinstein who had been his dissection partner in anatomy class, and the face of the man he had dissected. Barry's face appeared in the waves, with turquoise lips, and blood was dripping from his mouth and nose, then the face turned into Koba's face.

Then Koba turned into a centaur and was lifting Barry up onto his back and riding into the sky like he was taking a sacrifice to the gods, and there were clouds that became Klaus and Kara and Salaam and Mohammed, who received Barry and carried him back to Earth and gently laid him down on the sand. Barry was speaking to him, but he could not hear the words. And then Barry's body disintegrated into the sand, and Andrew tried to pick up the grains of sand and they slipped through his fingers.

Eve could see that Andrew was becoming frightened as he picked up sand over and over, and she pulled him toward her and hugged him. "Don't try to control it. Accept it whatever it is."

"But there are faces in the sand and in the water. You're a monkey," he said.

"So are you," she laughed. "So, I guess we're compatible. Now, what adventures would two monkeys like to take? Let's move."

Andrew could barely talk, so he nodded and got up. He looked at his watch and realized that only twenty minutes had passed since Eve had put the acid on his tongue, and it felt like hours. What if the panorama of images and thoughts would never stop? What if he would be trapped in this world of spinning, changing faces that appeared out of waves and sand?

He felt Eve take his hand and they started to walk. As they moved, new images replaced the faces in the waves, and Andrew felt like he was watching scenery from a speeding bus. They returned to the hotel, and Eve led him to the bed and held him close to her. He began to think about sex with Eve and her body touching his and their bodies tumbling down a hill enmeshed in each other's arms, but then his mind changed gears and he was tumbling down the mountain over rocks.

He felt Eve's hands pulling down his bathing suit and he could feel her hands on him and his hands on her but he was not sure what was real and what was in his mind. He felt her naked body moving on his and they were in a tunnel, turning and twisting around and around like a rope. He felt so close to her that he was inside her and she was inside him. They were becoming one body, part female and part male, and it was a revelation that they could exchange bodies. He was not sure if they were having sex, because he could not keep his mind focused. Instead he imagined that he was a bird floating above the ocean and watching everyone on the ground below having sex. They became part of a school of black-and-yellow fish changing direction every few seconds, moving one way and then the other. Eve said, "This is not happening."

He was not sure what she meant, but he shook his head. He rubbed her back with his hands and down to her thighs and he felt between her legs where their bodies joined together. The contour of her breasts was smooth, wet, and fragrant against his face and soft against his fingers.

"This is not happening," she repeated. He was not sure what was happening and what was not happening. He felt her hands and her lips on his mouth and the weight of her body on his. He tried to focus on Eve, being beside her, inside of her, part of her. It was something he wanted, but his eyes kept moving away from her to the stains on the ceiling that looked like a horse or the curtains over the window that danced like ballerinas. He heard a voice saying, "This never happened," and he was not sure what that meant. Finally, he felt her get off the bed and pull him toward the bathroom. He noticed that they were naked and their bodies undulated like the curtains blown by the fan above their heads.

They showered and watched the soap bubbles run down their face and shoulders to their legs with amazement, as if they had never noticed the colors in the bubbles of soap before or their reflections in the bubbles They held each other and turned around in the shower as the water created rivulets in the crevices between them. After the shower, they stood together in front of the mirror. As Andrew looked at Eve, her body deconstructed itself into pieces: face, breasts, and thighs like a Picasso painting. And his body, narrow face and dilated eyes, heaving chest and shoulders, quivering hips and a cock that changed size as Eve touched it. They were almost the same height. Their nakedness felt as much a curiosity as an erotic image. Andrew felt the enormous truth of what they had shared that could never be explained to anyone or doubted.

They put on their bathing suits and went to the front desk of the hotel. Mr. Patel was at the front desk, smoking. He was wearing a different dashiki that came almost to his knees and had a cup of tea in front of him. He asked them if they wanted to go to the underwater national park to see the famous coral and fish. He had a car that would take them and provide snorkels and masks for only fifty American dollars. Andrew was not sure if he would be able to swim, but Eve nodded and pulled him along to the car that would take them to the park.

The park was mostly deserted, and Mr. Patel asked how long they wanted to stay so that he knew when to return to collect them. "Only an hour," said Eve.

"Are you sure, Madame?" he said. "There is so much to see. I have paid the fees. It is our national treasure."

"Yes," she said. "One hour."

The underwater national park was not very remarkable from the beach. Just some benches to sit on and attach masks and flippers. After that, they followed a path down to the rocks. Andrew struggled with his mask, unsure how to fit the snorkel and mask together. He might have used up the entire hour puzzling the correct way to attach the snorkel and get it into his mouth if Eve had not come over and helped.

When they put their heads under the water, it was as if someone turned on the lights in a room that had been dark. An entire world of color and shapes appeared that had not been visible from the beach. Eve held Andrew's hand as they floated just above the coral, looking down on fish with pink-and-green spots, yellow-and-black stripes, gray-and-white splotches. There were caves where starfish lay against red-and-black coral and flowing fields of seagrass.

Andrew was happy to stay in one place on the surface, floating back and forth, breathing through his snorkel and watching the world beneath him swirl as fish raced by, feeding on seaweed and microscopic shellfish. He wondered what it might be like to live in one of those caves underwater and never know of life on the surface. How would you ever know what was real once you discovered what had previously been invisible? How would you know when to trust your feelings when they had previously deceived you? What if the person holding your hand, sharing the moment, who could validate everything you had experienced, had seen something different? What if that person said, "This isn't happening. This never happened." Who would be right? Did it matter?

Chapter 15

FTER AN HOUR, Andrew and Eve swam back to the shore. Mr. Patel was waiting in his car and took their swim fins and snorkels. "It is quite beautiful, is it?" Mr. Patel asked.

"Yes, I've never seen anything like it," said Eve. "Thank you for bringing us here."

"You are very welcome, Madame. I can show you many wonderful sights if you would like a tour."

"Oh, I think we'll rest now," said Eve. "Maybe later."

"At your service, Madame."

Mr. Patel drove them back to the hotel. As they took off their bathing suits and showered, Eve asked Andrew how he was feeling. He looked at her naked body next to his and it was shimmering and undulating. Five hours had passed since they had placed that half windowpane on their tongues.

"I'm good," said Andrew. "I'm feeling more normal, but more relaxed, and life is good. I can still taste the saltwater in my mouth that I breathed in through my snorkel. But I can control what I'm seeing now, and I like what I'm seeing." He felt his face opening into a grin and he felt an overwhelming sense of happiness washing over him.

"That's good," said Eve. "I want you to enjoy all of this." She turned toward him and danced a few steps, jiggling her breasts and hips.

"Mmm," Andrew said and he took her hand and led her to the bed. As he lay with her, he imagined Eve was a mermaid wrapping her body around his. He closed his eyes and let himself inhale her scent. But his mind was too explosive to remain focused. As he lay on the bed he noticed the stain on the ceiling becoming an elephant and then a giraffe and then an octopus.

Eve was looking at the curtains fluttering in the wind. Andrew tried to bring himself back to her. He wanted her and she wanted him but he felt her drifting away, like a raft pulled out to sea while he remained on the beach. They lay there naked for an hour, touching and kissing and holding each other, watching the ceiling move and the curtains become birds and butterflies. Finally, Andrew asked her if she wanted to fuck.

"I do, but..." And she paused. As the pause went on longer, Andrew forgot what he had asked her because his mind had already moved on. Then he remembered. He had asked her if she wanted to fuck and was still waiting for an answer.

"It's okay, I'm not sure I could do it now. Maybe we've already done it. I can't remember. But seeing you lying here next to me, you're so beautiful, like a mermaid. And I want to," he said.

"I do, too," she said. "It's not like Barry and I made any rules. We haven't actually had sex yet. And we've both had other people before. I've actually been with some girls too. Actually, just one," Eve laughed. Andrew heard Eve's words and wanted to respond but was distracted by the movements of the curtains and wondered whether they were alive.

"Hey, that's far out," he said, as much about the curtains as Eve's sexual confession.

"Barry knows about that, and he's okay with it," she continued. "He thinks it's sexy. But I'm not sure how he'd feel about you. You're not a girl, are you?" she said and she put her hands on his chest and ran them down his legs and between his thighs. "Well, I guess not," she laughed. "But I think you know how to make love the way that girls do, the way they like it. The way I like it."

Andrew wondered what Eve meant. He wasn't even sure that they had made love or how to make love like a woman. "I...I wasn't sure if we already did it. Did we? I remember us doing something and it felt like electricity going through me, and you said something about 'this never happened,' but I wasn't sure what never happened," he said.

"That's okay. I wanted you to feel something special. I was a bitch on the mountain. I was scared. I felt sick. I didn't want that to be what you remembered. I wanted to scrub your mind clean. That's what acid does. It scrubs your mind."

"When I was on the mountain, I imagined sitting on a beach because I was so cold. But this is even better than what I imagined."

Eve rolled over closer to him and put her hand around his head and pulled him close. "I don't know what's going to happen with Barry and me. Our Peace Corps mission is almost over. He can be weird at times, like a spoiled rich frat boy, but he has a good heart. So much happened, and he never really had a chance. He's going back home to San Francisco. He's invited me to visit. I've never been there but I've heard lots of good things about it. Lots of smart people with ideas about how to change the world. Make it better. So we'll see. This thing that we're doing here? It's a one-time thing. Just think of it as the dream you imagined on the mountain. It's better to think of it as a dream, as if it never happened."

They decided to get dressed and walk around Malindi. Andrew thought they should have been tired, but he felt energized. Now that the hallucinations had dissipated, he was more eager to explore the city. Malindi had cafes and shops that opened out onto the narrow sidewalks, and as they walked together arm in arm, they bumped into tourists from all over the world. In Malindi, the tourists sauntered without a clear destination, unlike the climbers on the mountain who had a clear path and a summit to reach. The Malindi tourists had faces reddened by sunburns and alcohol that were different from the intense, oxygen-starved faces of climbers on the mountain. Covering their reddened skin, the Malindi tourists wore straw hats and brightly colored African fabrics and white linen pants with drawstrings at the waist.

Eve waved to each couple they passed and some waved back and greeted them in German, French, English, or with a Swahili greeting of, "Jambo." Andrew observed this extroverted side of Eve that he had not seen during the climb and wondered how much of her personality was from the drug and how much was a part of herself she had kept hidden.

They walked into a café for a cup of tea. There was a thin, bearded Asian man behind the bar serving drinks and an African woman with an Afro holding a baby and talking to the man. Andrew thought she looked just like the woman from the bus. Or perhaps this could all be a hallucination. He hesitated to say anything, fearful to reveal his drug-intoxicated state. But then the woman noticed him and waved. He waved back tentatively.

"So you have found me," she laughed.

"Yes," said Andrew. "I wanted to thank you, but we had to leave on the bus. It was too dark. I never expected to see you again."

"Well, now you can buy me a beer," she said. "I'm Grace. And this is Amani," she said, pointing to the baby. "And this is Ali, my husband," she added and pointed to the bartender. "He picked me up at the bus station and drove me back to our home here. This is our restaurant. That man who grabbed your bag was a scoundrel. The bus station is very dangerous for Mzungu like you. But you were lucky to have a friend," she laughed.

"Yes, I was. This is Eve," said Andrew as he pointed to Eve. "We're visiting from the US. I'm a medical student and Eve is Peace Corps."

Eve nodded and said, "I guess we were meant to walk in here and see you. We were just wandering down the street and something drew us here."

"I have special powers," Grace laughed. "Or maybe you were thirsty and hungry. Now we must have food together. Please have some dinner with us."

"We were just going to have some tea," said Andrew. He was not sure his stomach would be able to digest food.

"We will just have some ugali and rice and a bit of meat. A traditional African dinner," said Grace. She looked over at her husband, and he nodded and walked into the kitchen. "Where are you staying?"

"The Rafiki Hotel," said Andrew.

"Ah yes, with Mr. Patel. He is our friend. And now you must tell us your story," said Grace.

Eve looked at Andrew and laughed. "Okay. Once upon a

time..." then she paused and looked at Andrew to continue. "Your turn," she said.

Andrew tried to begin the story, but his mind was still disorganized. And so he said, "We went swimming at the underwater national park today. We were floating on the surface of the water, looking down at this hidden world of colors and shapes that were moving in front of our eyes. Then we realized they were fish and coral and seaweed, all invisible from the beach, and it was like looking at them through a translucent stone, a moonstone. It was magical. We wondered what other magic could top what we had seen at the park, and then we were walking on the street and it was just like floating over the coral in the water, but instead of seeing fish, we saw people, and instead of coral, we saw a restaurant. We walked into this restaurant and it was more magic, because here you are, the lady who saved me, and the lady we wanted to find and thank, and you were shining like an electric eel. We did not even know your name before, but now we do. That was the greatest gift of all."

"I like that story," said Grace, "because it feels true even if it is somewhat short and simple. Now we should eat, and then I will tell you a story," she said as Ali brought four plates with cornmeal gruel, rice and chunks of beef, and bottles of beer.

Andrew was not sure that he would be able to coordinate the process of picking up the food, putting it in his mouth, chewing, and swallowing. He stared at the food for a few minutes while Eve stirred the rice and meat on her plate with a fork. Grace was breastfeeding Amani, and there was a silence as Eve stared off at a painting on the wall.

Then Grace interrupted Andrew and Eve's reverie. Andrew's mind was wandering and he was not sure what he was hearing and what he was imagining as Grace spoke. "Now I will tell you a story about a boy and girl. They are both on a quest, but they have been searching with their eyes closed, bumping into rocks and trees. Finally, they bump into each other when they jump into the water together and, at first, they see nothing, feel nothing. They are holding onto each other's hands as the waves move them back and forth like seagrass, but they cannot even feel each other's hands. Their hands are numb. Their bodies are numb. The waves on the ocean surface create a fog of sand and rocks. They are blind.

"They are holding onto each other and take a deep breath to avoid the water entering their nose and mouth, then dive down to where the water is still and the fish and the seagrass calm. This was the place they had been looking for, where colors and shapes dance before their eyes. Their bodies float free and they feel their two hands squeezing together. They can only remain a few seconds underwater before their breath is used up, but in those few seconds they experience a moment of great clarity that will guide their future.

"They return to the surface and fill their lungs with air, and when they look down again from the surface, all they can see is more swirling of the clouds of sand. They wonder if that moment of clarity had been a mirage. But they realize that their bodies suddenly feel all of the sensations that had flooded into them underwater. They go back to their hotel, make love, and then wander down a street until they walk into a restaurant where a woman with big hair is suckling a baby and her husband preparing a meal for them. The woman confirms all they had seen, and tells them the clarity would guide their lives toward their futures. She gives them a stone that allows the light to pass through, and a piece of coral in the shape of Neptune's trident that will protect them.

"This is the stone." Grace took off a necklace that contained a gray, translucent moonstone and gave it to Eve. "And this is the coral." And she gave a small, trident-shaped piece of bleached white coral that had been decorating the table to Andrew.

"Oh, I couldn't take this," said Eve.

"But you must. It is part of your story. It is your moonstone. But not the end of your story. You must keep it with you. It will give you clarity when you are lost." Grace paused for a moment and then looked at Andrew, "And you also. You must hold onto the coral. The three prongs of the trident will beat away any scoundrels."

Andrew rolled the piece of coral in his palm. It was small enough to put into his pocket. He liked the weight of the coral in his hand, and imagined that it was a real trident that would protect him. He took a deep breath and closed his eyes for moment, remembering the ancient gods Poseidon and Neptune. He opened his eyes and looked at Eve and she was smiling and putting the necklace with the stone around her neck.

Andrew chewed the beef off the bone and took a handful of corn gruel in his fingers and licked it with his tongue. He drank down one bottle of beer and then another. Ali and Grace were now standing and singing an African song and swaying with their baby held between them. Eve grabbed Andrew's hand and pulled him up so that they could all dance together. They swayed and danced as one for several minutes, and an older couple with gray hair and African shirts who had been dining in the restaurant quietly got up and clapped. Then Andrew and Eve danced out of the restaurant, waving as they passed through the door and continued down the street. Eve held Andrew's arm in hers, and they could have been boyfriend and girlfriend to any outside observer. Their interlocked arms as they marched together felt like the clarity that Grace had described in her story.

As the sunlight faded into night and was replaced by the lights of the town, their energy began to wane. They walked back past the restaurant to find Grace and Ali and thank them, but the restaurant was closed and dark. Then they went back to the hotel, found their room, got into bed, and fell deeply asleep without undressing. Mr. Patel had to wake them at ten the next morning so they did not miss the bus back to Moshi and the hospital.

The bus trip back was awkward. Eve moved constantly, changing positions, bending her knees up toward her chest then extending her legs out straight, resting her head against the window, pushing her elbow against Andrew's ribs, sleeping in short spurts and then waking and turning her head away when Andrew turned toward her. Andrew sensed a change in Eve's disposition and found himself turning over the coral trident in his hand as he speculated on what Eve was thinking. Andrew asked if she was okay once, and she nodded. "I'm just tired." But neither of them discussed what had happened in Malindi or what might come next.

They arrived at the bus station in Moshi in the evening and took a taxi to the hospital. Kara and Klaus were sitting in the waiting room of the hospital. The news about Barry was all good. Barry was to be discharged the next day. His chest X-ray was almost back to normal, and he could take medicine at home to remove any remaining fluid in his lungs. Kara and Klaus planned to leave for Denmark the next morning.

Kara took Andrew aside as Eve went off to visit with Barry. "How was the trip to Malindi?" she asked.

"It was wonderful. We saw the underwater national park and

the coral and the fish were amazing. I've never seen anything like it before," he said.

"Yes. That's good. And was there anything else?" Kara smiled at him.

"No, that was all we had time for," he said, ignoring the implications of her question.

"Very good. Klaus and I wanted to visit Malindi, but we had no money for another trip. But maybe you could visit us in Denmark. Have you ever been there? We have beautiful beaches also. And you know the women go topless," Kara added and laughed.

"I didn't know that, but I won't forget. I've never been to Denmark," Andrew said. He was curious about Denmark and the attitudes of the people about politics and healthcare, and it was also where they made one of his favorites, Carlsberg Elephant beer.

"Here is our address and telephone number. You can just arrive, and you will have a nice place to stay," said Klaus as Kara wrote down all the information on a piece of paper and gave it to him.

"Thanks. I'd like to visit you and Klaus and we could talk about everything that happened. I'll tell you more about Malindi too. There was a strange woman we met there," he said. "She was sort of a fortuneteller."

"Maybe we will be part of your good fortune and you will bring us luck also. Please visit us," she said. "Now that you are here, we will take our leave. We must pack for our trip tomorrow."

Andrew said goodbye and walked to Barry's room. The corridor had pink-and-white pastel colors on the walls and a black-and-white linoleum floor. There were no nurses visible, and

Andrew found Barry's room from the sound of Eve's voice as she told an animated version of their walk through Malindi at night. He listened for a moment as Barry told Eve about his treatment. Then Andrew knocked lightly at the door and entered.

"Hey," said Barry. "So you decided to leave the fish and come back here."

"It was a tough choice," said Andrew. "Probably one of the most beautiful beaches in the world."

"I've been pretty bored. I think the nurses are all retired nuns. They come in to do physical therapy every six hours and pound on my chest with rubber discs. Look at these welts. They're a bunch of sadists." Barry displayed two rows of angry red bruises and welts on his chest. He explained that he had contacted the Peace Corps, and they were recommending that he go home immediately. The Peace Corps was also going to send a Peace Corps doctor to check on him and make sure he was fit to travel. Barry wanted Andrew to recount what had happened on the mountain because he could not remember much of it.

"So, is it true that you carried me down the mountain?" he asked.

"I did some. And Koba carried you too. Do you remember?"

"No, I don't remember anything. Anyway, I heard that you saved my life. That's what everyone's saying. The doctors here said it: 'He saved your life. You would have died if he didn't carry you down.' So, I believe it. They see people just like me die on the mountain every year. Wow, I mean, what can I say, man? You fucking saved my life. I mean, whatever I have, it's yours. I'm not kidding. You name it and it's yours."

"Don't think of it that way," Andrew said, because he knew he had already collected on Barry's offer. He had slept with Eve.

He tried to change the conversation. "It was high-altitude pulmonary edema. I'd never seen a case of it. But really, I don't want you to think about it like that."

"Whatever it was, I was dying and you saved me. The grim reaper was coming after me. I owe you big time, man. But at least you went to Malindi with Eve. How was Malindi? Beautiful beach, from what I hear. Beautiful women too. But you had Eve. You can look but you can't touch. Anyway, you can't beat her for beauty."

"No, you can't; that's true," said Andrew, smiling at Eve. And in that instant, when their eyes met, there was an acknowledgment of the intimacy that only lovers can share.

"Yeah, well, I guess you'll be going back to Dar es Salaam tomorrow," Barry said.

"Yes, I have to finish up my clerkship. I guess you'll be leaving too."

"Yeah, I'll be leaving soon. Before I go, Eve and I have a lot of catching up to do. I'm ready to show her what I can do when I have enough oxygen. If you're going to be here tomorrow, maybe we can get dinner together, the three of us."

"I need to get the bus tomorrow morning," Andrew said. It was true that he needed to be back, but now he wanted to leave immediately so that he would not have to see Eve and Barry together.

"Yeah, everyone's taking off. All the excitement's over. I guess it will just be me and Eve. By the way, Kara and Klaus were wonderful. They visited me every day and got me food and whatever I needed. Kara tried to protect me from those nurse sadists. The Germans came by and so did John and Mickey and Salaam. They were all nice. I actually got to like Helga. But Kara's really a gem. And Klaus too. Great guy. Super. I invited them to visit me in San Fran. And that invite is also open for you, of course. Any time. Please come and visit. And Eve's going to come out and visit San Fran when she gets done over here. Maybe I'll be able to convince her to stay for a while. She really saved my life just like you did."

Eve knelt down and kissed Barry softly on the cheek as Andrew watched.

That was what he thought about on the long bus ride back to Dar es Salaam. That kiss on the cheek.

Chapter 16

ANDREW KNEW OF people with obsessions. He had seen them in the psychiatry ward. The man who washed his hands every hour and touched doorknobs with tissues to avoid the germs that were his obsession. Or the drug addicts, even after years of abstinence, who talked of how they continued to desire the heroin or cocaine that was their obsession. Or Shakespeare's Juliet, who described her obsession with Romeo: "Good night, good night! Parting is such sweet sorrow, that I shall say good night till it be morrow." And Andrew agreed that an obsession could be both sweet and sad, just as some of the best foods tasted better with a mix of sweet and sour or sweet and salt. Obsession could give the heart hope in spite of obstacles. In fact, he wondered if the obstacles were part of an obsession, and once they were overcome, the obsession would fade because part of its attraction was its apparent unattainability.

Eve now filled a part of his mind that he had not known existed, and he revisited her presence at odd moments without warning. And the feelings were both sweet and sad, particularly her comment that what they had done together "had never happened." What did that mean? Something that he revisited over and over again, she did not believe had happened at all. If she did not believe anything had happened, or didn't want him to have such thoughts, how could they ever be together?

Unlike an object of obsession such as gold or fame or revenge that required only the actions of one person to reach the goal, his obsession with Eve required her to reciprocate. Otherwise, it would have no meaning, no value at all. Even with determination and perseverance, it would all be for naught if Eve did not share his feelings. Yet, he believed she did. Grace had given him the trident and Eve the moonstone because their futures were intertwined. He needed to find her so they could continue the adventure that had begun in Malindi.

Everything went so quickly after he returned to Dar es Salaam and flew back to medical school. He had not been thinking clearly and had been feeling rejected when he'd seen Eve with Barry. But now he was beginning to have clarity, exactly as Grace had predicted. Still, he needed to move carefully, gather more information, and plan his next steps.

It was during a sleepless night at the end of his medical school cardiology rotation at the Denver General Hospital, six months after he returned from Africa, that he came upon a plan. He would visit Klaus and Kara. He thought perhaps they could help him answer the questions that occupied his mind in the early morning hours between sleep and dreams, as his yearnings for Eve surfaced and were on his mind as he awakened. Maybe they could explain why Eve had not written or called him. Maybe they could tell him what he should do now. He had a week's vacation between his medical school clerkships, that he had been planning to use to organize his interviews for residency positions, but perhaps he could fit in a short visit to Denmark. They had invited him to visit, but he had rushed back to Dar es Salaam and never followed up.

They were the only people he could discuss his feelings about Eve with. They knew her and would be honest about what she might want and how she felt about him. And they might have some information about how to contact Eve, where she lived, what she was doing. He remembered how Kara had walked with him down to the first hut, holding his hand when he slipped on the mud, and how she had made it possible for Eve to go with him to Malindi while Barry was still in the hospital. She must have sensed that they wanted to be together, that they were right for each other and needed to be together And so he decided it was worth a try. In fact, he wondered why he hadn't considered the visit sooner.

While he could not find any direct flights from Denver to Copenhagen, there were inexpensive flights to Brussels and he could take the train to Copenhagen from there. It would allow him three days to visit Denmark and he would still have time to work on his residency interviews. He made a long-distance call to the telephone number that Kara had given him just before they had left Africa.

Klaus answered. "Hallo."

"Hello, this is Andrew—from our climb in Africa?" There was a pause and Andrew waited to hear a voice, but when the silence persisted he added, "I was thinking of visiting you guys in a few days. I can get a flight to Brussels and then a train to Copenhagen. Is it okay?"

"Ah, Andrew. Yes, of course. This is a surprise. I have to teach my students. But Kara can greet you. Here is a telephone number for her. Please call her." Klaus gave Andrew another telephone number and Andrew hung up and called the number. This time, a woman's voice answered the telephone.

"Hallo?"

"Hello, this is Andrew calling from America."

"Andrew? Yah? This is Kara. How did you find me?"

"I spoke to Klaus. He gave me this number. I'm thinking of flying to Brussels in two days and then taking the train to Copenhagen to visit you and Klaus. I have just a few days. Is it okay?"

"Yes. That would be a wonderful surprise. You will need to take a bus to find me after you arrive in Copenhagen. I am just outside of Copenhagen. Not too far. I will tell you the direction. You can also call me when you arrive in Copenhagen." Kara gave him the number of a bus to take, where to find it, and her address.

Andrew took the plane from Denver to New York first. He was excited and nervous because he was not accustomed to making spontaneous decisions like this about trips or vacations. He would usually plan and read guidebooks and try to find the best deals. But this time he felt the need to just go and let events unfold as they would. His mind was spinning on that first flight as he tried to remember everything that he and Klaus and Kara had done together. He remembered how welcoming they were to him as he reached the third cabin, and how Kara walked with him in the dark to get help for Barry. Initially, he had thought of them as an innocent and naïve couple, but as he thought more about them, he realized that he had been wrong about that assessment. He had mistaken their acceptance of him and the others as innocence when it was really openness and a willingness to trust others.

By the time he arrived in New York, he had calmed down and begun to imagine what he might do in Denmark with them. He wondered how they would look and what their lives were like at home. People are different when they travel. They can experiment with a new personality. When they return home, they usually return to their prior identity and personality too, and Andrew wondered what that might be for Klaus and Kara. How different would they be from the couple he had met in Africa?

Andrew slept most of the way on the plane to Brussels with fragments of dreams, interspersed with questions he would ask Klaus and Kara about Eve. He would tell them about the bus trip, the psychedelic adventure on the beach, and how they wandered into a restaurant run by a mysterious woman who had helped them on the trip. Everyone had a story about how they met that seemed fated and inevitable. What would they think about a future for him and Eve? It would be a nice diversion from thinking about his future through the prism of his residency application, which posed hopelessly opaque questions about his accomplishments and aspirations. Internal medicine or surgery or critical care were all reasonable possibilities for him, and he had no idea how to dissect them from each other and make a choice.

While Klaus and Kara could not help him with his residency choices, they might be able to help him with Eve. He wanted their honest opinion about whether they felt that Eve seemed interested in him, and whether there was any hope for him. They had been with Barry at the hospital and they would be able to advise him about how to speak with Barry if Eve was still with him.

Andrew landed in Brussels and the trip to the train station was a blur of strange languages, luggage, passports, and sandwiches. The train ride was quiet and Andrew could stretch out his legs, read a book, or just lay his head back and rest. He liked the half-awake state on the train where he could open his eyes and see a new town with a brick train station, a name in Flemish, people on bicycles, trees, and cars, all flying past before he had a chance to register them in his memory. The passengers on the train all respected his privacy, but also were willing to answer any questions he had about travel or the train.

In medical school, each new clerkship had been like travel on a train, but instead of speeding past the stops, he would disembark at the surgery stop for a few weeks, watch operations, learn how to stitch, and then it was time to get back on the train. His next stop might be pediatrics, where he would learn about babies with fever or teenagers with acne. There were so many stops that it was easy to lose track of the destination, but Andrew enjoyed the novelty of each new specialty and the new faces he encountered. Andrew had been happy to be the passenger on the medical school train because the scenery was interesting, constantly changing, and there was continued movement forward toward graduation. Now, on the train to Denmark, he felt the same sense of momentum toward a destination that would include familiar faces but unfamiliar geography.

He got off the train at the main station in Copenhagen. He quickly noticed how much whiter, taller, and blonder than him everyone was. In Africa he had been the only white, the object of stares, laughter, and rumors. It did not matter if he was tall, fat, blond, or dark-haired. No one seemed to notice such differentiating characteristics. Even his somewhat dark skin color did not really matter, because he was so much whiter than the Tanzanian students. Here in northern Europe, he was also different, but in another way. His parents were both the children of immigrants who had come from different parts of Europe—Ireland, Italy, Russia, and Jews from Eastern Poland—and they had a very different genetic pedigree than the people of Denmark. In the US, his grandparents had not been considered white. That label was reserved for the descendants of the English, French, Germans, and other Northern Europeans. Now, in Denmark, he could begin to understand how such distinctions had been made.

When he got on the bus that Kara had identified for him, Andrew also realized that English was not the preferred language for the people on the bus, though most people seemed to understand it when he asked them questions. He mentioned to the bus driver what address he was looking for, and that he was not familiar with the area. Then he asked if the driver would inform him when they reached his destination. The driver nodded without speaking, and a white-haired man wearing a blue overcoat, who had overheard Andrew's request, assured Andrew that he would be on the lookout for Andrew's stop, which was a farming village not far from where the man lived.

The urban scenery—brightly painted three- or four-story buildings along canals, and people riding bicycles or walking along the street—gradually gave way to rolling farmland with cows and farmhouses. Andrew's fatigue from traveling lulled him into a state of peaceful lethargy, and he was jolted awake when the white-haired man in the long coat nudged Andrew to alert him to the approach of his stop. Andrew grabbed his backpack and climbed down the steps of the bus onto an intersection where two rural roads crossed.

There was a solitary white farmhouse with a red roof, red door, and a pickup truck in the driveway set away from the road. Andrew waited for several minutes to see if anyone might come out of the door or if a car might arrive to pick him up. When no one came along, he crossed the road and walked down the driveway to the front door of the farmhouse. There was no number on the door, but there was a cast iron bell hanging from a rope with a small hammer attached. Andrew stood for a few minutes, looking at the bell, and then struck it with the hammer. Before the loud clanging stopped, Kara's face poked out from the door. "You found our little hippie farm," she said. "Come in, come in, you must be very tired."

Kara hugged him and pulled him inside the farmhouse. It took Andrew's eyes a few minutes to adjust to the darkness inside the living room and notice two young blond women on a maroon sofa. One of them was feeding an infant. They got up and greeted him with handshakes and hugs. "This is Freja and Ella," said Kara, pointing to the two women. "Perhaps you would like some coffee or tea. We have wonderful, fresh milk too from our cows. Would you like coffee with milk? Or maybe you would like some beer or a soda?"

Before Andrew could collect his thoughts and answer, he had to overcome the temptation to just keep looking at the three women and decide if they were truly three distinct individuals or if they were a blurred image of one.

"Yes," said Andrew. "I'm thirsty. It all sounds good."

Freja and Ella began speaking in Danish and laughing. Andrew looked to Kara for some explanation. "Oh, they are just commenting how handsome you are. They do not see too many men with brown curly hair and a somewhat short, dark body. Most of our men are very blond, with straight hair and large bodies. We are bored of them. My friends are curious what you look like without clothes." Kara laughed and her cheeks glowed deep red, and Andrew also felt himself blushing.

"That would be very embarrassing," he said. "I would need at least two of your famous Carlsberg Elephant beers."

"So, you have heard of Carlsberg. We have some in the refrigerator," she said.

"Beer sounds good. It was a long trip, and I think I'm a little dehydrated."

Kara went to the refrigerator and brought him two bottles of Carlsberg. "Well, maybe I will want a sip of one of them," she said.

Andrew opened the bottle and lifted it to his lips. The cool liquid tasted almost sweet and the flavor deepened as it covered his tongue. He took another sip and could already feel the warm glow of alcohol spreading through his tired limbs. "Mmm, it's better than what we get in the US," he said. He looked at the three women in the room with him. They were gorgeous, and he was surprised at being the subject of their fantasies. He wondered if they had husbands or boyfriends, which reminded him to ask Kara about Klaus. He scanned the room again to make sure he had not missed Klaus lurking in the shadows. "So where's Klaus?" Andrew said.

"Oh, he's in the city. We have separated." Kara paused for a few seconds and took a sip of beer as Andrew expressed shock.

"I wondered about the different phone numbers. I thought maybe one was a work number. I'm sorry to hear this."

Then Kara continued, "It's okay. I'm living here on this women's commune. Klaus will see you tomorrow in Copenhagen at our apartment."

Kara had delivered the news with little emotion, as if she was discussing a change of furniture. "You two seemed so good together. You've known each other since you were children. I don't understand," said Andrew.

"Yes, well, we were somewhat shaken by the trip to Africa. We did not behave with proper courage. We were cowards, especially Klaus. He should have gone with you to help carry Barry. I said that to him, and we began to argue on our trip home. All of our years together, we would not argue, but once it started, we could not stop. It was like a flood that washes down so much dirt and broken trees and trash stored up for years. I didn't understand how Klaus could stand by and let you go off in the night on that mountain without helping. I wanted him to go with you, but he wanted to climb to the top of the mountain to show how strong he was. He didn't want to miss that chance. I felt such shame and realized he was not the heroic man that I had thought he was. I didn't want to be married to a selfish man."

"But it wasn't Klaus's fault. I don't think he's selfish. No one knew Barry was so sick. Not even me, and I'm in medical school. And it was so cold on that mountain and our brains lacked oxygen. We couldn't think right. This is terrible. I knew something was wrong. I had nightmares. I need to talk to Klaus. You need to get back together," said Andrew.

"No, I can't. Klaus was so angry with me. He said nasty things about me, and I can't forget them. He told me that I was lazy and had no ambition in life without him. He said that I was a lazy hippie. So now here I am, living on a hippie commune, and he's sure it's just to spite him for what he said. But he doesn't realize that I like to be part of a community where we grow our own food and make cheese from the milk. I don't need the money he makes. I don't need the apartment in Copenhagen." Kara walked over to the window and pointed out the cows and pigs and the vegetable garden that provided the food for the commune. Andrew noticed that Kara was wearing overalls and a plaid shirt that fit well with her new farming life. The kitchen had herbs hanging from hooks and a vat of soup was cooking on the oven, giving off an aroma of chicken and onions.

"But people say things that they don't mean when they feel hurt. You and Klaus are wonderful together. It was one of the reasons I wanted to come and visit you. I wanted to find out the secret to your successful marriage. I trust your opinion. I wanted your advice...about something personal."

Now Kara smiled broadly. "So perhaps it's a romance? Please tell me. I love to hear this."

Andrew hesitated and then took another large gulp of beer. He wondered if Kara would judge him severely and maybe even despise him for his intimacies with Eve while Barry lay in the hospital. Kara and Klaus had made the trip possible by volunteering to stay with Barry, and he had taken advantage. If she could become so angry at Klaus, how would she react to what he was going to tell her?

Kara waited. Andrew could feel her eyes pulling at him, twisting him and opening him like the beer bottle she was sipping. He sighed. "Okay, but please don't tell anyone."

"Of course. I'm a good secret keeper."

"When Eve and I went to Malindi Beach, we took LSD. I had never done that before, but she wanted me to experience it. I had never taken it. Have you?"

"Well, I'm a hippie. So of course, that's like our vitamin. But yes, I have taken LSD. I took it with Klaus on our anniversary. He became frightened, and I had to take him to the clinic for an injection. That was another sign that we weren't compatible, but I didn't want to see it. How did you like it?"

"At first I was scared," he said. "I had hallucinations. Eve's face became a monkey and then a cat. I could not control my thoughts. But ever since, I keep thinking about her. I never intended for anything to happen between us. I knew Barry was in love with her. I never even planned for her to go with me to Malindi. That's the truth. But Eve wanted to go and Barry didn't mind. He encouraged us." Andrew paused. He was losing the thread of the story and was not sure exactly what to say next.

"So, what happened?" said Kara. "Did you sleep with her?"

"Yes. But I'm not even sure what we did. That's the weird part. We were together in bed physically, and naked in bed, but I'm not sure we were in the same place mentally. I don't know what was real and what was in my mind. But I know that I wanted to be with her. So probably we did."

"Maybe you should not try to analyze it. If it was a good experience, that's all that is important, even if it wasn't the same for both of you. The point of LSD is to expand your mind, to break down the barriers and hang-ups that prevent us from experiencing life. I have some LSD here if you want to take it with me."

Andrew took a deep breath and imagined what it might be like to take LSD with Kara and perhaps some of her friends. What would they decide to do? He wondered where it might lead. But he did not want his mind to be jumbled again and to have to put it all back together. He wanted advice from Kara and needed their minds to be clear, and already he was getting clouded by the alcohol. "No, maybe some other time. Maybe we can just walk around."

"Yes, of course. You must be tired from all of your travel. You can finish your beer or just take it with us, and we can walk around our little farm."

Andrew swallowed the last sips of the beer and felt his mind relaxing. Freja, the woman who had been feeding the baby, brought him a sweet roll with cinnamon and sugar infused into the middle. "Thank you," he said. "Danish beer and Danish pastry. This must be real Danish pastry. We have something like this in the US, and we call it Danish. Did you make this?"

"Yes, we make all our food here," Freja said.

"Do you have a boyfriend or husband here with you and your baby?" Andrew asked, not sure what prompted the question.

Freja seemed confused and did not seem to understand the question until Kara explained it. Then she laughed, "No. I have my girlfriend Ella and my baby. We have no boyfriend or husband."

Andrew looked to Kara for an explanation, but she had gone into the other room to get herself some coffee. "Of course, there was man to make baby," she continued, "but he is not a husband. Just baby-maker. He's not here living with us."

Andrew ate the pastry, then he and Kara walked outside. There was a light breeze and Andrew could smell the pungent odors of the cows and pigs, but there was also the sweet scent of hay that was more pleasant. Kara's blond hair twisted in the wind and Andrew wished he had been ready with his camera to snap a photograph that would capture the beauty and sponta- neity of the moment. "Is it just the three of you working on this farm?" asked Andrew.

"Do you want to stay and help us?" said Kara. "We could have four. But this is a commune for women only. No men, ex- cept as visitors."

"I wish I could stay, but I have to get back to medical school. Sometimes I wish I could be a hippie and live off the land like this. But I want to be a doctor and help sick people, and there's so much for me to learn. What I saw in Africa was shocking: women with no prenatal care delivering malnourished babies.

One well-educated doctor could make a huge difference. I wish I had been able to do more to help."

"Maybe you will go back to Africa when you finish your studies. But maybe you will go back to her first. And maybe she will prevent you from following your dream."

"Who?" said Andrew.

"Eve, of course. Does Barry know?"

"I don't know. I didn't tell him. I wanted to, but I couldn't. And now I don't know where either of them live. Eve said our sex together never happened. What does that mean? Is that so we never tell anyone about what happened in Malindi? Or is it really how she felt? But people can sense these things. Do you think Barry knew?"

"Maybe he doesn't care. Maybe he accepts it. We have many open relationships here in Denmark now. Two men and one woman. Two women and one man. Three women and no men."

"He would care. Even though they were just beginning to date, he was already in love with her. He talked about it when we were walking down the mountain, when he thought he might die."

Andrew and Kara walked past the barn and out into the pasture. Kara's face glowed soft pink in the sunlight, and when she smiled at him, Andrew sensed that she wanted him to kiss her. He wondered if the conversation about Barry and Eve was partly responsible, or perhaps they were both lonely and there had always been an attraction between them.

A chestnut mare that Andrew did not notice when he had arrived at the house was walking along the white fence line. The horse turned and looked at them as if they might offer some food, and then continued walking as if it had given up. "What do you think?" asked Andrew. "I never sensed that there was much passion between Eve and Barry. But I'm not expert in such things. In fact, I'm a total novice. Did Barry say anything to you when he was in the hospital?"

"He talked about her several times," Kara said. "He wanted to marry her. And maybe I gave him a bit of a frown because he asked me how I liked being married, and of course I told him it was fine even though I was already fighting with Klaus. There was no reason to upset him when he was recovering from such an illness. But I also told him that I thought marriage could be a prison for women and that probably marriage will be gone in a hundred years, maybe sooner. Why should we be restricted to just one person to love? This is not practical. There are so many people that we can love and so many ways if we will only give ourselves the chance," she said. "It is the critical attitudes of society that stop us."

"What did Barry say when you told him that?"

"I didn't exactly say that to him. But he said that it was the image of her face that kept him from giving up when he was on that mountain and could not breathe, like the image of the Virgin Mary. So, I could not argue with that. Her image saved his life, just like her image seduced you in Malindi," she said. "But images can evaporate and disappear."

They walked around the barn and through the piggery. Kara showed him a sow with seven piglets. "This is what is real. Seven piglets suckling out the milk. They know if it is real." Kara took his hand as they walked and he felt her gentle squeeze. After they crossed a dirt road leading to a pasture and a small workshop, Kara stopped and looked at him. "Do you want to sleep with me?" she said.

Andrew did not know how to answer. He'd imagined they might drift into the question of sleeping arrangements when bedtime arrived. He had even imagined that all three women might be sleeping together in one bed and maybe they would invite him to join them. Or perhaps they would have a few more drinks before dinner and get a little drunk and one thing might lead to another, and in the morning they might wake up together and wonder how it had happened.

If he was being honest, he had been attracted to Kara from the first time he saw her with her backpack at the lodge where they met the other hikers, but thought she was too young, and later that she was too attached to her husband. But now that Kara had put the question bluntly to him, he hesitated. "I would like to, but I'm so confused about Eve and now with you and Klaus. I don't know if it would be good for us to sleep together until I figure some things out. And tomorrow I will visit with Klaus," he said.

"I thought perhaps you had come all this way to sleep with me, that maybe you realized when Klaus gave you a different telephone number for me. Did you?"

"No. Well, maybe. Not consciously. I like being with you. I can talk to you. I don't know," he said.

"Well, you can have your own bed if you want. We have an extra."

Andrew did not answer. He could not believe he was giving up an opportunity to sleep with Kara and to hold her in his arms and feel her body against his. He let the question float up like a balloon that was still visible in the sky, slowly floating away.

Kara showed him the workshop where they repaired the farm equipment and did woodwork. There were a variety of saws and benches and the workshop smelled of lacquer and sawdust. "We can make tables and chairs and cutting boards. We sell the cutting boards at the market," she said, and she showed him an example of one of the boards with several types of wood glued together and sanded smooth. "The wood is prettier when the colors are more different. See this one with purple wood and black wood and brown. It's prettier, isn't it?"

Andrew examined the grains of the wood and the patterns of colors. "Yes, it's more interesting than one plain piece of wood, but I think they are both beautiful. Each piece of wood has its own perfection." He leaned his head over to hers and their lips touched softly and then with more intensity. He put his hands on her face and down her neck, feeling the air going through into her lungs and moving her chest up and down. He felt the pulsations of blood in her neck and her breathing accelerating as he kissed her again and again.

They found a soft place where the sawdust had accumulated and lay down together. She let him put his hands on her legs and back and all over her and she writhed and gasped as he moved on top of her. He could feel her breasts heaving, and he pressed his thighs against her. The sawdust was creating clouds of powder as they moved back and forth on it. Andrew coughed once and then Kara coughed as the sawdust irritated her lungs.

"Maybe we should go back to the house," Kara said, coughing again.

"I think I may be allergic to this dust," said Andrew. They got up and brushed the sawdust off their clothes and hair, and Andrew gave Kara one more kiss. He brushed off the sawdust that was still clinging to her cheeks and pulled sawdust from her hair. As they walked back to the house, holding hands, Andrew began to wonder what all of this might imply about his feelings for Eve. If he was in love with Eve, how could he suddenly be so attracted to Kara? But the thought was fleeting and quickly replaced by the thoughts of Kara writhing under him, the removal of their clothes and the excitement of their bodies.

Kara's bedroom contained a simple double bed and bureau. She told him to take off his clothes and get into bed, and that she would need to go to the bathroom and would be right back. Andrew waited, assuming Kara was cleaning off sawdust or taking care of birth control, but then he heard her cough again. As he lay naked in the bed, the time began to extend and become too long and he finally got out of bed and knocked on the bathroom door.

"Kara, are you okay?" he said. She did not answer. "Kara?" He pushed open the door and she was sitting by the toilet on the floor, holding an inhaler. She was breathing quickly and wheezing.

"It's my asthma from the sawdust," she gasped. "Please get my injection." Andrew opened the medicine chest and pulled out a needle and syringe. He handed it to her and she quickly injected the medicine into her leg. Then she sat gasping next to the toilet, breathing into the inhaler. "I'm sorry," she said.

"What do you want me to do?" he said.

"Just a few minutes and the medicine will work," she said. He watched as her breathing began to slow and her color improved. "Now you can help me get up," and she extended her hand and he pulled her up to her feet. "I'm feeling better," she said. "Thank you. Sometimes my asthma can be bad."

Andrew helped walk her to the bed and she got in under the covers. She was mostly naked except for her panties. "Can you pile up the pillows? I need to sit up."

Andrew took the two pillows and found another on the chair and piled them together. Kara leaned back on them and smiled weakly. "Yes, this is much better. Well, that was exciting. Not exactly what you expected," she said, and she reached down and let her hand rest on his stomach. "Now I need to rest. Sorry. Is it okay if I hold you like this? It will help me sleep."

"Sure, okay," he said.

As Kara drifted off, Andrew felt his mind wandering back to their hike down the mountain and how he had perceived her strength, and now he saw her vulnerability that had been hidden from him. He thought about Klaus and how Klaus had probably cared for Kara during other attacks. It was what people who were married did for each other; it was part of the love and the sharing, and it made Andrew sad to think that he might be further tearing apart the fabric of her relationship with Klaus. He watched Kara sleep and her face looked even more childlike and angelic than when he had first seen her. Her fingers moved over his body as she slept, as if he were Klaus and she were familiar with him. As they lay there in the bed, resting, he felt an intimacy and trust that had begun when they walked up the mountain as new friends and then down the mountain helping Barry together.

He brought Kara dinner that night, explaining to the two other women about her asthma attack. They seemed to know about her asthma and were not very concerned. Kara used her inhaler a few more times in the evening and rested in bed. "I guess it was the sawdust and the excitement of being with you," she said.

In the morning, Kara felt better. "I guess I am not so allergic to you after all. I feel much better now," she said.

They ate a breakfast of fried eggs and bacon with coffee and fresh milk, "an American breakfast," she called it in his honor. She gave him the directions to find Klaus in Copenhagen. Andrew was to meet Klaus in his classroom and watch him teach, and then they would go to Klaus's apartment for dinner, and Andrew would spend the night there. When Andrew packed up to leave, he tried to kiss Kara on the lips, but she turned her head, hugged him, and presented her cheek for him to kiss.

Chapter 17

HEN ANDREW PUSHED open the door to Klaus's fourth-grade class, he was met by the curious eyes of a blond ten-year-old girl in a red sweater and jeans. The girl stared at Andrew without speaking for a few seconds, and then said, "Danger. Danger. Stranger. Stranger," as Andrew imagined she had been taught to do. Klaus hurried over to greet Andrew with an enthusiastic handshake and hug. Then he announced to the class that they had a special visitor.

The children in the class had been arranging pins on a map of the world based upon places they had visited. Klaus gave Andrew a green pin and asked him to stick it in the city where he lived. Andrew held the pin for a moment, trying to think about whether he should stick it into Washington, DC, where his family lived, or Denver, Colorado, where he now went to medical school. He even glanced at San Francisco, where Barry lived and perhaps Eve, too, if Barry had convinced her to stay. None of the children would care which place the pin landed as long as it was in the United States, so he stuck it in Denver, which was more or less in the middle of the country. The students paraded by to admire his pin.

"This is my friend from United States. You can ask him any question you want to know about the USA. As you can see, he lives in Denver, Colorado."

One boy wearing glasses and a shirt with a cow jumping over the moon wanted to know if Andrew was a cowboy and owned a horse. The boy had read about how cowboys in Colorado could ride horses and carried guns. He wanted to know if Andrew had ever shot anyone who was robbing a bank.

"Oh no," Andrew said. "I've ridden horses, but I'm going to be a doctor and fix up people who get shot. I don't want to shoot them." The boy frowned in disappointment, doubtless hoping for more gore and drama. Two girls were reading about coyotes and mountain lions and wanted to know if Andrew had ever seen them.

"Yes," he said. "Sometimes at night, I can hear a whole pack of coyotes singing." Andrew demonstrated how coyotes sang. "I get out my guitar and sing with the coyotes." The girls giggled and two boys imitated Andrew's sounds.

"You'll be taking over my job," said Klaus. "You have a much more interesting life than I do."

Andrew enjoyed watching Klaus with the children. Klaus was able to speak to them as an adult but also entertain them with stories and maintain order when they became noisy and disorderly. Klaus wore a tan sweater and he seemed taller and thinner than Andrew remembered, or perhaps it was his contrast with the small, ten-year-old children.

After school, Klaus and Andrew went out for coffee in a shop connected to a former lighthouse, with the coffee and pastry shop on the ground floor. Customers could walk up the stairs of the lighthouse to a small, round observation room and look out onto the ocean. Andrew and Klaus counted one hundred steps to the top of the lighthouse. "They must have constructed this staircase so that it would require exactly one hundred steps," said Klaus. "This is something that we Danes think about. It's a mix of aesthetics and humor. Do you like it?"

"This is a such cool place for a coffee shop," said Andrew. "I can't imagine living here and watching for the boats out in the fog. The water seems to extend for miles."

"It's the ocean. It was somewhat of a lonely life here, but some people were suited for it. We Danes like the privacy of fog. There was a loud foghorn before, but that's gone now. It was one of Kara and my favorite places. Kara actually wanted to run a coffeehouse like this where we would make pastry. But that is not a practical idea," said Klaus. He paused for a moment before he added, "So, how do you like Denmark so far? What would you like to see?"

"Anything, really. It's all so interesting. Mostly, I came here to see you and Kara. I'm sorry about what happened between you. Maybe you can get back together?"

"I don't know," Klaus said. He paused and rubbed his forehead and his eyes. "It was quite a shock. Of course, we're still friends. I speak with her almost every day. We were very happy to hear that you were coming here to visit us. We didn't have the chance for a proper goodbye when we left Africa."

"I wanted to talk with you too...about Eve, and about my trip to Malindi Beach. About what we did, about what happened."

"I don't understand," said Klaus.

Andrew looked out to the ocean for a few seconds. "I slept with Eve on the trip to Malindi. I didn't mean for it to happen, but we took some drugs. When I got back to Dar es Salaam, I couldn't stop thinking about her. I didn't tell Barry. He probably knew. I thought that maybe you spoke with Barry when he was in the hospital, and maybe he said something to you about Eve and me. I feel silly bringing this up with you now. You have your own problems to think about. But I don't know what to do and I keep thinking about her." Andrew watched Klaus's face, and he noticed Klaus's lips twitch, then Klaus turned his head away and rubbed his eyes again.

When Klaus turned back, he said, "I don't think I could help you. Kara is my only girl in my life. I have no experience except her."

Andrew could see that Klaus's eyes were watering and there were tears running down his cheeks. "I'm sorry," Andrew said. "I didn't mean..."

"It's just my allergies. Kara and I are different in many ways, except we both have allergies to trees, grass, and wood dust. But she has the heart of a hippie. She thinks everything can be solved if you just take someone to bed and make love with them. She does not believe in medicine or property or owning anything. She believes in sharing whatever she has. I'm not so free or adventurous. I'm a capitalist even though I'm a Dane. I believe in God and work and showing up on time and saving money to buy a house or clothes and following a plan. The trip to Kilimanjaro was our chance to see if she could be more organized and if I could be more adventurous and spontaneous. We failed. I didn't help you with Barry because it was not part of my...our plan. Our plan was to stay together and reach the top of the mountain. I didn't want to leave Kara. I was stupid. Kara was right to criticize me. She also criticized herself. We both felt like failures. Our trip was a failure because we couldn't learn from each other or from you. I should have helped you. I'm very sorry."

"No, it wasn't your fault. After all, you came all the way to Africa to be together. We just happened to be hiking in the same group, but you had no obligations or duty. Neither of you are doctors. It was up to me. There was no way for you to know that Barry would be so sick. In any case, Barry is okay, so it all worked out. There's no reason for you to split up over such a thing," Andrew said.

Klaus seemed unconvinced. He shrugged, turned, and went down the stairs to get more coffee and pastries. The steps were more difficult going down because of the unevenness and the poor lighting. As Andrew followed Klaus down the stairs, the slow pace and darkness caused him to breathe in the dankness of the passage; perhaps he also sensed the darkness from Klaus. "Kara likes these uneven steps," Klaus said. "She says they make you appreciate each one and each step is different. I think they are just an unnecessary danger."

On the first floor, they bought their pastries and more coffee and brought them back to Klaus's apartment. They sat down at the kitchen table and sipped coffee for a few minutes without speaking. Finally, Klaus said, "You wanted to talk about Eve? And Barry?"

Andrew considered what to say. Now that he knew Klaus and Kara had separated, his own questions about Eve seemed trivial. How could a brief few days together compare to a relationship of years? "It's just that I was so close to Barry on that mountain. I could feel the pulsations of his heart and his chest moving as he took a breath. We were that close. We were like twins in a womb. I could feel the life inside of him. I thought we might die together on that mountain. And then we both survived. I saved him. Well, Koba and I saved him. Then I went off on a trip with Eve and slept with her while he was recovering in the hospital. That was despicable. I fell in love with her. Now I want to be with her, even though I know it's wrong. Barry encouraged her to go with me. Maybe he knew it would happen. But I never told him, and he trusted me. You were there. You saw it all. Maybe you even knew." Now Andrew paused. He waited to see what Klaus would say.

Klaus got up from the table and went to a desk. He pulled out a letter. "This is a letter I received from Eve after Kara moved out. I'm not sure I showed it to Kara. Eve wrote it to thank us. It was very nice. You can read it."

Andrew pulled the letter from the envelope.

Dear Klaus and Kara,

I've been wanting to write to you, but somehow too many days have already passed and I am somewhat embarrassed now to be writing to thank you for something that happened a month ago. You stayed with Barry at the hospital and let me go off to Malindi Beach, which was so thoughtful. I really needed to get away, and Malindi was perfect.

But what I wanted to thank you most for was that night when Barry got sick. I remember how alone and terrified I felt. I knew no one. I was physically shaking so much after Barry left that I almost fell over. I was cold and I tried to warm up in my sleeping bag but it didn't work. I thought maybe I would die. And then you both came over to me. I was crying and you got around me like a cocoon. One on each side until I stopped shaking. You stayed with me until Klaus went off with the group to reach the summit, and Kara stayed with me until Klaus got back. It is something I will not ever forget. You did not know me and yet you treated me like a sister. I was too much in shock to thank you at the time but thought about it for the past month.

I hope you will consider visiting Barry and me in San Francisco for your next trip. We're living together, which was a surprise for both of us. We're both doing fine and would love to show you around this amazing city.

Your friend,

Eve

At the bottom was Eve's address in San Francisco.

Klaus closed his eyes for a few seconds, ate his pastry, and sipped his coffee. "I am somewhat poor at understanding love. Kara is much better. She would usually have to explain simple things to me about people and relationships. I am more mathematical. I add up the chips on one side of the ledger and the chips on the other. I compare them and can tell which side has more. If I am not sure, I can run an analysis and use statistics. I can calculate probabilities. That is how I like to make decisions. So, with that approach I would say that you saved Barry's life so you probably have more chips on your side. If you want her and she wants you, Barry should accept it. He can find someone else. But also, according to her letter, she is quite happy with Barry, so maybe she doesn't share your feelings. Therefore, there are some more chips on Barry's side. That is just a simple mathematical calculation. But of course, love is not simple like that. Calculations cannot measure love. What did Kara say?"

Andrew could not meet Klaus's eyes as he tried not to reveal what had happened when he visited Kara. "Kara wasn't sure. We talked about Eve. Kara asked me why I thought I loved Eve. She wanted to know when I first began to think about Eve. Was it when we climbed up the mountain or was it later at Malindi

Beach? The truth is that I noticed her right off, but I was afraid to show my feelings. I didn't expect her to feel the way I did. That was a surprise. I thought she and Barry were a couple and that she was just being kind to me because I was alone. But now I think there was a spark from the beginning, but maybe I'm fantasizing. How about you? When did you know you were in love with Kara?"

Klaus laughed. "It was in the third grade. There was a boy who pulled her hair and she got mad and ended up in some trouble. Her face turned red like a tomato because the teacher was blaming her. I went and sat with her later for lunch and I shared my cupcake with her and her whole face lit up, and it was so beautiful and just for me to enjoy. She got crumbs and frosting all over. Her face was a mess but it was even more beautiful, as if it was decorated. She looked at me and laughed, and I went to get her a paper towel and helped clean her face. I never like a mess. All the kids in class made fun of me. They said I was in love with her. Of course, they were right, and she was so happy to have me clean her face. It was contagious. I usually cannot experience happiness like that. I am somewhat more controlled. We have known each other a long time, and I still feel happy when I see her. It's hard to be apart from her."

"Maybe you can get back together."

"I don't know. We are both stubborn. And Kara is liking her hippie life."

"Eve is not like Kara," Andrew said. "Maybe she's stubborn, but she's more practical, not at all a hippie except perhaps her enjoyment of LSD. She can be mercurial and spontaneous and hard to predict. But I think deep down she wants to make things happen, to be in charge and make them work. I don't really know her that well, but I think happiness for her is about the freedom to think of new ideas and meet new people. I could help her with that, and support her. She doesn't like to see anyone mistreated. Neither do I. But I'm not sure she's happy or even that she wants to be happy. She'd rather be on an adventure. That's how we're different. I like stability in my life and I want to be able to focus on being a good doctor. She pushes me in another direction. And I think that's good. I want adventure in my life too, and I think Eve also wants stability. When we took the LSD together, I really felt like I connected with her like I've never been connected with anyone. I let go of reality for a while. We could see right into each other's brains. Do you know what I mean?"

"I'm not sure," said Klaus. "I think LSD can also create a transitory personality. Once it wears off, the real personality could be quite different. What you saw might not be the real Eve. Maybe you should gather more data? Maybe go and visit her."

"I want to visit her, but as you can see in her letter, she's happy with Barry. That letter pretty much answers the question I had."

"As I said before, I'm more analytical than Kara. I wouldn't reach a conclusion based upon a drug-induced infatuation. Or based upon a few lines in a letter. At least now you know her address."

"I don't know. It sounds pretty hopeless."

Klaus got up and asked Andrew if he would like to see the rest of the apartment. It was just one bedroom, a living room, kitchen, and bathroom. But it had been enough for Klaus and Kara. Now it seemed small for Klaus. He had a photograph of Kara and him together on a boat, their eyes sparkling in the sun. Next to it was a painting of a farmhouse similar to the one

Andrew had visited the day before. "I have some sausage and cheese and noodles," he said. "Will that be okay for dinner?"

"Sure, anything is fine. I'm not a vegetarian," Andrew said. They ate hungrily and drank a glass of wine and then a second. Andrew was feeling a gentle buzz and realized he was beginning to fall asleep at the table.

Klaus noticed that Andrew's eyes were closing. "You're tired," Klaus said.

"No, I'm fine," said Andrew.

"I have to get up at six to get to school in time. And I want to take you to the airport bus. Kara told me your flight is tomorrow. Is that right?"

"Yes. A short trip. But so nice to see you again. Okay. Where do you want me to sleep?"

"It's up to you," said Klaus.

"What do you mean?"

"You can sleep in my bed or on the couch. You have a long trip and I would like to make sure you can have a good sleep."

"The couch will be fine," Andrew said.

"Kara told me you kissed her."

Andrew took a gulp of wine. "I...I'm sorry about that. I never planned to kiss her. It just happened," Andrew said.

"It's all right. I want her to be happy. In Denmark we are quite liberal. She was not happy with me. Maybe she will like you."

"No. No. That's not it at all. I'm here as a friend. Anyway I think she's allergic to me or a part of me. She had an asthma attack right after she kissed me."

"Yes, she has very severe asthma. Sometimes we have to go to the hospital when she has an attack. I'm glad you were there with her. I worry about her because she does not take care of herself.

Well maybe no more kisses for the two of you," Klaus laughed.

"Anyway, you're the one she loves. I could tell when I saw you in Africa. And she still loves you. Maybe you just need to show her how much you love her," Andrew said.

"So you are a marriage counselor now?"

"No. I'm not an expert at all. That's why I came here, to get advice from you. But I just know that you and Kara are right for each other."

Klaus shook his head and got up from his chair. He shuffled into the bedroom and carried back out a gray woolen blanket and a small white pillow. "Are you sure you don't want to use my bed? It's much more comfortable than the couch," Klaus said.

"Klaus, look at us," Andrew smiled. "I'm used to examining people. I can measure the couch and our height. I know that at least I can fit on the couch, but your legs would be dangling over the edge. I'll be fine." Andrew took the blanket and pillow from Klaus and dropped them on the couch.

"All right then, six o'clock," Klaus said, and he disappeared into the bedroom and closed the door.

In the morning, Klaus drove Andrew to the airport bus and handed him his backpack from the trunk. They stood in front of the bus for a few minutes, and then, when the bus driver opened the door, they shook hands. There was an awkward moment of uncertainty.

"I think that maybe you're not so stubborn as Kara," said Andrew. "Just apologize. Tell her you love her, that you have always loved her," he said.

Klaus wrapped his arm around Andrew's shoulder for a moment, and Andrew patted Klaus's arm. Then he climbed up onto the bus and Klaus's face disappeared as the door shut.

Chapter 18

ANDREW DECIDED TO fly to San Francisco for the Bay to Break-ers race on a whim. It had been more than two years since his trip to Africa, and more than a year since his trip to Denmark. He had tried to stop thinking about Eve because everyone told him it would drive him crazy. Alcohol helped, but the effect was temporary and left him at a lower spot than where he'd begun. The truth was he would never stop thinking of Eve and the trip to Malindi: the bus ride; the border; the bus station; the hotel; the coral; the restaurant. It was all magical. He would hold the coral trident in his hand and think about what Grace had said to them in that restaurant. Grace had seen the same things that he felt. He thought Eve must be feeling them too, even if she was with Barry. People make mistakes, and the mistakes can be corrected with thought and planning, and a little luck, as long as the mistakes are not fatal.

Andrew had made a mistake that could have been fatal a month after returning from Denmark, when he was bartending at a friend's party. He would take a drink after he had served two or three, and didn't notice how his coordination was gradually deteriorating and the drinks he was serving were increasingly concentrated with alcohol. It wasn't until he got on his bicycle to ride home that he realized how drunk he was. As he pedaled, he swerved across the road. He could barely maintain his balance. When a car came up behind him, he tried to get over toward the edge of the roadway but instead the bike lurched in front of the car.

He woke up as the ambulance was driving him to the hospital. His memories of what happened after that were a series of fragments: Questions about his age and residence that he knew he should be able to answer but the answers escaped his memory before he could express them in words. He remembered the intern in the hospital telling him he'd have a scar on his forehead, but fortunately his hair would cover it if he did not become bald. The intern had laughed, and Andrew did not understand what was funny. He remembered the intern sewing up his forehead and how the anesthetic did not seem to be working.

But what was most disturbing was that, when the nurse asked him who she should call to pick him up and take him home, he could not come up with a name. There was no one. He had housemates and classmates with cars, but he did not want to bother them in the middle of the night. There was no one who would want to be called, who would expect to be called. He lay on an emergency room stretcher until daylight and finally called a housemate who picked him up, before rounds, and dropped him off at home. His paperwork from the emergency room said that he suffered a concussion and a closed head injury and that he should avoid anything that required concentration of attention, but everything he did in the hospital required concentration. He went to dermatology clinic for his rotation with a huge bandage wrapped around his forehead and scalp, and the attending physician sent him home because he would scare the patients.

For a while, Andrew had headaches and strange dreams when he rested. When he was finally allowed to go to dermatology clinic, all he had to do was describe rashes and write down what the attending was prescribing. Usually, the medications were steroid ointments of various concentrations, but even remembering those orders was difficult. And Andrew found that the rashes he was observing were populating his dreams. He began to drink to help him get to sleep, and to prevent the rashes from taking over his mind and his dreams.

He almost failed his next rotation, the psychiatry rotation, because he went to work hung over one morning before rounds. His faculty preceptor only allowed him to pass the rotation because he found Andrew's explanations of a romantic obsession psychologically interesting. The faculty member also extracted a promise from Andrew that he would get counseling and begin a wellness plan, which prompted Andrew to start running again. First just a mile and then two. He stopped drinking. He convinced his wellness counselor to climb Mount Kilimanjaro on a vacation to Africa.

Andrew graduated from medical school and began his internal medicine internship at Denver General Hospital. He gradually got used to the eighty-hour work weeks and patients calling him "doctor." As the year went on, he immersed himself in critical care medicine, which felt like the right specialty for his future after an internal medicine residency, because he could rescue some people from dying just as he had with Barry. He never wanted to be in a situation where someone was dying and he did not know what to do. With critical care medicine, there was always something he could do, some procedure or machine that might bring a patient back from the edge.

One day at Denver General Hospital, he was eating lunch in the break room of the ICU when another intern showed him a story about the upcoming Bay to Breakers race in San Francisco. The article described the growing notoriety of the Bay to Breakers race: the outrageous costumes worn by the runners; the hipsters; the Dykes on Bikes; the New Age health gurus; the radicals; the libertarians; the Black, Asian, Hispanic, straight, gay, women's and men's groups. Costumes were made of paper mâché or plastic, and included signs that the participants carried. The serious runners were given a less impeded path by being lined up at the front of the pack.

Andrew thought the trip could be a test of his improved wellness and his ability to move beyond his preoccupation with Eve by being in the city where she lived without calling her. Maybe he'd see her, maybe he wouldn't, but he would be going for the carnival atmosphere of the race and the excitement of San Francisco. And he might call Barry to find out if there were any lasting effects of the pulmonary edema or just to check in and reconnect.

And so he flew into San Francisco and found a room at the Sir Francis Drake hotel downtown. It was dark when he arrived, and the race would begin in the morning. As he stood at the hotel entrance, he watched a cable car climb the steep hills with tourists hanging on to the railings. It was an apt metaphor for his life the past two years—a slow climb up a steep hill with no clear destination in sight, hanging on to something that was always moving, with the future shrouded in fog. He watched the cable car disappear up the hill and went to bed.

Chapter 19

T HE MORNING NEWSPAPER described the upcoming race as more of an amoebic movement than a consistent progression forward for most runners, except for the serious racers, who started at the front. Andrew read the article and decided to get up front and enjoy the spectacle from the front looking backward, rather than from the back looking forward. He hoped that maybe he might bump into Eve, or perhaps Barry too, if they were watching the race. Even though he had copied the address that Klaus had showed him in Denmark, he had not sent a letter or even tried to explore exactly where it was. He was too fearful of the embarrassment of rejection at the doorway. A spontaneous meeting before or after the race would be less awkward than an obviously intended meeting. But he had not considered the thousands of people at the race and the difficulty of identifying anyone inside a costume or wearing a mask.

The race was as advertised—a long string of costumed people

on floats, runners of all ages and shapes, some with numbers on their backs indicating an official registration and others with their usual jogging shorts and shirts out for a Sunday of entertainment and exercise. Andrew realized that he would never be able to spot someone in the crowd. He gave up scanning and found a place near the front. As he was awaiting the start of the race, he looked over at the elite runners lined up at the starting line. These runners, who competed nationally and internationally, had been chosen based upon their previous race time and were competing for prize money. They represented European countries and a few African countries. Some of them had set world records for the marathon or other long-distance races and had names that were vaguely familiar.

Andrew suddenly recognized one of the African runners. He was wearing a jersey with the Tanzanian flag colors: green, blue, and black. It was Koba! Andrew remembered that Koba had been training for an international race when they'd first met on Kilimanjaro, but lacked the financial support to travel. Helga and Barry had offered support after the climb, and perhaps they paid for this trip. Somehow, he had made his way to San Francisco.

"Koba!" Andrew shouted as he got close enough to yell.

Koba turned and their eyes met. Koba's perfect ivory teeth gleamed in the sunlight as he smiled in acknowledgment of Andrew's call of his name, as if he expected him to be there. Andrew pushed his way closer to the front as the runners prepared for the starting gun. He reached out his hand between two runners in front of him and grasped Koba's hand, saying, "Jambo." Koba nodded while his coach, standing next to him with his gym bag, shook his head and scowled.

"How did you get the money for this race?" Andrew asked. "You had to travel all the way from Africa."

"It was the Germans. They have continued to sponsor me. If I win here, I can go to Germany and run a race in Berlin, and help advertise their gym. It's brilliant." Koba's face shone in the morning sun. When he looked down at Andrew's running shoes, he frowned and pulled a pair of running shoes out of his bag and passed them over to Andrew as his coach angrily shook his head.

"These are new shoes from one of my other sponsors. They will make you run fast," Koba said. "Give me those old ones."

Andrew quickly changed his shoes and gave his old shoes to the frowning coach. Andrew was surprised how well Koba's shoes fit him. The shoes were light and sleek with little padding—true racing shoes. He never would have worn running shoes for a race without having tried them on and run in them first, but he decided to take a chance since the improbable meeting with Koba suggested that luck and fate were somehow linked to these shoes. A few minutes later, the race began with the pop of a starter gun. Andrew felt the surge of the crowd around him as he was pulled along by the movement of the elite runners. He watched Koba move quickly out to the front, leaving the other runners behind.

The pace of the elite runners was too fast for Andrew, but he settled into a more comfortable pace as more experienced runners passed him. Koba's light, flexible shoes forced Andrew further forward on the balls of his feet, and he found his legs prancing smoothly and effortlessly along the San Francisco streets lined with spectators. He could see Koba and a few other runners up at the front, rapidly moving out of sight. A cool breeze filled his lungs as he began to breathe heavily. As he inhaled, he remembered Kilimanjaro and how he had gasped for air as they crested the lower peak in the dark. Now, as he ran, he looked at the throngs along the sidewalk, hoping to see Eve. It was almost as if finding Koba had made him think his quest to find Eve was also fated to succeed. He had no idea what he would do if he spotted her or Barry. Maybe he would run over to them and stop running the race. Or maybe they'd run together to the finish line.

Andrew found a comfortable pace and began to notice that the people on the sides of the road had thinned, and there were water stations and first aid tents. Now he could actually distinguish people in the crowd: an old woman in a sweatshirt with her miniature poodle; a middle-aged couple with tattoos on their arms; three Asian teenagers in overalls. Elite women racers ran past him and then older men with tanned legs rushed by. He could hear them breathing fast, smell their sweat, and feel the wake they created as they moved past. He entered Golden Gate Park and could feel the gradual slope of the road downward toward the ocean. Lush green bushes and trees replaced the rows of connected houses that had lined the street until then. Runners were sprinting past him, trying to secure a better finish, but Andrew was content to glide easily to the finish line.

He decided he would look for Koba at the finish and exchange shoes, and they could talk about the sudden success of Koba's running career and his German sponsors. Andrew was curious about the success of the gym and if the three climbers were still together. He thought he might even contribute a few hundred dollars to help sponsor Koba for a future race like the Germans were doing, now that he was earning an intern's salary.

As he passed the finish line, he noticed a crowd gathered around a first aid tent. It looked like someone was doing CPR, and Andrew decided to go over and see if he could help. Sometimes runners had heart attacks from overexertion, or they would become overheated and dehydrated. The crowd was dense and it was difficult to push through. By the time he did, the EMS crew had arrived and began loading the runner onto a stretcher.

Andrew turned to go back and find Koba, and that was when he heard his name being called. He looked to where the sound was coming from and saw a young man with light brown hair and a mustache, waving his arms. Andrew did not recognize him.

"It's me, Barry!" said the man.

Andrew squinted and began to see Barry's face as he emerged from the crowd. He was wearing a brightly-colored tie-dyed t-shirt and a broad grin so different from the expression of the critically ill man he remembered from Africa.

Barry hugged Andrew and lifted him up, as Andrew had once done to him on the mountain. "This guy saved my life," Barry announced to the remaining crowd. Some people stopped to look at Andrew, wondering what he had done, and if it had anything to do with the man getting CPR. "He saved my life," Barry repeated to anyone who would listen. The curious onlookers were not impressed and moved on. Barry finally released Andrew back onto the pavement and said, "I guess I shouldn't be surprised you'd be helping someone who just collapsed. What are you doing here?"

"It was the race. I was running."

"That's great. Who would have guessed? I was just watching the race, taking some pictures. They're always great at the end when people are sprinting toward the finish. I never thought I'd see you again. If you want, you can stay with me. I have a house here; it's not far from where we are now. Can you come over for a snack?"

"Yeah, sure," said Andrew. "But I just saw Koba. Do you remember him from Africa? He helped carry you. He's one of the international runners at the race. I borrowed his shoes. I need to find him and give them back."

"Are you kidding? Koba? Definitely. Let's find him."

Barry and Andrew walked over to a tent where the elite runners were resting. Koba was lying on a rubber mat as his coach massaged his legs. Barry bent down and shook Koba's hand. "Hey, bwana, good to see you."

"Jambo, mzee," said Koba. He pulled his leg away from the coach, stood up, and shook hands with both Barry and Andrew.

The coach frowned at the interruption, threw down a towel, and walked over to a security guard, who told Andrew and Barry they had to leave the tent immediately. Andrew quickly retrieved his running shoes from Koba's bag and exchanged them for the ones he had borrowed. He told Koba they would wait for him outside the tent as they were escorted out by the guard.

"I can't believe it! Koba's here," said Barry. "Damn, I wish I could have seen him run. I always knew he was an athlete. How else could he carry me down the mountain? He's a god. He had a medal and a ribbon around his neck. Maybe he won the race. Did you see it?"

"No, I was just trying to get my shoes." Andrew could feel the ocean breeze cooling and drying the sweat covering his body, and was beginning to shiver.

Koba emerged from the tent a few minutes later. "Jambo, Mr. Barry and Mr. Andrew," he said, his eyes sparkling with delight.

"Jambo," said Barry and he hugged Koba. "You've grown since I saw you, and you have a little beard on your chin."

Koba laughed. "I'm the same. I'm not sure you could see me so clearly in Africa. It was dark. You were ill."

"Ill? I was dying. You saved me. You both did. It was amazing."

"It was my duty. I am Maasai," Koba said.

Barry nodded. "How did you do in the race? Did you win?"

"First place," said Koba with a broad grin. He passed them his medal and they studied the finely-etched figure of a runner on the gold disc and handed it back. "Five thousand dollars," Koba added. They were all beginning to shiver as the wind blew through their shirts. Koba zipped up a windbreaker.

"That's amazing! Can you come over to my house? I live close by," said Barry. "I have a car and I could take you to see the Golden Gate Bridge."

"Yes, I would like to go on that bridge. I have heard it is the most famous bridge in the world. I was disappointed that the race did not end on that bridge. I would like to walk on it, maybe even run on it. But I have to be back in my hotel in one hour," Koba said.

"All right. Follow me. We'll have to go quickly," Barry said. Andrew and Koba followed Barry away from the race, up a steep hill past yellow, pink, and green homes connected together and lining the street. Wisps of clouds were beginning to drift by. "The fog is coming in," Barry said.

"Yes, it's like the clouds at the top of the mountain," Koba said. "Do you remember them?"

"I don't remember much about the mountain," said Barry. "Just your shoulder and Andrew's neck." Barry stopped in front of a faded yellow Toyota Corolla and opened the door with his key. "We have small cars here," said Barry. "They need to fit into small parking spaces between the driveways. I hope you won't be too uncomfortable."

"I can fit in the back," offered Andrew. "It's one of the benefits of short legs."

Barry drove the car through Golden Gate Park, where spectators and participants from the race were having picnics on the grass under the oaks and pines. "Here it is," Barry announced as they approached the bridge. Koba leaned his head out of the car window and stared up at the metal cables that formed majestic points and curves like a royal crown.

"Don't worry, I'll park at the end of the bridge so you can get out and walk back a little," Barry said. He found a place to pull over and parked the car. Andrew and Koba jumped out and began walking back across the bridge on the pedestrian walkway. People were walking in both directions, leaning over and taking pictures. Koba leaned over and touched the orange metal bridge support, slowly rubbing his hand against it.

"It's brilliant. Do you have a camera?" Koba asked Barry as he joined them on the bridge.

"Actually, I do have a small one in my pocket that I was carrying to take pictures of the costumes people wear during the race. Yes, we should take a picture, the three of us," Barry said, and he stopped a middle-aged woman in a blue windbreaker who'd had the same idea and was herding four noisy teenagers together. "Ma'am," Barry said, "I wonder if I could bother you to take a picture. These are my two friends who saved my life."

The woman raised her eyebrows and turned her head to examine the two men that Barry had identified. "Of course. That's quite a good reason for a picture, not that you need one when you're on the Golden Gate Bridge. Well, I'm sure there's a good story that goes with the picture. Maybe you could tell my kids so they'd stand still for a few seconds," the woman said as she grabbed Barry's camera. "So do I just press the red button?"

"Yes," said Barry. "Look through the little window and make sure we're in focus."

"All right, smile. One, two, three. Good, again...one, two, three. That should do it," the woman said and handed the camera back to Barry.

"Thanks," said Barry as he checked the camera and put it back into his pocket. A gust of wind lifted them slightly up from the pedestrian walkway and Koba stretched out his arms, letting the wind blow against his jacket.

"I can fly!" he yelled, running and extending his arms like wings. The wind lifted him like a kite, carrying him against the protective barrier. Andrew and Barry ran after Koba, grasping his jacket and legs.

"Geez, people get killed jumping off this bridge," Barry said. "What are you trying to do? It's hundreds of feet down into the water from here."

"I was really flying," said Koba, "at least two or three feet in the air. I've never actually flown like that before, but sometimes I have dreams of flying when I'm racing."

"Well, some dreams are better kept as dreams!" Andrew laughed. "Maybe we should head back to the car," he said. "I'm getting cold." They turned and walked into the wind back to the car.

Once in the car, Barry grabbed a notebook. "Koba, if you can write down your address, I'll send you the photo when it gets developed," Barry said. He handed Koba the notebook and a pen. Then added, "You too," as he turned his gaze to Andrew. "Write down your address next to Koba's." Andrew nodded. "And now where should we go? Do you want to see the cable cars? They're another famous part of San Francisco."

"No," said Koba. "I have to return to my hotel. My coach becomes very angry if I am late. I had to get up very early for the race and now I have to take my rest."

Barry drove Koba back through Golden Gate Park—the twisting streets that crested hills before plunging back down into neighborhoods with neon lights advertising dance clubs, bars, and Chinese food—until they arrived at Koba's hotel.

"Koba, before you go, I was wondering what happened that night after you helped carry Barry down to the first hut," Andrew asked. "I heard that you turned around and went back up to the top? Was that true?"

"Yes, I was very tired, but Miss Helga would sponsor me for my races and pay for the travel if I went back up to the top and wrote the names of Helga, Rolph, and Helmut in the book at the summit because she forgot to do it. Only guides can do that if the client is not present. And then I had to take a photograph and send it to them with their names. My uncle Salaam agreed and arranged it, so I went back with another group the next day. That is why I can travel to San Francisco and New York." Koba looked back at the Golden Gate, then continued, "Thank you for the visit to the Golden Gate Bridge. Now you have saved me like I saved you."

Barry laughed. "Thanks, but we're not *close* to even! I think I'd offered to support your running when we were in Africa, but I forgot about it then. I'd really like to do that." Koba nodded and waved at them as the doorman opened the hotel door.

⁘

Andrew and Barry arrived back at Barry's house after navigating through the city traffic. It was connected to two adjacent houses, and the entry was a narrow set of stairs leading up to a heavy wooden door. Barry opened it with his key and they walked through a hallway to an open living room and kitchen. There were dark ebony wood sculptures from Tanzania in the living room—a primitive standing woman and a man with arms and legs entwined in a vaguely sexual act. There was a brightly-colored framed African fabric on the wall. Andrew looked around for any evidence of Eve, and saw none. There were no photographs of her, and nothing at all feminine in the pictures or furnishings. Finally, Andrew decided to ask the one thing that had been on his mind since he'd first run into Barry down at the race. "So what about Eve? I thought the two of you were living together?"

Barry lifted his eyes up to the ceiling and inhaled deeply, as if the answer should be obvious. Finally, after a long pause, he said, "We split up. I guess I shouldn't have been surprised. I tried everything. I bought her clothes, jewelry, flowers. We went out to all the nice restaurants. We tried counseling. The problem was I'm not a woman."

"What do you mean?" said Andrew.

"She decided she was into women. It's San Francisco. If you're straight, you're in the minority here. I wasn't about to cut off my dick."

"I'm surprised," said Andrew.

"I can see why. She told me about Malindi Beach."

Andrew turned around and looked out the window. He had imagined this conversation with Barry. He had rehearsed what he might say on the airplane flying into San Francisco. He would describe the drugs and how they had altered his perceptions and disturbed his judgment. He would explain the disorientation of the moment and the hallucinations. Then he would apologize, express regret, and seek forgiveness. It was a long, convoluted explanation, and instead he said simply, "I'm sorry about that."

"It was all right. You saved my life. But what you did was wrong. I trusted you, damn it. I encouraged her to go with you."

"I know."

"When she told me, I was ready to beat the shit out of you. We were talking about trust. I was telling her that I couldn't trust her because she didn't tell me about a party she went to with a famous actor. I saw a picture of her in the newspaper with the guy, and that's how I found out. She laughed about it, and then asked me if there was anyone I really trusted, and I mentioned your name. And then she told me about Malindi. I was shocked. But then I realized that with drugs, the beach, Eve in a bathing suit...I get it. But still, I'm disappointed in you."

Andrew sighed. This was the conversation that he had dreaded, and he had no defense.

"Well, if you want to punch me, go right ahead. I deserve it," Andrew said. "As hard as you want." Andrew closed his eyes.

"No. No. I'm not going to punch you. If I'm totally honest, I had a feeling that when the two of you went off together something might happen. There was something about the look in her eyes. I thought I must be imagining it, and really I was so grateful to be alive and breathing the oxygen. But that's not why we broke up."

"What was it?" asked Andrew.

"I don't know. She's restless, impatient. She can't be happy the way most people can. She's always looking for the next new thing. She's into women now. Who knows if it will last? I wouldn't have minded it if she wanted to share. Threesomes are pretty hot. You know what I mean?"

"I've never had the opportunity," said Andrew.

"I don't really think she was telling me everything," said Barry. "She has a television show, actually just a few minutes early on Monday morning that's part of the news. But they pay her a lot. I think she wants to be a TV journalist. Or maybe she might want to be in movies. She's pretty enough and she can project as if she's in your living room. She looks great on TV. She's also talked about getting into politics. She's really good in a crowd. She could probably get elected to something, and she'd be good. People listen to her. And she picks things up fast. Do you want to see a TV clip of her?"

"Yeah," said Andrew.

Barry put on a tape, and Eve's face suddenly appeared on the screen. Her hair was short, and her purple lipstick accentuated her full lips. When it was her turn to speak, her mouth opened into a huge smile. She introduced herself, "This is Eve Vigil." She was wearing a dress with African patterns, set off with a milky, translucent pendant around her neck. She described population growth in California and how there needed to be a plan for sustainability for clean air and water. She talked about what she had learned in Africa and introduced a guest climate scientist and population ecologist. Andrew was entranced as he listened. Eve seemed knowledgeable and convincing. He noticed the pendant she was wearing, the one from Malindi, and thought this must be a message to him, even if it was subconscious. As he watched her, his body came alive and he realized how much he wanted her even after two years had passed.

"Wow, she looks terrific," said Andrew. "I didn't know she was a television star."

"She's good," said Barry. "Class A. I get it. I'm just a regular guy. I go to work at an office in a bank and decide who gets a loan to buy a house. I try to put in a word for the minorities because it's the right thing to do. Let's face it, the Blacks and Hispanics have been screwed, and they deserve a little extra help. I guess that's what going to Africa will do to you. My parents help me out because it's expensive to have a house in the city. This house is an investment for them. But all of this was not enough for her. So instead, she's living somewhere up in the Heights with another television lady."

"I'm sorry, Barry. But you seem to be doing well. Are you all recovered from that pulmonary edema?"

"Yes, I think so. I'm not climbing any more mountains. I told my parents about you. They were so grateful for what you did. And that you're a doctor. Right?"

"Yeah, well, just an intern. It still surprises me when people call me 'doctor.'"

"My parents were impressed. They wanted to meet you. Would you like to drive down to have dinner with them tonight? They have a great place in Atherton. It's just a half-hour away. I've already forgiven you for Eve, but we're still not even. I want to do something for you. I never thanked you properly. Really, anything you want. Just say the word."

"Thanks, but I'm pretty beat. Let them know I'd love to visit next time I'm out here."

"Okay, well, I'm not being a very good host. Would you like a beer or something to eat?"

"Maybe just a glass of juice. Orange juice if you have it?"

"Sure. Is that all you want? I could put some vodka or gin in it. I told you, anything you want."

"Just the juice. I'm a little dehydrated from the run. I went faster than I usually run. I guess those shoes that Koba loaned me were used to a faster pace and wouldn't let me hold them back. Orange juice would be fine...I'm not drinking alcohol anymore." Andrew thought about how Barry's gratitude made him feel uncomfortable, as if it was up to him to relieve Barry of the debt he felt. But it also gave him permission to ask Barry an awkward question. "And if you have it, I'd like Eve's phone number and address. I'd like to call her while I'm here," he said.

"Sure. I'm not too surprised. She's kind of an addiction. But you've been warned. She'll break your heart. Don't get your hopes up. As I told you, she's into her career first and women second. I'm not sure where that would leave you. She's changed. But if that's what you want, here it is." Barry copied Eve's phone number on a piece of paper and added her address. "Her place isn't far. Just a few miles away. Tell her I said hi and that she should come by. I still have a bunch of her stuff."

"Okay. I will if I reach her. I guess I'll go back to my hotel, take a shower, and change," Andrew said. "I'm still in my running clothes."

"Let me add my number, too. You might want it in case things fall through with Eve. You can stay here if you want and save some money." Barry wrote down his phone number under Eve's. "Maybe all of us could get together. Suggest it to Eve." Barry forced a smile. "Are you okay? I'm worried about you. This thing you have about Eve—it might not be what you think. It could drive you to a dark place. I've been there."

Andrew folded up the paper with Eve's information and the phone numbers and put it in his wallet. He wasn't sure what he would do with it, but now at least he had it. He sipped the orange juice and soon found himself gulping it down. "I didn't realize how thirsty I was. I think I'm okay. I've had some tough cases as an intern, made some mistakes, people died who I might have saved. After a while, that can accumulate. You can get depressed. But I'm feeling better. San Francisco, the run, and seeing you and Koba have all been good. And this juice is the best."

"It's fresh-squeezed. You can have more. It's just in the fridge. No reason to hold back. And even though you're not asking my opinion—I want to say something. Don't take it the wrong way."

"Sure, okay," Andrew said.

"When we were up on that mountain, it was like I was look-ing down at the three of us. I realized that so much of my life was silly and wasted, and there we were, about to die. And I thought about what my last pictures would be, or music, or words. I had this idea that whatever was last in my mind might be frozen with me, so I wanted it to be something good. I heard some music from the Grateful Dead in my head, but then came the faces of everyone I've ever loved. They just flashed past me. My grandmother, my grandfather. My parents. My brother. Eve. I even saw your face and Koba's face and some of the others from the hut.

"I realized that we need to have them all with us, like a can-teen of water when we're hiking. Not physically but mentally, so that if one of us gets to the top, we all feel like we made it. Fuck that book with the names. And if one person gets sick, we're all sick. I think that's what you need to get you out of those dark places. Not alcohol or drugs. They just take you deeper. You need to find the people and the places and the music and the experiences that will keep the lights on. Keep on trucking. You know what I mean?"

"I think so. Yes. I'll try to do that. And you're right about the alcohol. Thanks, Barry, it's really wonderful to see you. I'll give you a call before I leave." Andrew walked to the door, and Barry put his arms around him and gave him a bear hug.

"I really meant what I said. Anything you need, let me know."

Andrew felt a sudden pressure to leave and call Eve. The phone number in his pocket was like the heat from a fireplace burning against his skin. He had to see her. They needed to talk.

※

Eve was in her apartment. She relished the quiet when she had the place to herself. The idea of a roommate seemed sensible when she and Anne had discussed it. They both worked long hours, and Eve had to be at work early while Anne had evening hours. By sharing the rent, they would both be able to afford an apartment with a great view, a health club, and separate bedrooms. Eve was not interested in sharing a bedroom with Anne, even though there had been a night when they'd gotten drunk and tumbled into bed together. There seemed to be some chemistry between them, but Eve was not sure she wanted to be in a relationship. Roommates would be just fine. She was glad to be free of the restrictions on her life that living with Barry had imposed. Even though she enjoyed the financial support and the companionship, it had become increasingly clear that they lacked the chemistry for a successful relationship. Barry was too needy and uncomfortable with the freedom that Eve wanted. It was better this way.

※

Andrew called the number from his hotel room and waited as it rang once, twice, three times. Eve picked up on the fourth ring. "Hello," she said, half-yawning. Still, Andrew recognized her voice.

"Hi Eve, it's Andrew," he said. He waited. There was a pause—one second, two, three—and he wondered if she was surprised, confused, or maybe the call had disconnected.

"Andrew?" she finally said. She seemed to be trying to wake herself as she puzzled at his name.

"I'm in San Francisco. I flew in to run in the Bay to Breakers.

I saw Barry at the finish line, and he gave me your number."
Andrew blurted out the explanation so that Eve would understand that he knew she and Barry were no longer together.

"My goodness. What a surprise. Where are you now?"

"At my hotel, the Sir Francis Drake."

"That's not far. I have a meeting in an hour to go over some
material for a shoot tomorrow morning. I'm doing some television work these days. Would you like to meet after that, if
you're not too tired? Say about four or five?"

"That would be great. I'd love to see you," he said.

"Good, I want to see you too. You must be just about done
with medical school."

"Yes. I'm an intern now, officially a doctor."

"Already? Congratulations. I guess we're all becoming grown-
ups," she said.

Eve described a Japanese tea house not far from his hotel
where they could also get sushi. She would make a reservation
and meet him at five.

When Andrew hung up the phone, he laid down on the bed.
His head was swirling with the events of the day, the race and
all of its exuberance and emotion, the chance meetings with
Koba at the race, and later with Barry and now the call to Eve.
He let his head sink down into the pillow and imagined his future conversation with Eve. He would tell her about visiting Kara
and Klaus in Denmark, and how the trip to Africa had affected
their marriage.

Then he'd ask her about her work and give her some up-
dates on his medical education as an intern and how he was
leaning toward critical care after his internship and maybe pulmonary medicine. He would mention his recent volunteer work
at a farmworkers' clinic and how much he had enjoyed helping

people who really appreciated what he was doing for them, where money and payment were not part of the equation.

Then he might bring up Eve's relationship with Barry, and that he felt badly for both of them, and see how she reacted. He'd play that by ear. Maybe then he'd talk about Malindi and how much he had thought about what it meant over the past two years. Or perhaps it would be better to show her that he had followed her advice, and act as if it never happened, just start fresh. Of course, Eve might get tied up with her work and not show up at all. He had to be prepared for that, too.

Andrew got to the restaurant early. He wanted to have time to find a table where it would be quiet enough to talk and be comfortable in the restaurant. He noticed that most of the people at the other tables were young professionals dressed in gray and black casual business clothes. The waiters and waitresses were thin, Asian, and dressed in simple white shirts and blue pants or kimonos.

When he saw Eve open the door and walk into the restaurant, Andrew was struck by her presence, and that people at the tables near the door turned to look at her and then kept staring. She was in a blue satin dress with a small black jacket, and her earrings caught the light and sparkled. Her hair was cut shorter than what he remembered from the television clip he'd seen at Barry's. As she looked around the room, Andrew stood up so that Eve could see him, and she waved and continued toward him. When she got to the table, they hugged briefly and she gave him a slight kiss on the cheek before releasing him and taking her seat.

"I don't want to get my lipstick or makeup on you," she explained. "This is such a wonderful surprise. How was the race? Did you win? I'm going to talk about the race tomorrow on TV.

So, tell me about it. It's a great San Francisco tradition."

Andrew was surprised at the energy and enthusiasm radiating from Eve's face and voice, and he would have been content to continue to sit in its glow if not for her sudden silence as she waited to hear the answers to her questions. He stumbled for a moment and laughed nervously. "Ha ha. I could never win against those professional runners. I actually did better than I thought I would. I finished number 477 out of five thousand," he said.

Eve nodded. "I've run in that race. That's great, top ten percent. Your name will be in the Chronicle."

"Really? In the newspaper? Well, I started with the elite runners. I saw Koba, our porter from Africa, there. He's the runner who did win. Remember how he helped carry Barry down with me?"

"Of course! What a surprise. I'll have to mention that in my story tomorrow." Eve paused as a waiter delivered a small pitcher of ice water and two thin glasses to their table.

Andrew filled the glasses and continued, "He's an international runner now, and I talked with him before the race. He even loaned me his new personal running shoes. Then, all of a sudden, everyone started running. I was there with all the great runners for the first few minutes, and they sort of carried me along with them until I dropped back into the pack with the normal people. Well—there were people roped together as centipedes, and there were the Dykes on Bikes, so when I say the 'normal' people, it's a bit of an exaggeration. Let's just say they ran at a slower pace. But I think the good start really helped."

"Isn't that how life is? Your prospects really do depend on where you start, and who you run with, and we don't all start at the same place," she said. "Yet some people are able to overcome a tough start."

"I noticed that with the farmworkers at the clinic where I'm volunteering. They're starting at the back of the pack. They work hard just to survive. But they seem to have a positive attitude and they're grateful for all the help we give them, and some of the kids become nurses, even doctors. I even had one follow me around the hospital one day as an observer." Andrew paused. The conversation was heading in directions he had not exactly planned, but Eve seemed engaged and excited to see him. He watched as she nodded and smiled at him as he discussed his work with the farmworkers. But he wanted to hear her voice, so he shifted topics and asked, "What are you doing with this television stuff? I didn't know you were interested in television."

"I never was. But I had a friend who works for one of the stations. They needed someone for the early morning show. It's only five minutes and I talk about social issues, business, and politics. It's pretty broad. But it's exciting to be on live television. I like dressing up."

"Better than safari clothes?" Andrew said. He was imagining Eve's wardrobe and what she might be wearing on television.

"I have to look good. People notice everything—my shoes, my makeup, and every word I say. I have to think on my feet. I'll see where it goes. I'm not sure that this is what I'll be doing a year from now, but it helps pay the rent and I've become a bit of a celebrity. People notice me when I walk into a store or restaurant."

"I noticed. When you came in here, people were staring. I thought it was because you looked so great."

Eve blushed. "I think they just recognize me. But it's fun, and I get to talk about topics that are important. At 7:00 a.m.

people aren't too choosy or discriminating. They're willing to listen to anything that will help them wake up."

Andrew looked around the restaurant, wondering if a waiter might take their order. He switched topics, fearful that the time for their conversation might expire before he brought up what was most on his mind. "So…Barry told me you're living in the Heights."

"I love living there. I have a roommate to share the rent. She's the friend who told me about the television job, and she understands about the schedule and why I have to get up at five in the morning. She's been teaching me about the television business."

Andrew took a breath. He had planned to bring up their time together in Africa, and whether she had been thinking about it as much as he had. A waitress came to the table and interrupted his thoughts. She was wearing a blue kimono with white flowers around the edges. She asked if they wanted tea and Andrew looked over at Eve for some advice. "Should we share a pot of tea?" he asked.

"Sure," she said. "I like the green tea."

The waitress looked over at Andrew, and he nodded his agreement. The restaurant was a narrow hallway, with small tables along the sides and a few larger tables at the entryway and at the back. There was bamboo edging the walls and fabric from Asia decorating them. Andrew noticed that most of the customers at each table had a pot of steaming tea and small gray ceramic teacups.

"This restaurant is great," he said. "I never would have noticed it just walking by."

"That's San Francisco. There are so many little nooks and crannies where restaurants have jammed into the small spaces. So, what are you doing these days, other than working?"

"I'm trying to survive internship, working a hundred hours a week. Some days, all I can think about is sleeping. I like what I'm learning, but I don't want medicine to be my whole life. I need to find a specialty where I can work hard but have time for a life too. I want time outside of work, maybe time for a family someday," he said.

Eve began to speak but stopped when the waitress brought the tea.

"Would you like to order food?" asked the waitress as she put out the tea.

Andrew looked at Eve for direction and she nodded. The waitress put two menus down in front of them and bowed her head gently before turning to go.

"So, you want a family?" Eve mused. "I couldn't imagine that. Life is too uncertain. How could you commit to children when we don't even know if people will be living on the earth in the next fifty years? We could blow ourselves up tomorrow or poison ourselves slowly. But tell me more. Did you have someone in mind, or are you just going to order up the wife and kids like the California and dragon rolls on this menu?" she laughed.

"I don't know," he said. "I like kids. I enjoyed watching them play during my pediatrics rotation in medical school. We actually had to play with them in the children's psychiatry rotation. The parents were so devoted to them. I think it makes you a better person when you have kids. You have more at stake about the future," he said.

"Women have always been defined by their role as mothers and wives. I don't want to be defined that way. And women end up sacrificing their careers and their opportunities to support their husband," she said.

Andrew looked down at the menu as a retreat from Eve's

accusatory stare. He did not want to get defensive or in a debate about the roles of men and women in society. It was not an argument he could win. The menu was a nice refuge. "Hmm, the sushi looks great," he said. "I like the idea of a dragon roll."

Eve smiled and Andrew surmised that she noticed how he had avoided an argument. "So I visited Kara and Klaus in Denmark last year," he said, changing the subject again to something neutral and more engaging.

"Oh, that must have been fun. I've never been to Denmark. How were they?" Eve said.

"They were going through a bit of a rough patch. I guess they had been having some problems before they went to Africa. We all went to that mountain for different reasons—to fix something, or find answers to a problem, or to explore and have an adventure. When Barry got sick, Klaus and Kara felt they should have done more. So, instead of bringing them closer together, the trip pushed them apart. They separated. She's living in a farmhouse with some other women. It makes me so sad. They've been together since elementary school. It's terrible for them to be split up. And maybe it wouldn't have happened if Barry hadn't gotten sick."

Andrew was not at all certain what would happen to Klaus and Kara. They were very different in their approach to life and what they wanted. Would they focus on their differences, or would they be able to look past them and find what brought them together? Andrew was worried about them. And he did not want to discuss his own contributions that might have pulled them further apart.

"Actually, I got a letter from them just a little while ago, maybe a month ago," Eve said. "I guess they've gotten back together. They mentioned you, and asked if I'd seen you. Now I can say 'yes.' Maybe you helped bring them back together. What did you do?"

"I doubt that. Just normal tourist stuff. We talked."

"Whatever it was, I think you did some good," said Eve. "Kara wrote that they were thinking of opening some kind of café or pastry shop with magazines and books for sale and live music and book clubs at night. Klaus could keep teaching, but he'd help out at night. They talked about coming out to San Francisco to study our bakeries and cafes. I'd love to see them and show them around. I think they could have a successful business model."

Eve snapped her fingers to emphasize her enthusiasm for Kara and Klaus's idea, and Andrew noticed people from the other tables looking at them. A waitress came over and asked if she needed anything. "No, no, we're fine," Eve said.

"That's good to hear," said Andrew. "You never know what choices people will make when unexpected events offer opportunities. Sometimes they don't make sense. Koba has dreams of flying when he runs, and when Barry and I drove him for a little tourist visit to the Golden Gate Bridge, he almost flew off the bridge when a gust of wind lifted him up. He was so excited to be lifted off the ground that he put out his arms and tried to fly. People can get killed that way."

"He's a normal teenager. That's just the point. People want to see things or do things that have been impossible where they live. They want to experience life and see what it has to offer them. Maybe even try to fly through the air. So much of what we do in life is constrained by social conventions and fear of shame or embarrassment. Speaking of that—I had a visit from those two cousins, John and Mickey. Do you remember them?"

"Yes. They seemed a bit out of shape for climbing the

mountain. They never talked much to the rest of us in the group, and sort of kept to themselves. I could never figure out why they had come to Africa or why they wanted to climb the mountain, but each person is different, I guess."

"It turns out they had important things they might have discussed but were afraid to. They're gay and have been in love with each other forever."

"Really? John and Mickey? But they're cousins."

"Cousins fall in love, too. They didn't want to share any of what they were going through with the rest of us. Apparently the mountain climb was sort of a dare and a test, or at least that's what they told me. They came here to San Francisco to do things they don't feel able to do in their home countries. They've been in love with each other since they were teenagers. They just didn't know it then, or couldn't accept it," Eve said. "They called me and we had dinner. Barry came too. I'm surprised he didn't tell you. He was quite the promoter for San Francisco. They looked much more gay when they were here: leather jackets; tight jeans. They even talked differently."

"Wow," said Andrew. "I never saw that one coming. They seemed totally straight. And they're...together?"

"Yes. They were so cute. And they were very apologetic to Barry about not helping more. They asked about you, too. They both thought you were cute."

"Really? I never even noticed them looking at me. I thought I was pretty good at reading people. But I guess we were all so caught up in our own survival up there on the mountain, we kind of lost track of everything swirling around us until we had no choice. I wonder what happened to those other people in our group, the Germans. They were a strange bunch, particularly Helga."

"That's another funny story. After you left with Barry, we had a lot of time to be together, and of course no one could sleep, and Helga told me all about her dream for a gym. I got a letter from Helga a few weeks after we got back to the US. She wanted me to help her advertise the new gym that she started with Helmut and Rolph. They wanted me to send pictures we had taken of them. I had a few that we took near the bottom and one outside the third hut. They wanted a letter from me to post on the wall about how they had climbed Kilimanjaro and then carried Barry down the mountain and saved his life. They were also trying to write up a story for their newspaper."

"That story is not exactly true. I hope you refused."

"Oh, I wrote something about the trouble we had, and I sent them a picture of Barry at the hospital. He agreed. And remember, they helped carry him from the second hut down to the first. But I did feel a bit used by them," Eve said.

"They were just out for themselves. They didn't care if Barry died, as long as they reached the summit. Now they want to change the story and look like heroes because it's good for their business. They were selfish and wrong about what Barry needed. Did you know they made Koba go back up the mountain to write their names in the book at the summit because Helga forgot to do it? At least now they're helping to pay for his travel to races."

"That seems like a fair bargain. I try not to judge. They made a compromise and no one knew what would happen when you and Barry walked out the door that night. It's something I've learned doing the news. You never know the whole story unless you really dig into it. Most people don't do that. They don't really experience the depths of life; they just float on the surface. That's one of the problems that Klaus and Kara have. They're naïve. They have never been on their own. They met when they were very young. First, they had their parents to take care of them, and then they had each other. You can't really grow until you face the world on your own. You should understand that. You've been on your own. And so have I. It can be frightening and lonely. But it's also liberating. You have to find your own inner peace and happiness before you can find it with others."

"It sounds like you've become a Buddhist. Next thing I know, you'll be at a monastery."

"No, I need people. I wouldn't mind being able to sit in a corner by myself and read for a while. There's so much I want to know about economics and politics and education. I feel ignorant when I interview people who have developed these amazing programs. I wish I could understand how their minds work. But my mind is too curious for me to empty it completely and meditate. That would be torture. I need to talk to people. I need to be active and do things, change things."

"Seems like you keep in touch with people. I've never been able to do that."

"I like people. I'm curious about them. Maybe that's why I like to do stories about people on television. Climbing Kilimanjaro was rough. I wasn't myself. I kind of became lost and disoriented when Barry got sick. Maybe it was the altitude. I don't know. But I like to keep in touch and write back…if they write to me. Our lives have a tendency to spiral and intersect over and over," Eve said, and she stared at him and smiled. "Just like you're here now."

"I should have written. It was awkward. I actually wrote several times but never mailed the letters. I'm sorry." Andrew could not hold her gaze and looked down at his plate and sipped his water.

"Well, I should have written to you too. I was embarrassed. You had seen me abandon Barry several times, on the mountain and then when we went to Malindi. And I put up a wall between us after Malindi and tried to pretend nothing happened. I worried you would not trust anything I wrote to you. So it was easier not to write anything. I'm sorry about that."

The waitress returned, and they ordered a dragon roll, an eel roll, and a plate of tuna sashimi to share. The waitress gave them each a bowl of miso soup, and Andrew found himself lost in the swirls of mushroom and seaweed and bits of tofu. He wasn't sure how he would be able to tell Eve about his feelings for her. It seemed too sudden, too abrupt, too desperate. She seemed so enthusiastic about being by herself and all of her opportunities.

Eve sipped on her soup and then continued, "I'm definitely not a Buddhist. I need the stimulation of other people and ideas. That's why television feels so comfortable. There's always someone with a microphone asking me to comment on a problem or idea. I like having my voice heard. I've even thought about politics, but I don't like all the lobbying and campaigning that goes with it."

"But what about personal relationships? I don't mean to pry, but how are you feeling since you and Barry split up?" Andrew said.

"That was a mistake from the beginning. Barry is a sweet and generous guy, but we're going in different directions. He wants stability in his life, and I want to shake things up. I want to make people think, question, tear down what's rotten and decaying in the world and build up something new that's fresh and vibrant and better than what we had in the past. The world needs to change. I want to be with people who share that vision.

Barry is pretty happy with the state of the world. I'm not."

As Andrew sipped his miso soup, he doubted that he could be what Eve desired. He wanted to make the world a better place too, but he wanted to do it person by person, curing disease or preventing illness and injury. He wanted a home that could be a refuge from the life-and-death decisions that were a part of medicine. He wanted a life outside of medicine, with love and beauty that would counteract the darkness and suffering of illness and hospitals that he encountered every day. He wanted to be engaged in the world and make it better, but he did not want to destroy it in the process and have to rebuild it.

"I agree. The world needs to change. We have the same goal, except I'd probably start with helping people one at a time. I'd be satisfied if I could cure a few sick people, maybe save a few lives every year. Bit by bit, I'd make the world a better place. That's how I'd do it, because I don't know any other way. It might sound trite, but I think we need more love and compassion in the world. That was one of the things I thought about up on the mountain," Andrew said.

"What a romantic," said Eve as the sushi arrived. "Thank God for romantics. You may save the rest of us realists from killing each other."

As they ate their sushi, Andrew found himself staring at Eve, watching her eat. She was eating most of the dragon roll and the tuna sashimi they were supposed to share. At first, he was surprised. But then he smiled because he was enjoying watching her eat and realized that she probably did not have much time to calm down and eat and talk. Her face was relaxing and softening as they sat together. He took the dragon roll and the last piece of the tuna sashimi and ate them and she laughed, "Sorry, I'm being such a pig. We were supposed to be sharing and you just let me eat it all."

"I'm just happy that you're enjoying it." As he watched her, his face glowed as if the world had more possibility now than it had when he entered the restaurant.

Eve interrupted his reverie. "What?" she said.

"Oh, I'm sorry. I was enjoying watching you. You really love that sushi. I was just thinking about the last time, when we ate together in Malindi. I didn't mean to stare," he said. "And I was noticing your necklace, the one from Malindi."

Eve laughed and her eyes seemed to become larger and sparkle. "I wear it all the time. Speaking of Malindi, the strangest thing happened to me a few days ago."

"What?"

She hesitated for a moment and then said, "I need to show you something. Do you have time to walk back with me to my apartment? It's not far."

"Sure," said Andrew.

Andrew paid for the tea and sushi and they walked out of the restaurant and up a hill, turned a corner, and then went up another hill. They arrived at an apartment building and Eve entered a code that opened a door into the vestibule. They went up an elevator to the third floor, and she led Andrew into the apartment. Andrew was surprised at the décor, part modern Scandinavian with carved wood chairs and tables, and part early-1900s European impressionism, with prints by Miro, Picasso, and Chagall, and copies of Georgia O'Keeffe's flower paintings.

"Sorry for the mess," said Eve.

"What mess? This is beautiful. What a view," Andrew said as he looked out the window at the Bay Bridge and the water of the San Francisco Bay in the distance. Eve came over to him and they looked out the window together. "The water reminds me of Malindi. Do you remember this?" He showed her the piece of coral in the shape of the trident that Grace and Ali had given to him. "I carry it in my pocket for good luck all the time," he said.

"That's funny. I want to show you something." She pulled a small moonstone out of the drawer. It was slightly tinted blue, but clear enough to allow light to pass through it. The stone was attached to a leather cord. Eve put the cord around Andrew's neck. "It's for you. It came from Africa a few days ago," she said.

"Really? How do you know? Was there a letter or anything with this?" Andrew asked.

"No letter, just the box and the stone on the cord. But I know it's for you. It's from Grace and Ali. I wrote to Mr. Patel with a letter for Grace. She had said they were friends, and I had his address but not hers. I was thinking about you, but I didn't know what to do. I was embarrassed because I had written to everyone else, but not you. And I wanted to do it but so much time had already passed. I guess I was afraid you would despise me. You had seen me at my worst, when I was falling apart on the mountain and I abandoned you and Barry that night when you both could have died. And even though Malindi was magical, I barely spoke to you on the ride back to Tanzania. But I think it was because I was just scared. I realized you brought something out in me that made me feel safe and that I could still be myself. And that was exciting and terrifying. So I wrote to Grace. I thought she might have some suggestions. She seemed to have recognized how we connected and the clarity of our futures. I know we were both a bit altered and I'm not sure what she really said or even what it meant. But I figured, what did I have to lose? So I wrote her a letter, mostly about myself and what I was doing, but also about you and how I had lost touch with you. And she sent me that moonstone. I knew it was for you and I wasn't sure what to do with it. I think it was her way of telling me to find you. What do you think?"

Andrew went to the mirror. It had been two years since he and Eve had stood together like this at the Rafiki Hotel, and he felt himself immediately transported to that moment, to that time when "nothing happened." He studied Eve's face and could feel her drawing him forward with her eyes and the subtle tremor of her lips. He turned, bent slightly, and kissed her neck below the stone. Eve took a breath. He kissed her neck above the stone and then under her right ear and then under her left ear. He watched her to see how she reacted. Was she pulling away, or drinking in each kiss like a drug and wanting more?

Andrew covered her face with small kisses, and she laughed. "Andrew, what are you doing?" she said.

He took her hand and led her to the bedroom, and she floated down on the bed as if in a trance. He touched her face lightly and then began to undress her and kiss each part of her body that became exposed. She moved her shoulders to free her arms and breathed in as his hands touched her breasts. "Mmm...mmm," she moaned.

He had been thinking about this moment for two years, trying to remember Malindi and what they had done and what they hadn't done. He wondered if she had been having dreams about this moment too, or was she just having a spontaneous reaction to his presence and his hunger? He lingered on her shoulders and on her arms, and kissed them as he removed her bra. He kissed her breasts as his eyes explored them, and then moved down her chest as he slipped her out of her dress and underwear.

Andrew paused and his eyes explored her body as if it were a newly unwrapped gift. Each ridge of her hips, each movement of her chest, each shadow where clothing had covered skin could have been a brushstroke of a Renoir masterpiece. Eve's eyes stayed closed as she remained motionless in front of Andrew, waiting for his next touch. Andrew decided to let his lips and tongue follow every ridge and every curve of her body. He was a bird fluttering over her; he was an eel with electric touch; he was seagrass undulating in the currents.

"You make love like a girl," she whispered. "I like it."

Andrew was not sure how a girl made love to another girl, but he decided that if it was what she liked, he would imagine he was a girl with a body that was the mirror image of hers. He took off his clothes until they only had their twin necklaces shimmering in the light, and he rolled onto her, legs to legs, arms to arms, chest to chest, and did not move for several minutes except for his lips that continued to lightly touch hers, to remind her that he was there. And then he bent one leg and then the other, as Eve pushed her thighs up against his and pointed her toes down like a ballerina. She pulled Andrew down off of her and he slid down beside her. They were both on their sides, eyes open, breath passing through whistling lips. "I really missed you," he said finally.

"Don't talk," Eve said. She rubbed her hand over Andrew's hair, twisting her fingers into his ringlets and then down to the back of his neck as he began kissing her neck again, and Eve turned until she was on top of him, and she put him inside of her.

"Don't move," she said. They lay like that with only their hearts beating and their chests rising and falling against each other, their hands slowly exploring each other—backs and thighs and arms and shoulders, whatever they could reach, even grasping at the air. Eve could feel her body rising and filling as she shook with uncontrollable urgency. She could feel him inside of her and she could feel their bodies swelling together. She wanted to move, to let the orgasm build and explode, but not yet. She held him, and he moaned and his hands clutched and scratched at her back. "Not yet," she said as his back arched.

"I can't hold off much longer," he said. She began to move slowly now. She lifted her head and pushed his chest down as she rose up over him. She lifted her hips and felt him now, hard and swollen inside of her.

"Not yet," she repeated.

When it happened, it was like a storm in the desert that arrives with a few small drops of rain and then the dust and the wind and the lightning and thunder all explode together, until the storm finally passes and leaves the ground wet and replenished.

"Whew," she said. "I've never...."

"Me either," he said.

They spooned together, listening to each other breathe, holding on as if they would never separate, as the light faded and darkness filled the room. Andrew felt his body floating on a sea of gentle waves that would lift him with each of her breaths and lower them down together as she exhaled, slowly returning them to the bed and the room. Neither one of them wanted to talk. But eventually they began to move, to recover their individual bodies and to dress.

"I have to go," she said. "I have an appointment. Let's get dressed, and I'll walk you out."

Andrew got dressed quickly, but his clothes did not seem to fit anymore. His body felt different and his clothes seemed to belong to another body. She kissed him on the cheek as they went down the elevator, and then on the lips. When they got to the entrance of the building, she paused and looked at him as if she was suddenly seeing him for the first time, as if the fog had lifted for a moment and she had an unexpected clarity for her life ahead. She clutched the moonstone on her neck as the moment passed.

The fog swept in from the ocean, obscuring the bay and the hills beyond.

Andrew embraced her, kissed her, and said, "This happened." He stepped back and waited.

"I'll call you," she said.

Epilogue

ALBUQUERQUE 1986

EVEN THOUGH HE'D been a father for eight years, Andrew still experienced a momentary shock when he saw the children lying on the queen-sized bed and realized they were really his—expecting him to take care of them, tell them stories, feed them, put them to bed. The children accepted his authority about truth, fairness, and discipline with little argument. They might question a food he put on their plate or a decision about a family outing or a rule about limiting television watching. But they never questioned his right to be the authority—unlike the nurses in the intensive care unit, who would routinely remind him to wash his hands before and after every change of gloves for every patient, even if he never touched the patient, because that was the protocol and no logic or argument would sway them.

At least with the children, he could make up new rules, offer bribes of cookies and milk, and make a plan depending on his mood at the moment. At bedtime, as he struggled to create a story from thin air, he often felt like he was walking that path in the dark on Kilimanjaro with Barry, trying to feel the texture of the trail with his feet as the story rushed ten yards ahead of the words leaving his tongue. Sometimes, he would become lost and wander aimlessly down various dead ends before giving up and kissing the children goodnight. But sometimes, he created stories where he truly connected with the children, where their eyes opened wide in wonder as creatures emerged from his imagination and jumped into theirs, where danger appeared around every corner, and heroes came alive and did battle with evil villains.

Bedtime was the best and worst of times. The children were tired and might erupt with tears from the most minor of frustrations, a lost stuffed animal, a noise in the yard, a room that was too dark or too light, and he would have to calm the situation or even threaten discipline. Or his story might fail because he lost the thread of the plot or the characters never began to breathe. But at other times, the children would suspend their critical thinking and accept creatures who could levitate and speak in rhymes and riddles that appeared magically. Andrew had to create a story that would satisfy eight-year-old Lira's logical, scientific mind and five-year-old Michael's wish for superpowers. And so, Andrew's stories often mixed magical realism, where almost anything might be possible, with a routine day in school or a walk in the garden.

The children were washed and smelling of shampoo, toothpaste, and skin lotion as they waited for him. Lira tracked his movements with her dark brown, almond eyes, and with the slightest smile from her pursed lips when he kissed her forehead. Michael stood up and jumped into Andrew's arms. Andrew caught him and placed him gently on a pillow as Lira watched, pondering whether she would get up and jump too or whether she was too old for such silliness.

Andrew's stories usually followed a pattern, starting with children innocently walking to school or to a park, when they would encounter some kind of danger—a deep hole leading to a cave, a tornado blowing out of the sky, or perhaps an alien lost in his spaceship, asking directions. There would be a princess to save, or a diamond that was lost, and ultimately there would be a struggle requiring heroic actions as the forces of good battled the evil villains. And good always won over evil.

Sometimes Andrew wondered if he was setting up his children for future disappointment, because in the real world good did not always vanquish evil; heroes did not always appear when they were needed; villains were not easily recognizable or were hidden from view. A few days of work in the hospital intensive care unit could provide ample evidence of how terrible diseases ravaged the nicest people and miraculous cures brought by heroic doctors and nurses were the exception rather than the rule. No one told the stories of the treatment failures and subsequent suffering.

As the children lay on their pillows, the scent of their wet hair blunted the antiseptic odors that had been absorbed from the Betadine and alcohol sponges on his hands over the previous twenty-four hours in the intensive care unit. Andrew wondered if his children would always think of him when they smelled hospital antiseptics, as if the smell had been imprinted in their brains with his image.

The muscles of Andrew's neck loosened and relaxed and he felt a gentle wave of gratitude and contentment with the children in his arms, their chests pressing against his. They were waiting for him to conjure up a world that would transport all of them off to sleep.

"So, what will it be tonight?" Andrew began. "Do you want to travel to Mars and Venus and meet Martians and ogres? I can teach you how to speak like a Martian by clicking your tongue. Or you could grow gills and live under water with whales, sharks, and starfish and electric eels. There's an underwater boarding school where they teach fish how to get off of hooks."

"No, Daddy. You promised you would tell us a true story tonight. Not a make-believe story," Lira said. Her soft cheeks began to glow salmon pink as she became insistent. "You were going to tell us about the time you climbed up the highest mountain in the world and saved Barry."

"Yes, Daddy. The mountain story," said Michael. Andrew noticed how Michael's hair spiraled in brown ringlets, much like how his own hair had been when he was a child. They also shared the same gray-green eyes. Lira was much fairer, like her mother, with light skin that easily burned in the sun.

Andrew sighed. He wasn't in the mood to relive that endless night with Barry after spending a night without sleep in the intensive care unit. There were two patients who refused to die but also refused to live. They dwelt somewhere in between life and death, like Barry had on that mountain. Sometimes a patient would carry two identities, one living and one dead, and the identities would rotate as if they were connected at the waist like Siamese twins. Andrew had been holding on to each of his patients' living identity with all his strength. But in these patients, one body system after another failed—the brain, lungs, kidneys, the heart. Like a series of battles, Andrew would rush from one organ system to the other, trying to limit the damage that one failing organ could do to another. A failing heart would starve the kidneys of vital blood; the kidneys would not be able to filter the toxins that the body produced; and the brain would become confused and comatose. The sequence could vary, but the result was the same—more medicines, more tubes, more specialists who would tell him how to fix the kidneys or lungs or the heart, but not how to save the patient. And the ventilators and medications and blood transfusions only prolonged the agony.

One patient was a teenager who had been hit by a car while riding his bike on a dark, busy street. Andrew could imagine Michael as this boy in a few years. The driver never saw the boy before his two-thousand-pound Ford pickup crushed the boy's one-hundred-pound body. The boy's face could have graced one of Michelangelo's angels with his innocence, repose, and beauty. But the rest of his body was broken beyond repair: his lungs were crushed; his neck was broken; his liver was ruptured. The boy would soon be departing with his angel wings.

Another was a woman who had poisoned her liver and brain with an overdose of Tylenol and aspirin. She was at home writing letters of explanation to her friends and family about the logic of suicide and her misery of slipping into depression followed by mania, how she had ruined everyone's lives, time after time. The paramedics brought her in because, halfway through the letter to her teenaged daughter, she realized she had made a terrible mistake and called 911. Her pen trailed off the paper as she lost consciousness. But the paramedics brought her in too late. The vital enzymes that sustained her had stopped working.

Andrew couldn't stop thinking about that letter and how logic could sometimes create fog rather than clarify when it

came to love and family. He would often hear about the decisions that patients made that seemed logical and innocent, but
would transform a routine day into the most important day of
their life. That was what had happened with Barry, due to some
uniqueness or vulnerability of his body that could not tolerate
high altitude. The truth was that one never knew when a routine day would become the stuff of story and memory, when or
where our bodies would crumble like fragile sandcastles in the
ocean waves.

"Are you sure you want that story?"

"Yes, please, Daddy," said Lira. She locked eyes with him
and her lips moved slightly upward as her neck muscles and
shoulders shrugged as if there should be no argument.

"Well, okay, I'll try, but I'm very tired tonight." He paused
and tried to remember how it had all started and what parts of
the story he would include, which parts he would alter, what
magic might unexpectedly appear, and which parts of the story
would need to be eliminated. And so he started, "Once upon a
time, Barry and I were up on the top of the highest mountain in
Africa. It was so high that no plants or animals could live there.
Clouds would drift around the top of the mountain like whipped
cream. Only a few insects could survive for long. It was so cold
that water would turn to ice if it spilled on the ground.

"There was snow and wind blowing through the cracks in
the wood of the hut where we were staying at night, so everyone
in our climbing group was shivering in sleeping bags, trying to
keep warm. We were trying to sleep because it was dark and we
were about to head off in the middle of the night on the steep-
est, coldest, darkest hike of the whole trip, up to the top of
the mountain where we could see for one hundred miles when
the sun rose. We could even see the future from the top of the

mountain. There was a book at the top where you could sign your name, and you'd be on a list of the people that God would interview when he needed some more angels."

"Daddy," said Lira. "Is that true? Is there really a book?"

"Yes, there is a book...." Andrew's mind drifted to another book, the Bible, in which it was written who would live and who would die and if by fire or ice or starvation. He had seen it all in the intensive care unit—the fire of fever, the icy skin of shock, the starvation of cancer—and he thought about what kind of god would write such a book, as if people could do something that would alter their fate. Or, was it all about acceptance of one's fate? But Andrew had seen how, occasionally, people seemed to cheat fate. Sometimes an antibiotic cured a deadly infection, and sometimes what had been written could be unwritten.

Andrew thought about how the people climbing the mountain to sign the book at the top thought that they would also write their own story. But he knew that was not true. One person never wrote a story alone. In his story, three strangers set off in the night. They fell onto the frozen ground. Andrew never got to the top of the mountain to sign the book. Instead, he had to carry Barry down the mountain.

Andrew told the children the true story about Barry, about how Barry could not breathe, how he collapsed and how Andrew and Koba carried him, pushed him, and rolled him, because they knew that truth was not written at the top of a mountain at sunrise, in a book. It was written in the arms and legs and beating hearts of three people struggling to find their way in the darkness.

"Why Daddy?" asked Michael. "Why did he have trouble breathing?" Andrew had noticed that, recently, Michael's favorite word had become "why?"

Michael smiled at Andrew, and Andrew noticed his son's missing front tooth. He thought about the temporary gap in Michael's mouth and how it reminded him of the temporary freedom of children to ask so many questions and fill the gaps in their knowledge, while adults were supposed to have all of those gaps filled and hesitated to reveal ignorance. Only the mad geniuses and scientists could recreate the ignorance of childhood, so that they could ask the important questions to solve the world's most difficult problems. He wanted his children to remember his stories, where knowing an answer might not be as important as asking the right question.

"I don't know why," Andrew said, "but I knew I had to help him get back down the mountain. It was the only way he'd be able to breathe. And so I carried him just like I carry you when you're tired." Andrew sighed as he told them about pulling Barry through the snow, about almost giving up, and about Koba lifting Barry up into his arms and carrying him down the switchbacks to the hut. And how they made a stretcher and finally arrived at the hospital where Barry was cured.

"Daddy, did you ever see Barry again?" Lira asked.

"Yes, he lives in San Francisco. He's fine. I saw him once, but I haven't seen him for a long, long time. He works in a bank."

"Is he your friend?"

"I think so. Yes, he is, but I just don't see him or talk to him. I guess I should. Sometimes it's hard after you save someone."

"Why, Daddy?"

"I don't know. Maybe it's just too much responsibility, a debt they can never pay back, an imbalance between two people. It's a good question."

"But we get picture cards from San Francisco every year. They're on the refrigerator," said Lira. "One has that golden bridge. Is it from Barry?"

"Yes, Barry sends us New Year's cards with pictures. But I think the picture of the Golden Gate Bridge on the refrigerator is from Klaus and Kara, our friends from Denmark. They were visiting Barry in San Francisco. Your babysitter, Ola, is Kara's aunt."

"I love Ola," said Lira.

"Me, too," said Michael.

"Yes, we all love Ola," said Andrew. "Thank goodness for Ola. She'll see you tomorrow after school. And now it's time for you to go to sleep."

"No, Daddy. We're not tired. Please, one more story."

"I think we're all too tired. But we can lie here for a few minutes."

Andrew rested his eyes and felt himself drifting off as the children became quiet. His story for the children had removed the thoughts of his dying intensive care patients from his mind, and he found himself thinking of San Francisco and the day he had run in the Bay to Breakers race and found Koba and then Barry and finally Eve, as if they were prizes in a treasure hunt. He thought about how that one day had changed everything.

The children were breathing slowly, almost asleep. Andrew was getting ready to carry them to their beds when he felt movement on the other side of the bed. "Mama," said Lira.

"Yes, darling. How was Dad's story?"

"Good. It was about Daddy carrying Barry down Mount Kilimanjaro in Africa. He saved Barry. And there was a book at the top."

"That sounds exciting," she said.

"Was it a true story, Mama?" said Lira.

"Yes, sweetie pie, Daddy knows lots of true stories. He saves people every day."

"He had to carry Barry. Can you snuggle me?" said Michael.

"Me, too?" said Lira.

"Me, too?" said Andrew.

"Mmmmm. Everyone needs to be snuggled," Eve said as she encircled them with her arms and pulled them toward her.

"Mommy," said Lira, "can you tell us a story tomorrow?"

"Sure, darling, if I get home in time. I have another council meeting and sometimes it goes on late into the night, like tonight."

"What's a council?"

"Those are the people that help Mommy run the city."

"Are you the boss of them?"

"Yes, just like I'm the boss of you and Michael. But they don't always listen to me. Just like when I tell you to go to sleep, you don't listen either."

"Can you put them in time out?" said Michael.

Eve tickled Michael and then she tickled Lira. The children laughed and they all settled back on the pillows for one last snuggle.

Andrew was often surprised at how Eve could move so quietly in their room and get into bed without his realizing it until he felt her there beside him. She would do it sometimes when he had gone to bed early and was waiting for her to finish some work or come home from a council meeting. She could magically transform from the efficient mayor of Albuquerque like a cloud passing quietly overhead, unnoticeable until it blocked the sun.

When she had run for mayor, she'd been the dark horse

against old Harry Gaines. She was the newcomer to Albuquerque, a recent California transplant with unfamiliar, radical ideas. Andrew had encouraged her, because he knew she was not going to be satisfied with the life of a stay-at-home mother. It had been hard enough to get her to give up her old life and move to Albuquerque with him when he began his critical care training.

The pregnancy was a surprise, but Eve had been eager to have the baby and get married. Andrew had not expected that. But Eve explained that she was ready for an adventure. That was something she hoped that Andrew would understand. And life together would be a series of adventures. They would share parenting and work it out together. Andrew agreed, without knowing exactly what that meant.

After Lira was born, Eve volunteered occasionally at a homeless shelter and a home for abused women. She was concerned about the lack of city services and the lack of voice for women in the city. After Michael was born, she made friends in the neighborhood with other parents and attended community political action groups. When Michael was two, Eve realized that she wanted to go back to work. Her friends encouraged her to run for city council or mayor. Andrew had thought that the run for mayor would allow her to meet new people and become more active in the community, even if she lost. He never expected her to win. But when Eve got onto television for the debates, her youth, preparation, and enthusiasm was too much for old Harry—the seventy-year-old former mayor. The city was ready for a youthful, innovative change.

After Eve won, Andrew wondered what they would do for childcare. Between his medical practice and her full-time job as mayor, they needed full-time help at home. That was when Kara and Klaus sent them Ola, Kara's aunt, who now cared for the children and prepared meals for the family for the week. Ola was taking classes at the university when the kids were at school, and somehow it all was working out.

Now the children were a clump of hands and arms and legs in the middle of the bed. Andrew felt Eve's arm reach out to him and he grasped it for a moment before releasing it. Eve's hand reached a child's arm or leg as if they were fish floating by at the underwater national park in Malindi and she was grabbing at snappers, turtles, and the electric eels. Finally, it was time.

"I'll take Lira," said Eve. "You take Michael."

"Okay," he said. They carried the children to their beds, pulled out the blankets, and lay them softly on their pillows.

"How'd the story go?" she said to Andrew as they returned to their bed.

"Fine. They wanted a true story, and so I told them about Mount Kilimanjaro and Barry. I wasn't really in the mood for that story. I have enough true stories in the ICU every day. But Lira insisted. It was okay. I hope I didn't scare them. You never know what's going through the kids' minds," he said.

"Same problem I have with the city council," she laughed. "I have no idea what's going through their minds either, but I'm not as creative as you. I should bring you to one of my meetings. I get so frustrated sometimes."

The bed was still warm and rumpled. Andrew laid there on top of Eve and she rolled around playfully, pulling his clothes off and making him want her while she hesitated and watched him squirm. She pulled the covers over their heads until all was darkness. He kissed her and she rolled over on top of him. They made love, and then he held her close.

"Did you ever imagine this?" he asked.

"What do you mean?" she said.

"This life, these children, your job as mayor, mine as a doctor, everything that happened since the Bay to Breakers race. Everything that happened since Africa. We met on a mountain, and you had a boyfriend. And I saved him. Our story would have made more sense if I'd saved you."

"Ah, but you did," Eve said as she laid her head back against the pillow. Andrew felt her breathing soften and slow, carrying him away with her to that cove, to where they could float softly among the zebrafish, the red-and-black coral, and the seagrass.

THE END

ACKNOWLEDGMENTS

I would like to thank Julie Mars, Emily Colin, Frank Huyler, Ethan Sklar, Cameron Crandall, and Al Bradford for their helpful advice. I would also like to thank Deborah Helitzer for her encouragement and constant support. I would like to thank Ethan, Ariel, Nyika, and Jos and Julian and Mira for listening to my stories over the years. And, finally, I would like to recognize my father, Albert Sklar, who shared his stories of World War II and the heroism of his friends, and my mother, Selma Sklar, whose love and curiosity about the world have been my guiding light.